ENDURING LOVE

Keith Gawen

Note for Librarians: A cataloguing record for this book is available from Library and Archives Canada at www.collectionscanada.ca/amicus/index-e.html
ISBN 1-4120-9831-9

Printed in Victoria, BC, Canada. Printed on paper with minimum 30% recycled fibre. Trafford's print shop runs on "green energy" from solar, wind and other environmentally-friendly power sources.

TRAFFORD™
PUBLISHING™
Offices in Canada, USA, Ireland and UK

Book sales for North America and international:
Trafford Publishing, 6E–2333 Government St.,
Victoria, BC V8T 4P4 CANADA
phone 250 383 6864 (toll-free 1 888 232 4444)
fax 250 383 6804; email to orders@trafford.com
Book sales in Europe:
Trafford Publishing (UK) Limited, 9 Park End Street, 2nd Floor
Oxford, UK OX1 1HH UNITED KINGDOM
phone +44 (0)1865 722 113 (local rate 0845 230 9601)
facsimile +44 (0)1865 722 868; info.uk@trafford.com
Order online at:
trafford.com/06-1587

10 9 8 7 6 5 4 3

Authors Introduction to Enduring Love

$\mathcal{A}$fter nearly four Years of war, the people are tired. Tired of food shortages, tired of living in damaged houses, losing close friends and relatives and even being killed or injured. It seems never ending. Then, gradually, it becomes apparent the Allies are prevailing. The U Boat menace has been defeated, the North Africa campaign has been won, and our armies are advancing up the spine of Italy. There is a feeling that final victory is in sight, particularly now a huge army has landed in Normandy on D Day.

Churchill has said, "It is not the beginning of the end, but the end of the beginning" Nevertheless, the war still has several surprises to run before final victory belongs to the Allies. As spring turns into summer in 1944, the first of a new menace appears in the skies over the people of London and the South East of England.

Dedication

In memory of my sister, Patricia, and her part in the war.

ENDURING LOVE

Chapter 1

*S*t Marks Parade, an imposing row of ten shops each with a two storey flat above in the growing suburb of Sidhurst, stood higher than the older lock-up shops around it. Set with a wide pavement, quite novel for the 1930's, there was plenty of room for passing window shoppers to stand and gaze. Over the flats the windows were constructed in the new all-metal design, small panes framed and set into a brick façade. The rear of each flat had a back door to a small landing with an iron external fire escape. From this vantage point you could see beyond the tiny garden, just big enough to hold an Anderson shelter, over the churchyard to an avenue of detached houses, fifty yards away.

In the front, a smartly painted front door was the 'posh' entrance to each flat. Adjacent to it the larger shop door filled the space to the next flat. The front door opened inwards to a straight staircase to the first floor flat. They were quite luxurious when first completed in 1935, but the ravages of the 'blitz', and poor repairs to the damaged front meant the windows no longer fitted, and the plaster on the walls was patched and discoloured, the décor never having been properly attended to after the damage.

Nevertheless, the flats were comfortable and provided good accommodation. The main stairs opened directly into the living room which was large with plenty of room for the traditional three piece as well as a dining table and chairs. At the back was a small kitchen with a glazed back door leading to the fire escape platform. There was a southerly aspect, so every day the afternoon sun warmed it making it a pleasant area for working, but too hot in the summer. Most residents kept it open all day in warm weather. Two bedrooms on the second floor, and a good sized bathroom completed it. The residents definitely felt themselves a cut above the people living in the older Victorian 'semis' across the High Street.

In Flat No.4 St Marks Parade, Elsie was awake although it was only six thirty. She had been having a bad night. The War had gone on far too long, and everyone felt depressed and tired. For Elsie it was worse than most. Her husband Bill had been killed in the night raids in November 1940. He was never from her thoughts, and as the sun streamed across her bed, it only brought out her grief and loneliness. Almost ever day she cried into her pillow. The mornings were the hardest time of the day, and usually she had to force herself to get up just to divert her mind from the grief that was always with her.

The time slowly passed, but she made no move to throw off her depression. Half awake, she heard the telephone in the sitting room below start to ring. In her mind she cursed it. "Who in the name of Heaven is 'phoning me at this time?" It was now 7.45am. The ringing continued, demanding her attention. Still cursing, she reached out and grabbed her dressing gown and staggered to the door, down the small stairs to her drawing room, and picked up the receiver.

'Hallo!' she almost shouted at it.

The familiar voice of her sister Margaret greeted her. 'Happy birthday, Elsie!, Hope I haven't called you too early, but I wanted to catch you before you left for work!"

Elsie quickly swallowed her irritation.. In her grief for Bill she had totally forgotten what day it was and replied. "Thank you, my dear. It was good of you to call. I needed to hear your cheerful voice this morning. D'you know, I have been in such a state lately, I had forgotten what day it is! All I know is it's three years since Bill died, and I still miss him so much."

Today was the 11th June 1944, and her 42nd birthday. Bill her husband had been killed in November 1941. He was the manager of the Sidhurst Dairy and they had lived in the Company house all their married life, since just after the Great War. Bill, an A.R.P. Warden, had been on duty with his friend Jim when a stray bomb fell on one of the terraced houses in their patrol sector. He had left Jim to mind their beat, and hurried off to the scene where he was the first to arrive. Hearing cries for help he rushed into the house and managed to pull an old lady to safety. Then, knowing her daughter lived there too, dashed back to rescue her While he was inside looking, the whole house collapsed, burying Bill under the rubble. By the time more rescue reams arrived and pulled him out, Bill was dead.

The daughter was away in London!

Elsie was so shocked that for several days she could not take it in. How could a man who had survived the trenches in 1917, come home virtually unscathed, be taken by God now? Every time since, when there was knock on the door, she remembered the kind policeman who came to break the news. No matter how hard she tried to divert her attention, Bill's death was always uppermost in her mind wherever and whatever she was doing. The elderly lady Mary Windlesham that Bill rescued was taken to hospital, badly hurt and Elsie never saw or heard from her and believed she died later of her injuries.

Margaret was still talking. "Isn't the news good. We thought the Second Front would never come, and now our troops are already making their way inland from the beaches." She sounded excited, and went on "And did you hear the wireless this, morning. They have reached Caen."

At this point she realised that her sister might not be so enthusiastic about the news.

"Of course, Brian isn't anywhere near, is he? Have you heard from him lately?"

Brian was Elsie's son, a young officer serving with the Royal Artillery in Italy, and the main reason why she kept going. Always the apple of Bill and Elsie's life, he had become all the more important since his father's death.

"No, not this week." replied Elsie. "His last letter came on Saturday. He is still in Italy as far as I know, or was last time I heard. The censor crosses out anything in the slightest way revealing, you know."

Brian was a good son. He wrote every week regularly, and Elsie counted the days. She knew, as with all the young men fighting abroad, he was probably in constant danger, but preferred not to think about it except when the postman put a letter, or more often a bunch of his letters, through her door.

Or, sometimes to her intense annoyance, he put them through the letterbox of the shop next to her front door.

The shop concerned belonged to Jim Shaw, appropriately named Shaw's The Chemist. Jim had been, and still was, the other A.R.P. warden who accompanied Bill on the night he was killed. They had been close friends, and on his death, having a vacant flat, offered it to Elsie. She had to vacate the company's house, although they put her under no pressure to move out, it was inevitable. When Jim offered it to her, she jumped at the chance. She had first met him one evening when Bill brought him home for coffee after a dart's match.

"This is Jim Shaw, Elsie love," She looked up from her easy chair to meet possibly the most ugly face she had ever seen. Fortunately she showed no emotion. Jim's face was misshapen with bright red patches of healed scars, and his cheek on one side was almost non-existent giving him a twisted mouth. But his eyes were full of life and glowed in the fire light with vitality and determination.

"Pleased to meet you, Jim." she answered, trying hard not to appear shocked.

Jim had been here before. "Don't take any notice of the face, Elsie, I'm used to it's effect on people. One of the fortunes of war, I'm afraid to say." Elsie vaguely remembered Bill has once said something about Jim being a Great War casualty.

"Copped it in the head at Cambrai with the Tank Regiment. Finished my war for good. At least I got away with my life!" Elsie said nothing not knowing what to reply. "If it wasn't for the occasional headache I would be as right as rain now." Elsie caught Bill's expression and interrupted Jim's flow.

"I've got some coffee on, Bill, would you both like a cup?" They both nodded. "Very kind of you Elsie" said Jim. Bill motioned him to sit in the other easy chair and sat himself on the small sofa. While Elsie departed to the kitchen, the two men compared notes on the evening's darts.

Elsie soon returned with two steaming cups and a small one for herself.. They all chatted until Jim excused himself, and left to return to his father's shop in the High Street.

Later that night, she tackled Bill about Jim.

"How on earth did Jim survive such dreadful wounds, Bill?"

"Most of the right side of his face and head were blown away by a shell, and he was lucky he was treated quickly by a good casualty doctor. He spent some months in hospital in France before he was well enough to return to England. I think he had terrible pain and many operations over some years before he was finally discharged from hospital. He still gets frightful head aches, so bad he can't go to work. He takes aspirins to help deaden the pain but, however poorly he feels, he always tries to get to the shop to help take his mind off it."

"What shop's that?" asked Elsie

"Shaws, The Chemists on St Mark's Parade." said Bill. "You know the one. Actually his father owns it. They moved there from the small shop, which is now a sweetshop, near Woolworths when St Marks Parade opened in 1935. Jim will have itwhen his father dies. He is quite old now, and really Jim has almost taken it over already."

Although the dairy was not too far from St Marks Parade, Elsie had never been to Shaw's. She always went to Boots, at the other end of the High Street, and had never seen Jim when she was out shopping.

"Why haven't I seen him before? asked Elsie. Bill thought for a moment.

"Probably because he rarely goes out. He is too embarrassed to be seen much in public. You can hardly blame him!" Their conversation moved to more domestic matters.

Bill never mentioned Jim's wounds or appearance again, except on one occasion when some unpleasant youths mocked him in a pub. Bill sorted them out in a flash, and took Jim out of harm's way. Jim had been devastated when Bill was killed. He would never forget Bill's last instruction to him.

"Look, Jim, we can't both go. I'll see what I can do. You continue our patrol and I'll see you after the raid, if not before." He never saw Bill alive again.. Now he could not get rid of an idea that plagued his mind

"If only I had gone with Bill, and not stayed behind as he instructed, I might have saved him. Anyway, why could it not have been me who was killed? My life is of little value anyway, and I would be rid of the incessant pain that racks me unmercifully!"

After Bill's death, he had become very fond of Elsie, although he didn't speak to her often. She, like Bill, never mentioned his appearance, and even in her own grief and low times, always chatted to him. He would liked to have become friends, or perhaps even more, but she was so committed to her son, Brian. He felt it was not the time to make a positive approach, and his scars and appearance, he was sure, would deter her, so he kept quiet, and just hoped something would happen. She had taken up his offer to be his tenant, and he lived in his own small detached house in Amhurst Square, about half a mile from his shop.

Margaret was still chatting. "Look, I know you are in a hurry to get off to work, so I'll leave you for now, and come over in a day or two when I have a free morning. Have a happy day, and I'll speak to you again soon. Bye Elsie." She heard the 'phone put down. Elsie slowly replaced the receiver, and went into the kitchen to make some tea. A quick glance at the clock told her it was only eight o'clock, so she had time to dress and have a leisurely breakfast before catching the bus to work.

It was becoming a beautiful morning, and although it was Monday, she felt better. After a light breakfast her mood became more positive. Occasionally her depression lifted, and she felt it might be one of those times. Bill would want her to get on with her life. He had never been one to look back, and it was up to her to put the past behind. The war looked to be turning our way, at last. The Allies were flooding in to Europe, and it just a matter of time before peace came. Brian was alright in Italy, and even there, the campaign was going well. Yes, she must look forward!

By half past ten she was dressed and ready for work. The postman left nothing. She saw him pass her door just before nine, so she made out a short shopping list, grabbed her purse, ran down the stairs to the pavement, and set off down the High Street. She had only gone ten yards when she realised she had forgotten her ration book. Swiftly turning, she ran back up the stairs and took it from behind the mantelpiece in her sitting room. Running down again, she paused only to check the front door was firmly closed.

"Good morning Mrs Winter, how are you today?" She recognised Jim's voice. "Isn't it a beautiful morning?" He was sweeping the pavement in front of his shop. A task he carried out meticulously every day when it was dry.

"Hallo, Mr Shaw." she answered quietly. "Yes, it is. Do you know I left my ration book behind again!"

"Oh no," said Jim. "I'll have to tie it to your arms next time!"

Elsie saw he was intent on his work and anyway, she didn't have time to chat if she was to get her shopping done. She wanted to tell him about all the aircraft she had watched go over the morning of D Day, as they were calling it, but hadn't time. She hurried off thinking she would chat to him about it tomorrow. He was still a Warden and would know all the details. She completed her shopping and stood at the stop waiting for the 51 bus to take her to the camp in St Pauls Cray where she worked in the canteen. At almost exactly 10.30 she walked passed the guard on the main gate who nodded in recognition as he raised the barrier to admit her, and into the camp.

The men at the camp were very excited. The camp housed an anti-aircraft battery. She had noticed on several occasions that the soldiers serving here were older men. They had been called up late, and given less exciting jobs away from the front line. Many were married, but some unrestricted by attachments, gave her the eye, and would have gone further, if she encouraged them. With the excitement and her birthday, she was in a brighter mood than usual, and it did not go unnoticed by the men queuing up for their meal at the counter.

"You look happy today, and pretty with it!" commented one cheeky Bombardier, turning his arm so she could see his two stripes.

"That's enough of your cheek." she said tartly. Not put off he pressed ahead.

"I'm free this evening. Would you like to come to the flicks with me? There is a good film at the Odeon this week."

She had every intention of going to the Odeon that evening with her friend Betty. He was an attractive man and although she might have been tempted years ago, she knew she could not even consider such a thing. Bill and Brian were still too close and dominating her mind.

"Very kind of you to ask, but I'm afraid I can't this evening."

"Well, another time then, but I can't wait for ever, you know." replied the Bombardier.

He acknowledged the rebuff gracefully and taking his meal, went off to join his mates on one of the long tables.

"He must be lonely," she said to herself. "Away from home all the time and nothing much to do now the blitz is over. We hardly ever see a German aircraft these days. They must become very bored, and it would not have done any harm."

As she opened her front door there was a letter from Brian on the mat. After she made some tea, she settled down in her arm chair to read it. He was well, had not forgotten her birthday, but otherwise he had no important news, which was good. It meant he was safe! Reading Brian's letter sent her off in thought about him, Bill and her life with him, and she lost count of time. When she looked up at the clock, it was already 7.20, and she was supposed to be meeting Betty outside the Odeon at half past!

Betty stood waiting under the entrance to the Odeon waiting. It was unusual for Elsie to be late, and she was just wondering if she was alright, when she saw her slim figure tripping hastily along the pavement towards her. Betty and Elsie had known one another for over two years. Completely different in every way, they had quickly become good friends. Elsie was so steady, reliable and steadfast whereas she was flirty, changeable, and had no scruples. Several years younger than Elsie, she loved men, and had few morals. She knew Elsie disapproved, but didn't care. Just as long as she had a man around, and she had accommodated many in her time!

"Sorry I'm late Betty!" gasped a very out of breath Elsie as she approached. "Had a letter from Brian and lost count of time!

We haven't missed the start have we?" Betty looked at Elsie and thought how attractive she looked, all flushed and pretty in a blue dress. If only she would look occasionally at another man. Plenty, she knew, looked twice at her, but she was oblivious. What a pity, thought Betty, and they walked together into the foyer to buy tickets.

"How about nipping into the Black Lion for a quick one after the film, Elsie? It will hardly be dark, and it's not cold."

Elsie considered the idea. "Well, yes, if you like. I have felt a lot better today, and nearly left you for a Bombardier who wanted to take me here this evening!"

"Well, why didn't you!" said Betty. "We could have met here and I could have told you what I thought of him!"

"Not likely" retorted Elsie "and have you take him off me! I'm not that stupid!"

They both laughed and were 'shushed' by the people behind them, so concentrated on watching the film.

Both enjoyed the film very much. It was an American romantic comedy and had many scenes of luxury and sophisticated life in Hollywood. "Just what I need!" said Betty.

"My God, Betty," exclaimed Elsie "There'd be no stopping you if you ever got there!"

They jumped out of their seats just before the National Anthem, and got out into the High Street without having to stand still for it.

In five minutes they had walked down the High Street with the warm June air cooling their faces as dusk came down. Betty walked straight in the door of the Private Bar, the only one open to gentile ladies after nine o'clock, and ordered a glass of cider for Elsie, and mild and bitter for herself. She came over to the leather easy chair that Elsie had pulled up next to hers, and sat down. For a moment neither spoke until they had sipped their drinks.

Betty broke the silence. "You'll never guess, Elsie," she was obviously excited and dying to tell her news. "You know I have been away for a couple of days." "Yes, I know" said Elsie. "Well, I got engaged!"

Elsie was taken aback. She knew she had been to visit Douglas on shore leave from the Navy at Portsmouth, but did not expect anything like this.

"He's been promoted to a be a Petty Officer, and we'd been for a meal at a lovely pub. After coffee, he suddenly produced this ring and proposed! Look!" and she flashed a silver ring with a small diamond.

"I knew in a second he is the one, and accepted immediately!"

Elsie thought for a moment. She had met Douglas last time he came to see Betty in Sidhurst, and she didn't know what to say. Douglas seemed O.K., but a typical sailor, wife in every port type, full of fun, but as a serious husband? He was not what Betty needed, and she should have known better than to commit herself to a man without any real thought. Although she had only known Betty in the two years they had worked together at the Camp, she knew enough about her to realise this was typical of her impetuous nature.

She had to respond, so said warmly "Many, many congratulations Betty. To think I heard the news on my birthday. Now, let me buy you a drink to celebrate!"

She got up to order just as the barman called "Time gentlemen, last orders, please!" She quickly got the drinks and returned to thr seat "Better drink these up and make our way." Then she said to Betty. "Once again, the best of luck and congratulations to you both. I'm sure it will be a success!" A lie, but what else could she say, and who knows, it might work.

They quickly drank up and left the pub walking along the High Street to where Betty would catch her bus. Betty prattled on about Doug and was obviously quite overwhelmed by her engagement. Elsie was concerned for Betty's future but tried hard not to show her feelings.

At the bus stop in the still warm half light, Betty asked "D'you think Brian will be sent to France?"

"I don't think so." said Elsie "Although I never really know where he is, he must still be in Italy, as that's where his letter came from."

"I do hope he will be alright and write again soon." said Betty, as her bus came in to view. She raised her hand to stop it and climbed aboard.

"See you tomorrow Elsie. Goodbye, sleep well." Elsie turned and walked slowly back to her flat.. She pondered the future for Betty and Douglas, and thought about the day she and Bill had become engaged. Finally her mind turned to Brian, and she prayed to God to keep him safe and well.

Although she did not feel very tired, she undressed and got ready for bed. It had been an eventful evening. She was still thinking about Betty's news and how long it would last, and drifted into sleep

It seemed she had only just gone off when she became aware through a sleepy haze, of the sound of an aeroplane engine. That in itself was not unusual because there were often planes passing over during the night. This was different! The sound she was hearing was unique. Instead of a steady roar, the sound was pulsing like Bill's old motor bike. It got quickly louder, coming closer all the time. She got up and looked out of the window over the High Street. Out of the dark sky she saw a small aircraft, and it was on fire! She distinctly saw flames pouring out of the back. It flew low over the houses towards her, and she instinctively ducked down in case it crashed into the house opposite, but it didn't. It carried on, flying fast and straight until she lost sight of it behind the church. "I hope the pilot manages to get it down and isn't hurt." she said to herself. It occurred to her it could not have been German because there had been no air raid siren.

"Must ask Jim about it in the morning" she thought, and getting back into bed, pulled the clothes over herself and went back to asleep.

The next morning she made a point of coming down the

stairs just at the time Jim was cleaning the shop front.

"Good morning Mr Shaw." she greeted him. "Did you hear that 'plane last night? It was on fire. I saw it from the bedroom window!"

Jim had not. He had gone to bed late, and as always slept like a log until about six when his alarm clock shook him into consciousness He had to rush to get to the shop by half past eight.

"It must have been a bomber returning from a raid" he replied. "What time was it?"

"About half past one, I think." said Elsie."

"Yes," he continued, "That would fit. I'll see what I can find out at the Wardens' Post when I go on duty this evening."

He went on with his sweeping, and Elsie went back upstairs to get ready for her day at the canteen.

It was an uneventful day. No one seemed to have heard or seen the 'plane on fire', which disappointed her, and she was till thinking about it as she reached her door

"Is that you, Mrs Winter?" said Jim's voice.

"Yes, Mr Shaw." Jim came out of his shop entrance. "Wait a moment while I take off my coat and I'll be with you."

Jim came out of his shop to meet her. "I thought you might like to know what I found out about the 'plane you saw last night." He paused for a second to get his breath.

"It was not a 'plane, it was something else!" She began to be interested at the tone of his voice.

"I went up to the Post as usual this morning to enquire, and they were all talking about it. Unfortunately, what you saw is secret, so I can't tell you!"

"Why on earth, not?" Elsie was indignant

"Well," he continued. "It was something new, and although we were given some information, we must not repeat it in case it is not correct."

He sounded very mysterious, and Elsie wondered what ever it could be.

"A rocket plane perhaps?" she suggested.

"I don't think so. We'll just have to wait until it is officially announced. That's all I can say." He went back to his shop leaving Elsie thoroughly irritated. Why had he bothered to say anything! She went upstairs pondering his words. He had obviously stayed behind to tell her as he was usually gone before she got home from the canteen. But tell her what? Whatever he knew he couldn't repeat. A bit odd really

****

Chapter 2

*I*t was a normal day at the canteen on Wednesday, but all the ladies felt there was something strange in the atmosphere. The men came in for snacks as usual, full of their normal chat, but everyone felt a sense of urgency. It was as if they were expecting something. Nothing out of the ordinary was said, but something was up! They all knew it. Just before they finished clearing lunch, their Manager, Ted Thatcher came in to the kitchen.

"Could you call all the ladies in for a moment please, Joan?" Joan was the senior employee. "Then close the counter shutter for a few minutes, I have something to say to you all. Tell any men to return in a few minutes."

Once all his staff assembled he looked at them a bit sadly, before speaking.

"Could I have your attention, please, for a few minutes. I have a sad announcement to make. I have been notified by NAAFI headquarters that 39 Battery, who you know occupy this camp, are being moved immediately, and as a result, this canteen has to close down. What is worse is that I have to tell you that it will close permanently on Friday, when the Battery departs. Unfortunately, I have nothing more I can add, but I expect you have noticed the activity in the camp and are not really surprised."

For a moment there was a shocked silence. "So, we are sacked are we?" asked Joan. "When do we leave?" Elsie thought of Betty. "What about the staff who are not here? It's Betty's day off. How will she know?"

"I shall be advising her by telephone immediately, as soon as I have finished talking to you, and any others who are not here."

There was a hubbub of noise, and Joan held her hand up. "Yes, Joan" said Mr Hatcher.

"What about our pay? Where will we get another job? Many of us depend for our livelihood on the canteen work?"

"Everyone will get this week's pay plus a further week and any holiday pay owed. Also, I have details of possible employment for anyone who likes to speak to me afterwards. I'm afraid I can do little more. I have my orders, and am in the same boat. I shall be looking for a job myself from Friday, like you!"

Elsie realised there was nothing they could do. "Can I see you after, Mr Hatcher? I will consider anything you have."

"Right, Mrs Winter," said Mr Hatcher. "Come to my office with the others and collect your last pay packet, and I'll tell you then. The same goes for anyone else interested."

"Where are 39 Battery going?" asked someone.

"That I don't know, and if I did it would be secret, but I imagine it's France. After all, what is there here for Ack Ack guns? We haven't had a German plane over for months. I imagine they need all hands in Normandy." Everyone agreed. That's where they were going!

As the news sunk in, Elsie realised she had to find employment quickly. The rent had to be found to pay Mr Shaw. He gave her very generous terms, and the worst thing would be to have to admit she hadn't enough money to pay her weekly dues. "Yes", she thought, "I must consider whatever Mr Hatcher has to offer very carefully."

"Ah, hallo Mrs Winter," said Mr Hatcher as she came in to collect her pay packet. "Firstly, thank you for all the work you have done here. I'm sorry to see you go. You are one of our most dependable staff, and I shall miss all you've done to keep the canteen a welcoming place for our men."

Elsie was a bit embarrassed. She didn't realise she was appreciated. Perhaps he said that to everyone, but he continued. "Some of the men have, especially Bombardier Lawson, asked me to thank you on their behalf. Now this employment I have. I'm afraid it is not much, but if it will help for the time being -- - " His voice tailed off. Elsie nodded, and he carried on.

"It is from the Personnel Manager at Klingers. You know, the large factory at the roundabout on the by-pass. They have a number of vacancies. Factory work, of course, but perhaps it might suit some of you. Anyway, if you're interested, telephone him, his name is Mr Perkins at Sidhurst 4578. Here, I've made a note of it for you." He handed her a small piece of headed NAAFI paper on which he had written the name and number. "Say you have been recommended by me. He can ask me for a reference if he needs one. I also have an application form for you to complete and take with you."

She took the form he handed her, and replied. "Thank you Mr Hatcher. I'm sorry to have to leave. I have enjoyed working here, and as for the cheeky Bombardier, never stops trying does he!"

He stood up ending the interview, and shook hands before ushering her out. "Goodbye Mrs Winter, best of luck. I know you'll get something soon. There are plenty of good jobs in the area."

She didn't hang about at the camp, there was no point. She was home soon after five, and decided to telephone Klingers immediately.

"Klinger's" answered the telephone operator. "Can I speak to Mr Perkins, please" asked Elsie.

"Hold on a moment" said the girl

"Perkins speaking" said the telephone.

"Good afternoon Mr Perkins, my name is Mrs Winter. I have been recommended to speak to you about a job by Mr Hatcher at the Camp that is closing shortly."

"Oh yes" answered Mr Perkins. "You are the first to call. Did he give you an application form?"

"Yes, I'm just completing it now."

"Good. Now, can you come to our offices for an interview? Tomorrow afternoon would be possible, say 2.30? I can show you what we do and the positions open."

"Yes, thank you" replied Elsie. "I shall attend at 2.30 as you suggest."

"That's settled then," said Mr Perkins. "Just call in at our offices and our receptionist will show you where I am. Goodbye."

Elsie slowly put down the receiver. Already she had an interview. Would the work be acceptable? Wait and see. She knew they produced carbon products, but what that meant she had no idea. Tomorrow would tell!

She had hardly finished when the 'phone rang.

"Hallo Elsie, Betty here. I've just been sacked, and imagine you have too!"

"Yes, I have Betty. I've just spoken to Mr Perkins at Klingers. Are you going to contact them?"

"Yes, of course." replied \Betty. "I'll telephone immediately. Are the others going to try there?"

"No idea, Betty, I didn't wait to ask. As soon as they paid me off, I came straight home and called .him."

"I'll get on to him now. Bye Elsie."

She wondered if all the staff would do the same and was glad she got in early. At least she would have a chance, and hoped Betty would too.

Betty rang back about twenty minutes later as Elsie was having a quiet cup of tea and reviewing the day's happenings. Quite a day! Not what she expected when she set out for work!

"What time is your interview?" asked Betty.

"Half past two with Mr Perkins. Did you get one?

"2.45, must be the one after yours. Shall we get the bus together?"

"Good idea," answered Elsie, "why don't you call here at two and we can get the bus down. It's only about ten minutes on the 51."

"That's agreed." said Betty. "See you tomorrow, and we can have a good chat on the bus about Klingers before we meet Mr Perkins. Bye."

For the rest of the day she tried not to worry about losing her job, but found it hard. To occupy herself she walked down the High Street passed the Police Station to the Labour Exchange. For about twenty minutes she checked all the vacancies, but nothing appealed to her, and no one paid much attention. As she was going to Klingers tomorrow, she decided not to make enquiries, and walked out of the office saying to herself she would return after the interview if it was no good.

It was a sunny evening, and she made a light supper from the leftovers of the previous day, and sat in her little garden. It was very quiet, and the warm sun sent her into a doze. Let tomorrow take care of itself, anyway, I feel better in myself, and perhaps a change of work will do me good. At six o'clock she went up to her sitting room and listened to the news which was full of the advances being made in Normandy. Soon becoming bored, and it only made her think of Brian, she had a bath, washed her hair, and sat on the little landing outside the kitchen, and enjoyed the sun going down over St John's Church. About nine o'clock she decided to have an early night and was soon in bed. By ten thirty she was fast asleep.

When she awoke it was just light enough to make out her bedroom curtain flapping in a slight morning breeze. Something had brought her into immediate wakefulness. It was the sound of an air raid siren in the distance.

"That's odd." she said to herself. "Haven't had a raid in ages. Must be a stray German plane somewhere coming our way?" She lay back and relaxed again. The siren alone meant very little these days, and sometimes it went off just to show it was still there!

Then, the local siren on the Police Station in Sidhurst followed much louder, making her sit up. Something <u>was</u> happening! She sat listening. Then she heard it! The same sound! Like a motor bike coming towards her, as she had heard on Tuesday night. This time it was light. She must see it!

Jumping out of bed she ran to the window in the direction of the sound, and there it was! A small sleek aeroplane moving very fast and low across the lightening sky. Flames were coming from its tail, and it had short stubby wings. It looked like a flying bullet, except for the fiery tube over the tail. It had no cockpit which was strange. She felt no fear, and as on Tuesday night watched as it flew on over the shops and St John's Church into the distance and out of sight. What on earth was it?

Almost at once, she heard another in a slightly different direction. It did exactly the same, and she saw it carry on towards London, again very speedily. All at once there were three or four in succession. She could not take her eyes off them and the noise was becoming nearly continuous, one hardly disappearing before another took it's place.

Then, the telephone rang. "Hallo, Mrs Winter here." she answered.

"Is that you, Mrs Winter." It was Mr Shaw's voice. "Have you been watching them?"

"Yes, of course, they woke me up. What are they?"

Another roared overhead, drowning his voice, and passing on.

"Get down to the shelter immediately. They're flying bombs. The things you saw on Tuesday night and I couldn't tell you about!"

"They don't seem dangerous to me!" said Elsie.

"Well they are!" He sounded concerned. "Once the engine stops, they come down and explode as soon as they hit the ground. You'd better go down to the Anderson until I come in to the shop."

"I can't," replied Elsie. "The shelter is full of junk, smelly and dirty."

"Alright, but go down to the shop back door. You'll find the key under the mat, and go into the little room between the shop and the rear kitchen. It's in the centre of the building and the safest place. If one falls on St Mark's, it will demolish it and you as well!"

"Oh, all right" agreed Elsie, "But I must get dressed first. I'll wait for you downstairs."

There seemed no danger, and she was still fascinated by the 'flying bombs'. She stood and watched them going merrily across the sky and onwards. She was watching quite happily, when as one passed over, the engine suddenly cut. It continued on its way gliding lower and over the houses along the High Street and out of sight. A few seconds later there was an enormous explosion, quite close, and she saw at once a spout of smoke go up. "Better get down to the little room as Jim Shaw suggested," she said to herself. "Curiosity could kill the cat!"

As she quickly changed into suitable clothes and had a quick wash, the flying bombs were still passing over, and she could hear the ambulance bells. She felt quite calm, a little breathless, and almost heady with the excitement of it. Grabbing some milk and tea, she made her way down, took the key, through the back door, and in to the 'little room' There was a chair to sit on, and she waited rather impatiently for Mr Shaw to arrive. It wasn't long, and fifteen minutes later he rushed in the front entrance, and to where she was sitting. He looked worried sick!

"Are you O.K. Mrs Winter? I have been worried that you might be frightened in the flat on your own, and by the way, isn't it time you called me Jim?"

"I'm fine Jim. Until you called, I was enjoying watching them fly over. Now, tell me all you can about what's going on. Please call me Elsie. As you say we have known each other for a long time now!"

"These things are being launched from the French Coast.

They are pilotless aircraft guided to London, and they have a huge bomb in the front meant to destroy London when they land. I first heard about them on Wednesday, but it was top secret. Not now! Everyone will know, and it is already on the BBC news! All the ack ack has been moved to the coast as there is not much point shooting them down to crash on to houses."

"So that explains where 38 Battery has gone! Not to France, but to strengthen our defences along the sea! No wonder they were in such a hurry yesterday. By the way, er - Jim, I have lost my job at the camp. The canteen has closed, probably permanently, but I have already got an interview today at Klingers – that is if it is not cancelled."

But Jim was not listening. "Now Elsie, you must stay here until it quietens down. These things can't go on for ever. I'll get some more furniture to make it more comfortable, and when Joan comes in. you and she can get together until the all clear goes."

She could see he was worried. She, however, was not!. It seemed far less serious than the Blitz three years ago, and she felt totally unafraid. So she sat there obediently, more to please him than in fear of this new menace.

By the time Joan appeared about nine thirty, she was bored stiff. Jim had gone home to sort out his own household, and left her under strict instructions not to leave the little room. "You never know when one is coming." he told her. "Because they glide the last distance, they are on you and exploding before you are even aware of it!" He dashed off, and she made herself comfortable in the easy chair he had brought in from the back kitchen. After a while she started to look around the shop. At the back was the kitchen looking over the small garden with the Anderson shelter. The room was neatly fitted with shelving and two cupboards, in which she found a set of crockery over the sink. Then her little room which appeared not to be much used. Along side was the dispensary, where she presumed Joan, the pharmacist worked, and in front, the laid out shop. It was well planned, and she could imagine herself working in it.

She was still examining the stock, when there was a ring on the shop bell, and someone rattled the door. "Is there anyone there?" shouted a man's voice.

What should she do? She went to the door and shouted back. "There's no one else here at present, I'm taking shelter and live in the flat above. Is there anything I can do?"

"I need some bandages and first aid materials for the incident up the road. Can you help? I will pay Jim later. I'm Doctor Hargreaves."

"I'm sorry I don't know where anything is, but I know you, so I'm sure Jim won't mind. Come in and I'll take a note of anything you take for him." She slid back the bolt on the door and let Dr Hargreaves in.

He quickly picked out what he needed from the stock shelves, and Elsie jotted down what she could on a pad she found in the dispensary. He put them into his bag. "Thank you very much. You may well have helped to save someone's life. We have run out at the First Aid Post. Didn't expect this!"

Elsie nodded. Dr Hargreaves hurried off to his car parked outside, and was off down the road to the site of the bomb. Elsie wondered if she had done the right thing, and hoped Jim would approve. If not – well, she'd done it now so it was too bad!

Jim and Joan arrived soon after. Joan was early. She knew there would be a rush when the raid started, so had caught an earlier bus from her home outside Sidhurst. Elsie related Dr Hargreaves' visit, and waited for Jim's reaction. He was delighted.

"Good thing you knew Dr Hargreaves, Elsie, he is a very good customer when he is short in an emergency. He will be back as soon as he's finished, have no worries. You did the right thing and I'm glad you were here to help!"

Of course, when Joan came in she heard all about it, and

beamed at Elsie. "Saved me having to sort out what he wanted, So, good luck to you!"

Elsie set about making something for a late breakfast from food in the larder in the flat. While up there, she had time to see flying bombs were still passing over,. She guessed they were, because they had begun to hear muffled explosions in the distance. They were landing nearer than at first, but not enough to be concerned.

After they had finished the meal she had made for them, and in spite of Jim's protests, she returned to her flat. Apart from the fact she had done nothing to clear it up after rushing down to shelter, she knew she ought to telephone her sister. She would be worried, and was owed a call anyway.

She asked the operator for Margaret's number, and sat comfortably in her armchair while the operator found the number.

"Gravesend 2116" said Margaret answering the 'phone.

"Hallo Margaret, it's me, Elsie. Are you alright in Gravesend, or are you getting these horrible flying bombs as well."

"Yes we have had some, but I believe you are getting a lot, if the BBC is correct. We can see and hear them, or rather the explosions, but none have come our way yet. How about Sidhurst? Have you had any in the town?"

"Well, one fell just outside somewhere beyond the other end of the High Street earlier, but that's all so far. I am taking shelter in Jim's shop downstairs. He has been very concerned, but we are all safe at the moment."

The line was briefly interrupted by the operator. " Sorry, please finish your call as quickly as possible as the lines are very busy with emergency calls." Elsie had never heard that before, and said "I'd better go, Margaret. Glad to hear you are unaffected in Gravesend. I'll give you a ring another time. Bye"

"Bye Elsie. Thanks for ringing. Talk to you later. Bye." And she was gone.

Elsie had done what she wanted to, and went back to cleaning and tidying her flat. She hadn't normally time to give it a good clean, but as she was off until her interview in the afternoon; she was able to be more thorough than usual. It soon looked vastly better than it had for some weeks.

Meanwhile, the bombs were still passing over the shops, but not so many, and she hoped they would soon stop.

She thought about her interview with Mr Perkins at Klingers, and realised she had not yet filled in the form he gave her. She found her fountain pen in the bureau, and sat for a few minutes filling in the details asked for. It was not difficult, and Elsie had a Grammar School education,. Once completed, she tucked it into an unsealed envelope and put it in her handbag ready to take with her.

About a quarter to two, Betty arrived as agreed, and after sitting down for a few minutes comparing Application Forms, they set off to catch a bus down to Klingers. It was a simple enough journey, shorter than to the Camp, and they walked in to Klingers Reception area at ten to two. She had not appreciated how imposing the building was when you got near to it. It was a large yellow brick building, and the reception was quite grand and very modern. She realised it was built just before the war.

They walked together to the desk where a glamorous receptionist was idly pretending to use her typewriter.

"Can I help you?" she asked Elsie, who was leading.

"We have appointments with Mr Perkins," said Elsie. "My name is Mrs Winter, and this is Miss Manners. My appointment is at 2.30 and Miss Manners is at 2.45." Betty came from behind Elsie.

" Hallo Joan," she said to the receptionist."I thought you worked here."

The receptionist Joan, replied "Knew you would be in soon, Betty. I think most of the girls from the Canteen are coming in sometime today."

"What's Mr Perkins like, Joan?" asked Betty. Joan looked at her a bit askance.

"I think you will find him very nice. I'll tell him you are both here, although you are a bit early. Sit over there until he is ready to see you." She picked up the telephone on the desk and pushed one of the plugs into an extension.

"Mr Perkins, sorry to interrupt. The two ladies from the camp for your two thirty and two forty five appointments are here."

Elsie didn't hear the reply, and Joan announced. "He will call for you when he's ready."

They sat quietly and waited, not saying anything that Joan might hear, as she was an unknown quantity.

"What did you do at the Canteen, Betty." asked Joan from the other side of her desk.

Betty hesitated then said "I was assistant to Mr Hatcher, the Manager!" A lie thought Elsie. In fact, she'd been longer at the Canteen than Betty, but this was Betty's way of boosting herself. Then she added, "and he relied totally on me."

"I'm sure he did" replied Joan. "So what sort of job are you wanting here?"

"I have no idea, but it must be something worthwhile. I'm not going to take any old thing after my responsibilities in the Canteen."

At that moment she caught Elsie's eye and winked at her. "You have to make yourself important, don't you." she whispered quietly to Elsie so Joan couldn't hear.

The door at the far side of the lobby opened, and a tall man in a flashy dark suit came over to them. Elsie thought he looked a spiv and took an instant dislike to him.

"Good afternoon, ladies." he simpered at them. Obviously he thought a lot of himself.

"You might as well both come in together. I can show you the factory, and then we can talk separately after you have seen what you will be doing. If there are any more applicants in the meantime Miss Young" he said to Joan, "please bring them along too."

While Betty and Elsie got up, he set off at brisk pace through the door he had just entered. They followed behind looking as the posh lobby changed to a dirty looking factory floor where many girls and men were busily engaged in operating noisy machines. The lighting was poor, Elsie noticed, but no one seemed to mind. Loud music was blaring, and many of the workers were singing to it at the tops of their voices. Elsie didn't know what Betty thought but she instantly disliked the idea of working here.

Elsie thought the man must be Mr Perkins, but he hadn't been courteous enough to introduce himself to them. Meanwhile they passed out of the area and entered what was obviously a packing section. There was a long line of girls, no men, standing alongside a set of rollers. From a small square hatch at the end came a stream of varying sized packages. As soon as one reached the first girl, she grabbed it, selected a carton from the stack behind her, and put the package in to it. Then with gummed paper and string, tied the box neatly, sealed it, and stamped it with wording she could not decipher from where they watched. In the meantime as more packages came through, the next girl took one as she became free, and so on.

"This is where you will work." said the smooth man

"The vacancies we have are on the night shift where we are 30% undermanned. Or should I say 'underwomanned'." He laughed at his futile joke.

"If you're interested, I'll ask one of our Supervisors to show you the ropes, and she will also tell you the rates of pay. The amount you earn depends on the number of parcels the team can complete in a shift, so the more you do, the more you earn. I should tell you that the day team make more than anyone else in the factory, except management, so I suggest you consider the offer carefully before you decide."

He beckoned to a rather grim looking lady standing slightly to the rear of the rollers.

"This is Joan Penny, our foreman, or should I say 'forelady'"
Again he chuckled at
his own weak humour. "She will explain and answer any
questions."

He spoke to Joan. "Here are two possible members of the
night shift, Mrs Penny. Would you be kind enough to show them
the ropes, and answer any questions they may have."

Joan looked at them and smiled. Her grim expression was
now quite different, and she spoke in a friendly way.

"Not much to show you really. Klingers manufacture carbon
parts and ingredients, and we do the packing so they're ready
for despatch. It's quite easy, except you have to keep up a good
speed. Once you know which size carton to choose, the rest is
just practice. Here, I'll show you."

She walked over to the rollers, and picked up a pack as it
travelled towards her. Deftly she held it, selected a carton from
behind her, and had it wrapped and strung in a few seconds. It
looked easy, and probably was once you were proficient. Elsie
thought it was really boring. The thought of doing that all night
was quite abhorrent!

"That's all there is to it." said Joan Penny. "Once you are quick
at it, you will get excellent bonuses, especially on the night shift
where the pay is higher anyway. We are flat out at the moment,
and some of us are working seven days a week! Now, back to
Mr Perkins, and you can ask him anything else". Mr Perkins
came over. "Right, ladies, let's go back to my office and we can
get down to details."

Elsie looked at Betty and spoke first. "I don't think this
sort of work is for me Mr Perkins, so if you don't mind, I'll not
waste your time any more. Thank you for seeing us, and I'll leave
now."

Mr Perkins looked a bit taken aback. Perhaps he thought
everyone would just love working in Klingers factory. "Come on
Miss Manners, we'll talk in my office."

"Bye, Betty," said Elsie, and walked back to the reception

lobby. She gave a quick wave to Joan at her desk, and went out to get the bus home. Not the sort of job she wanted at all!

She was back at St Marks Parade by four o'clock, and as she arrived at her door, Jim Shaw saw her and came out. "How did you get on, Elsie? he enquired. She heard the sound of a 'doodle bug' as everyone now called them, approaching. It didn't stop, and she walked over to him.

"Not the sort of work for me, Jim. It was night work as well, so I'm afraid I didn't even wait to get all the details. I left Betty still being interviewed, but I think it is the most boring work I have ever come across!"

"What are you going to do now, then?"

"I suppose I shall have to go down to the Labour Exchange and register on Monday. I'm sure there will be something more suitable than Klingers!"

"If you've a minute, come in. I have a proposition to put to you." He led the way into his shop, and through to the back kitchen. "Now, let's have a cup of tea and a chat."

He made a pot of tea and took two cups from the shelf to which he carefully added milk. "You do take milk, don't you Elsie?" She nodded as he began.

"After your episode in the shop yesterday, I had a word with Joan about my plans for the future. I need someone to serve and help with stock,who is reliable, trustworthy, and used to handling a till. I know you can do all these things from your experience in the dairy. Bill often used to tell me how efficient and helpful you were. Now, how about coming to work for me? Joan is all for it, and likes you anyway. What d'you think?"

Elsie was delighted. She enjoyed her work in the dairy, and although it would not be with Bill, she knew she could do it once she was familiar the goods Shaw's sold. "Yes, Jim, I d love to! When would you want me to start, and what pay would I get?"

"Well," Jim rubbed his chin. "I've been thinking about that. "Suppose I give you your flat free, and pay you in addition the same wage as you were getting at the Canteen. Would that be

alright? Of course," he continued, "I will give you more once
you have settled in provided we get on well, and you take to the
work."

Elsie was thrilled. The flat free <u>and</u> the same wage as the
canteen paid her!

"Jim," she replied, "That would be marvellous. I will start on
Monday, if you want me to"

"Right," he said. "That's settled. Now, don't be late on Monday.
Nine o'clock prompt!" he laughed.

"I'll be off then Jim. I'll look in tomorrow for a few minutes,
to get acquainted with the shop in action, and start properly on
Monday. Thank you very much. I think I shall enjoy working at
Shaws!"

She went up to her flat and was surprised not to find a letter
from Brian on the mat. One was about due, she thought. Now
for a nice bath, but I'd better 'phone Margaret first. I can tall her
my news about working for Jim.

Once again she heard the rumbling burble of a doodle bug
approaching, and ignored it. As the V1 came nearer, she picked
up the telephone and said "Gravesend 2116, please!"

"2116" said Margaret. At that instant she felt an enormous
hand lifting her out of the chair, and a split second later the
sound of tinkling glass that she knew was her window falling
to the floor, then a terrific 'whooshing' sound. Pieces of debris
fell on her, and the room was full of dust.

"Hold on Margaret!" she managed to mouth the words in a
whisper, "I'll be with you in a minute!" She heard Margaret gasp
at the other end.

"Whatever was that, Elsie?"

Elsie gathered her composure. "A doodle bug has exploded
very near. I'll have to go. Sorry, I'll call you again as soon as I
can."

Dashing to where her front window had been, she leant right
out to see what had happened. Rising over the roofs of the shops
on the other side of the road opposite St Marks Parade, was a
huge pall of smoke. She could hear voices crying, shouting, and

people were running along the High Street towards the smoke. What could she do? Debris was still falling, and she saw pieces of wood, bricks and slates clatter as they fell on the road outside Jim's shop.

"My God," she thought. "How can I help?" People filled the street, and there seemed little point in joining them, so she turned back to view her living room. Dust had now settled – everywhere! Glass littered the floor under the window, crunching as she walked over it. Lumps of plaster had fallen from the ceiling, and there were several pieces of glass sticking like daggers in the wall. She looked at them and shuddered. They could have impaled her if she had been in the way!

All at once there was a banging on the shop door. Looking out of the window again, she saw a man knocking on her door. Seeing Elsie looking out, he called to her. "Is Jim in the shop?"

"He's gone for the night," called down Elsie. "Can I help?"

"We desperately need bandages and plasters! Can you get some for me?"

Elsie wondered if she could get in. Then it occurred to her, she could, with the key Jim kept under the mat. "Wait a minute! I think I can get some for you. I'm going down to the shop now, and will open the front door."

A good thing she did, because when she came through from the back kitchen, she could see the shop door was badly damaged, and if the man had pushed the remnants of the door, he could have walked in quite easily. She pulled the remains away, and opened the door frame by undoing the bolts, and let him in.

Quickly she found the bandages and sticking plaster that had been replenished since last time she found them for Dr Hargreaves, and he was off, running back to the bomb scene. "Thanks very much!" he called as he ran off. "Will come back later and sort our how much we owe you. " My name's Fred. I'm at the First Aid Post. Jim knows me. Bye!"

A few minutes later, Jim arrived. He looked shaken, and much relieved to see her in the shop trying to make sense of the chaos. Stock lay on the floor mixed with broken glass, and broken cupboards. There was dust and plaster everywhere!

"Thank God you're alright Elsie! I had visions of you lying hurt or worse, in the flat! People said it had hit St Marks Parade!"

"No, luckily it didn't, but it must be a shambles behind the shops across the road!"

Jim looked out into the High Street. A man ran past. He saw Jim and called to him. "We need help! Can you come? There are people hurt, and a building has collapsed!"

Jim said to Elsie. "Look after the shop Elsie, I must go and see what I can do. Have some tea ready, we may need it!" He ran after the man, and Elsie started to see if she could do anything to clear the debris.

For what seemed an age she looked at the mess trying to decide what to do. Finally she decided the first priority must be to clean the shop floor. Who knows, more stock might be needed. Going to the cupboard at the back, she found a soft broom, returned with it, and began to sweep up the floor. Hardly had she begun when Jim appeared puffing with exertion.

"Elsie, could, you come out and help me, please?"

"Yes, Jim" she called back and ran out to see him crossing the pavement holding an elderly lady with blood streaming down her face. Moving quickly to help, she put her arm round the casualty and between them they helped her into the shop. But where to put her? Except for one small space already cleared, the whole shop was in chaos.

"Can you fetch a chair while I support her?" said Jim. Elsie moved as fast as she could and collected a chair from the dispensary. She placed it carefully behind the lady.

"O.K. Jim, let her down slowly." Jim slowly released his grip from her waist, and sat her on the chair.

"O.K Mrs Seymour, let's see what we can do about that cut. We'll try and get you cleaned up a bit."

With a gesture to Elsie meaning 'watch her', he went to one of the shattered cupboards and returned with a dressing and bandage.

"Elsie, get a bowl of warm water and a towel. You'll find one at the back by the wash basin."

Elsie realised he knew exactly what to do, and moved busily to his bidding. Meanwhile the lady was less dazed and joined in the conversation.

"I was just coming passed Woolworth's when I was knocked to the ground. Something fell on my head, and the next thing I knew, Mr Shaw was helping me out of the gutter. Was it a bomb?"

Elsie returned with the warm water, and Jim started to examine the wound on her head from which blood was dripping steadily to the floor.. Elsie could see there was a deep long cut, and it looked rather nasty. Jim continued to give instructions.

"Just dab the cut very gently and carefully, Elsie, while I prepare a dressing. I think from the look of it she will need stitches, but a temporary dressing should stop the blood until the First Aid team arrive. Would you look in the High Street and see if they are in our area yet?"

Elsie went to the door again. She could see rescue teams, ambulances with lights flashing and the High Street alive with people. Some had bandages on their arms and legs, and others were unkempt and white faced. Many were still covered with dirt. She went up to a man who appeared to be organising, directing people to various places. As she came up to him he asked

"Do you need help? Is there anything I can do?"

Elsie answered promptly. "We have a casualty at Shaw's, and Jim says she will need stitches. Can you tell me when the First Aid team will get here?"

"They are just over there, at the back of the shops at the moment. I will give them a call and get someone over immediately. Don't worry, it will not be long. Is the casualty alright at the moment?"

"It's an old lady. She was knocked down in the High Street and has a severe cut on her head. Mr Shaw has put a bandage on as a temporary dressing."

He turned to to issue more instructions.

"Tell Mr Shaw someone will be over immediately." He moved away from her and set off to sort out a group of workers who had come down the High Street.

Elsie went back to the shop and reported to Jim. He had bandaged the lady's wound, and was finishing washing the blood and dirt for her head, neck, and blouse.

"Elsie, have you a spare blouse or something for Mrs Seymour to wear. I have done my best to improve her appearance, but her blouse is badly stained?"

His voice trailed off and she replied immediately.

"I'll go upstairs and get one"

Mrs Seymour was embarrassed. "There is no need to go to that trouble." she said to Jim. "I shall be perfectly alright now. You can let me go."

"Certainly not!" said Jim firmly. "Your wound needs further attention, and I'm not letting you go until the First Aid men have had a look at it. They will be here in a minute or two. Isn't that so, Elsie? Meanwhile Elsie will make us all a nice cup of tea. I could certainly do with one myself."

Unbeknown to Jim, Elsie had already put on the kettle, and knew it must have boiled.

"One will be ready in a moment" she announced. "Do you both take milk and sugar?"

"No sugar for me, dear, thank you." replied Mrs Seymour immediately

Jim interceded. "I think you should have some, even if you don't normally. You can miss it in the second cup if it is too much for you to stand!"

Elsie made the tea and brought in a cup for each of them. Jim took the sugar bowl and put three spoons of sugar into one and stirred it thoroughly before handing it to Mrs Seymour. She accepted it and taking a mouthful, swallowed it with a grimace.

Jim dived behind the counter again and came out with a

bottle of tablets. Mrs Seymour was beginning to shake, and Jim had noticed the first symptoms of shock.

"Here, Mrs Seymour, take a couple of aspirins. They will settle you down." Mrs Seymour swallowed them obediently. "Thanks Mr Shaw"

A voice hailed them for the doorway.

"Is this where the casualty is?" A large man appeared with 'Red Cross' on his sleeve

"I'm one of the First Aid team. Is this her?" looking at Mrs Seymour.

"Yes, "said Jim "This is Mrs Seymour. I think she needs a few stitches, and is shocked from her fall in the High Street."

The large rescue man went over to Mrs Seymour. "How do you do Mrs Seymour. Pleased to meet you. I'll help you to the ambulance outside, and then we're off to hospital to get that cut seen to."

Lifting Mrs Seymour to her feet, he was about to help her out when she stopped him and turned to Jim

"You have been very kind, both of you, and I feel much better. I shall not forget how you have helped me, goodbye and thank you!" She walked gingerly out of the shop on the arm of the First Aid man.

Just after she went out, Elsie remembered she had not got the blouse. Thinking about it she knew none of hers would fit Mrs Seymour. Men didn't think about such things!

"Now what, Jim?" asked Elsie

Jim surveyed the shop with a sort of sadness. "To think I spent all afternoon putting stock on the shelves and tidying up! Now I'll have to start all over again!" Elsie thought about her own plans for Saturday.

"Look, Jim, I'm not doing anything over the weekend. Why not let me start tomorrow, or even this evening. I could get the shop looking clean and tidy for tomorrow." She looked at Jim. His face was white with the strain, and the terrible scarring on his face had turned bright red,. He was both stressed and tired out.

"Well, tell the truth, my head aches as usual when I do anything extra. I couldn't stay for long, but if you want to help, please do, and your employment starts now!" He grinned at her in a cheeky way. It only made his face more grotesque.

"Leave it to me." replied Elsie. "If you can just give me a quick run down on where the stock goes, I'll try and get things tidied, at least enough for Saturday, anyway. It will be a good learning exercise, as I shall find where most things go." She was quite excited at the thought of working in the shop.

Jim went round what was left on each shelf and cupboard, putting one item of each piece of stock in the correct place. It only took a few minutes. Then he turned to her

"That should help Elsie. Anything you aren't sure about put where you think fit. If the place is tidy and clean, we can open as usual. I'm sure customers will accept that we are not straight after today's bomb. Now, here is the shop key. The emergency repair teams will be round before dark to do temporary repairs, and make everything secure and weatherproof. Please see them when they come, and of course, they will fix up the flat as well. I have to go home now." He reached up to the cupboard that Elsie now knew held aspirins, and took a bottle.

"These should clear my head. See you in the morning. Telephone if you have any problems. Thanks for your help today, it was very much appreciated. I think we shall get on well!"

Elsie was left to try and put some semblance of order to the shop. The first task was to clear the floor, so she could sweep it up. Any stock she put to the places Jim had indicated, and in half an hour she had the floor swept clean and the oilcloth lightly mopped over. Next she went to each cupboard checking it would hold stock on each shelf, but not worrying about any doors that were damaged. It took her about an hour to get it looking acceptable for the time being. She was beginning to feel very tired, and at six o'clock, decided she had done enough. She sat down on the chair to rest. "I know" she said to herself. "A cup of tea!"

The back kitchen was still a mess, but she managed to sort out a cup, the rest of the milk, and made a pot of tea that she took into the shop and drank two cups while contemplating the day's events.

"Anyone at home!" called a rough voice.

"Why, "replied Elsie, "What d'you want?"

"Emergency Repair, here. Anything need doing?"

"Come in! Am I pleased to see you! The shop door needs fixing, and something must be done with the window frame to secure the shop for the night, and then there is my flat upstairs. I haven't even looked at that yet!"

A worn out looking young builder type entered the shop. "We'll do what we can, love. Are your electrics O.K.?" Elsie hadn't given it a thought. She had made the tea on the gas cooker.

"Don't know," she answered.

"O.K. dear, we'll check each room and also your flat. Come on Tom. Let's do here first, in case there's a problem. We can fix it before dark." Tom came in behind him. Tom was much older, and touched his cap politely to Elsie. "Evening ma'am, are you alright. Must have been a nasty shock!"

Elsie nodded and the two men went round checking the lights and sockets. This they did by the simple method of the young man licking his fingers and stuffing them in to each light socket, saying "Switch on!" Whereupon Tom moved the switch. "O.K., that's live!" called the young man and moved on to the next light.

Elsie watched in amazement. "Don't you get a shock?"

"Yes, that's how we know it's live!"

They went to the power sockets. Elise wondered if they would sue the same method! They didn't! The old man produced a plug and light bulb on the end of a flex, and tried each one in turn. In a few minutes they completed all the shop rooms, and Elsie took them through her front door, and left them, performing the same ritual in the flat. In about ten minutes they returned.

"All well! No problems we can see. Call us if you have any trouble. Come on Tom, next door now!" They were gone. A few minutes later, two more men arrived on a lorry loaded with plywood, battens and various paraphernalia. "Come to board up the shop and secure your door, Ma'am." Without a by your leave, they set about knocking out the broken door, removing the remnants of glass from the shop window, and filling the gaps with sheets of plywood that they cut to size and nailed up. The speed they moved was incredible. Elsie was soon left in the dark shop and had to use the lights. Upstairs now, and the same procedure again. Half an hour later the two premises were secure, watertight, and very dark!

She felt safe and more protected, and could now relax and went up to see what had happened in her flat!

The scene when she entered her living room was horrific to a neat tidy person like Elsie. She was really tired, and all she could do was toy with some of the bits on the floor, putting them so they did not block her walking through. Next, her bed upstairs. She realised she would have to make it possible to sleep in it. She took off the exposed eiderdown and sheets, shook them out of the window, and remade it as best she could.

The effort of completing this normally simple task seemed to drain the last drops of energy from her, so she laid down on her bed for a few moments rest before starting again. At least, she thought, I am safe and relatively sound. She lay back for a few seconds, put her head on the pillow and fell into a deep sleep.

****

Chapter 3

*H*er eyes were still closed, but already Elsie could hear the now dreaded sound of another doodle-bug coming over. As if to protect herself, she turned over and pulled the sheet right over her head. The V1 went on to London, as nearly all did, except the one yesterday! "Oh my God, I start work at nine, and the flat is in a terrible mess." She sat up and slid her feet out on to the mat by the side of the bed. She felt a gritty roughness, and a piece of something sharp hurt her toe. Staggering to her feet, she picked her way carefully across the room and looked out of the window. It was a perfect June morning. The birds were singing in the trees at the end of the garden. If it hadn't been for yesterday, all would have been well with the world. As it is, there is work to be done and now!

She didn't even bother to make her usual early morning tea, but instead, collected a soft broom from the cupboard in the kitchen, and started to sweep the dust, plaster, pieces of glass and debris of every concoction into a big heap in the centre of each room in turn. Taking her dustpan and brush, each pile was taken up and tipped into the unused coal scuttle. She was about to take it down to the dustbin when she realised she was still in her nightdress, so left it in the kitchen. She then spent half an hour working her carpet sweeper over every bit of floor in her flat. Only then was she satisfied enough to put the kettle on and make a pot of tea. She felt better now. Elsie was a clean and tidy housewife, and until the flat was ship-shape and pristine again, she would not be happy.

It came to her that she felt fine, full of vitality and no thoughts of Bill, or Brian. It obviously needed a crisis to shake her out of her depression! Suddenly she thought of Margaret and the interrupted telephone call when the bomb fell. Her sister would be worried, and waiting to hear from her. Quickly, she went to the 'phone and asked the operator for her number.

"Is that you, Elsie? Are you alright?" was her sister's greeting. "I have been thinking about you, and wondered what happened!"

"Yes" replied Elsie, "I'm fine, now, but it was a bit hectic yesterday. All the windows were blown out, and some ceilings were damaged. Jim went out to help, and came back with a lady who had been badly cut and shocked, and gave her First Aid. I helped, and had a quick start to my new career. Did I have time to tell you that I have been fired from the canteen, and start working for Jim in Shaw's this morning?"

"Well, that's a surprise! "commented Margaret, "I know you loved it working in the dairy, so perhaps it will suit you. Did Jim ask you or you him?"

"He heard I had lost my job at the camp, and waited until I returned from an interview for factory work which I declined, and he asked me in for a chat, and offered me work with him. It's more money too, so all in all, I think if we get on, it could be what I want."

Margaret felt a difference in her manner. "I must say you sound brighter than since Bill died. Perhaps this has been waiting for you!"

"I don't think so. To be honest, Margaret, the doodle bug has roused me from my depression. I actually believe, the crisis has done me good, and helping Jim makes me feel wanted again. D'you know, I have hardly thought of him or Brian, since these bombs started. Now, how are you? Is Arthur O.K.? "

"Yes, thanks, we are both fine. Arthur is terribly busy at

the Bank, and hopes to be appointed Manager shortly. His boss died a few weeks ago, and he thinks he has a good chance of taking over the position. It would be a raise for him because the Gravesend Branch is one of the biggest in this part of Kent."

"I hope he gets it, Margaret. He has worked hard, and deserves to move up." She didn't really believe it. Arthur, to her mind, had always been a steady rather then hard worker. She was sure, had Bill lived, he would have been high in Manor Dairies by now, as all the younger men had been called up, but it was not to be.

Arthur and Margaret lived very comfortably in a detached house on the outskirts of Gravesend. They never had any children, and being the elder sister, it was too late now. Still they were happy together, or so she believed, and that was the most important thing.

"Glad all is well with you. Margaret. Must go now, I have much to clear up before I start in the shop this morning. Call me when you have a minute. Bye."

Elsie stood for a moment before she put the receiver back. Arthur and Margaret had a very cosy life, and she often thought how lucky she was. But did Margaret ever see real life? Certainly Elsie did and knew she would be utterly bored being a middle class housewife doing the social round. Rough her life might be, but she liked it that way.

By the time she finished talking to Margaret, it was nearly eight thirty. She had a lot to get through before nine, and she rushed round the bedroom getting dressed, before starting to wipe off some of the dust lying on top of the furniture and china. She heard Jim arrive, and begin his morning routine, sweeping the shop front, and went down a few minutes before nine to start her first day as Shop Assistant at Shaw's the Chemist.

"Morning Elsie!" he greeted her. "Sleep alright? You looked really tired when I left yesterday evening, but you did an excellent job in the shop. We can open in a few minutes I think, and do any more clearing up still needed before the main rush starts."

"Thanks Jim," answered Elsie. "I slept like a log. All the excitement tired me out, and I fell into bed once I had the flat cleared up. Now, what do you want me to start with?"

Jim stopped sweeping and came into the shop. "Just tidy up, and dust off the tops of the counters. As soon as Joan comes in, she will show you where things are. In the meantime let me run through the working of the till, so you aren't embarrassed the first time someone buys something. I'm sure it is exactly like the one you used in the dairy."

So the day began. Soon after nine thirty Joan arrived, and then Elsie's tuition really began in earnest. Elsie was intelligent, and after a few customers had come and gone, she realised she was going to be good at this! By ten o'clock she was immersed in the shop, and Jim brought out a white coat so she now looked the part. She felt at home. Joan was really sweet to her, and commented that Jim seemed happier than of late.

"He has needed someone to assist him in the shop for ages. Can't think why he didn't take someone on before." She looked sideways at Elsie. "Perhaps he was waiting until he could get you!" She grinned, and Elsie didn't know if she was teasing or not!

After the first flush of customers, there was a lull. Then the first customer she knew personally came in. It was Mrs McIver, who lived in Church Road, just over the back of St Mark's Parade. She looked surprised to see Elsie behind the counter.

"Hallo, Mrs Winter, didn't expect to see you here! Are you helping out after the bomb?"

"Well, no, I've started to work here. Jim needed someone, and as I had finished my job at the Army Camp, he asked if I would like to join him!"

She often exchanged pleasantries with Mrs McIver either when they met in the High Street, or at church on Sunday mornings. She was an older lady, and 'a bit posh', but was always very kind to Elsie, and helped her a lot when Bill was killed. Elsie liked her, and knew her son was in N. Africa with the Desert

Rats. Her husband was a doctor, and they lived in a big house with a large garden.

"Can you have this prescription made up for me, my dear/" she asked.

"Yes, of course, Joan is already here. If you care to wait a moment, I'll see how long it will be."

She went into the dispensary and gave Joan the prescription. "How long will this be Joan?"

"Let me see." said Joan, looking down at the doctor's scribble. "I'll make it up now. Tell Mrs McIver she can wait. It will only be two minutes, or she can come in on her way home from the shops."

Elsie passed on the information to Mrs McIver. "That's fine, Elsie. I think I'll wait, and we can have a chat." She sat on the chair by the counter.

"Now, how is Brian? Have you had a letter from him recently? Gordon is in Cairo at the moment. He has been made up to Sgt Major, and moved to Headquarters. I don't know what he is doing, but he's been attached to some new outfit. He can't tell us what it is about, but he thinks he may come back to Blighty for training before long!" She obviously was itching to tell someone about him!

"That is good news, Mrs McIver. No, I haven't heard from Brian for over a week. He usually writes regularly, so I am a little worried. There will probably be a letter on Monday."

They continued chatting, until Joan came out with Mrs McIver's medicine. "There you are Mrs McIver. Take it as before. That'll be one and six, please." Mrs McIver handed Elsie the money, said goodbye to them both, and left the shop.

Elsie thought about Mrs McIver's son Gordon. He must be about the same age as her, and she always thought him a very handsome man. She wondered what he was like now he was older. They had met when he was in his teens and she was helping in the dairy shop. Perhaps she might see him if he was returning home soon. Mrs McIver for her part, was thinking about Elsie as

she walked along the High Street. Elsie was an attractive woman.
It was time she shook off the sadness from losing Bill. Time
she found another man! She really did look pretty in her white
chemist's coat, and many men would think the same! Jim, she
knew, had a soft spot for her, and always had, even when Bill was
alive. Her thoughts fell into place. No wonder Jim had employed
her. She would not only be a huge asset in the shop, but did he
have his eyes on her for more? Time would tell.

Around eleven thirty, Joan came out from the dispensary.
"Elsie, I am sorry. We usually have a cup of something at
eleven. D'you want to wait until lunch, or have something
immediately?"

"What time is lunch Joan?"

"We shut for a while at one o'clock, but if people try the door,
we restrict the break to half an hour. If not, we open again at
two."

"Let's wait until lunch break, Joan. What do you do usually?
I could make us a snack in the back, but would need to go out
and get some food first"

"Tell you what, Elsie. Why don't we split it in half? If you pop
out now and get some soup and some rolls, there is butter in the
kitchen, and we can eat for a while, and then I could show you
the ropes in the dispensary. Not that you can dispense anything,
but you would know how everything works and where I put made
up medicines etc."

"Good idea!" replied Elsie. "The more I learn, the more help
I'll be! I'll nip out now and get something nice for us!"

Elsie waited until Joan came out of the dispensary and came
to the counter. "Here's two shillings" said Joan, taking the money
from the till. "Get a receipt, and Jim will approve it." Elsie took
the florin Joan handed her, and went out into the High Street.
As usual she could hear a doodle bug somewhere in the area,
but ignored it. The sound died away, and a minute or so later she
heard the explosion as it hit the ground somewhere. Everyone
was getting quite blaze about them now, she thought. Unless it
has your name on it, it's somebody else's worry!

She went down the High Street across to the dairy and spoke to the girl behind the counter. It had expanded since she worked there with Bill. They stocked a far wider range of milk products and food, and it was always very fresh. Many things were home made. She loved the potato scones, and sometimes there were some 'under the counter items'. The girl, of course, knew she had worked there when Bill had been the Manager, and welcomed Elsie like an old friend.

"Hallo, Elsie, Haven't seen you for some time. Thought you would be at the canteen at this time of day?"

"No, Barbara, I finished there on Thursday. I have started at Shaw's today. Unless they can't stand me, I shall be working there until further notice!"

"Don't fancy coming back here do you?" joked Barbara

"Not unless Mr Farnes pays me enough!" laughed Elsie. "He'd have to out bid Jim's offer!".

Mr Farnes took over from Bill, and was a very go-ahead person. Elsie was not that keen on him, but then she was comparing him with her husband. No contest as far as she was concerned!

"Have you any cream and jam sandwiches, Barbara?" asked Elsie. She knew the dairy still had a few.

"Well, not officially" replied Barbara, "But for you I think I can find one! Wait a minute" She went to the back of the shop and returned with a cake box that Elsie knew contained a sandwich. They were one of the few luxuries still available at the dairy. Not real cream, of course, but delicious!

She returned quickly to the shop. Going straight in to the little kitchen, she made a pot of tea, sliced a loaf she found in the bread bin, ran up to the flat and took a tin of sardines, and in a few minutes had two plates of sardines on toast, with the sandwich to follow. That, and two apples she took from her fruit bowl, made their lunch. Not very luxurious, but they both enjoyed it. While they were eating, Elsie asked Joan about Jim.

"Why has Jim decided to employ an assistant now? He never had one before did he?"

"He did once." replied Joan. "But she was not very good, didn't seem to learn the job, and started to get off hand with customers. Jim told her off, and she immediately left and went to join the A.T.S. We haven't heard from her since. That was some months ago, now. You know, of course, that Jim gets headaches." Elsie nodded. "Just lately they have been getting worse and more frequent. Sometimes I have had to stay after my normal hours because he was forced to go home to rest. The aspirins he takes to deaden it don't appear to be working so well. I told him he must lighten his load and not spend all his time in the shop, and suggested he find another person to help. Then you became available – pardon the expression – and he asked me if I thought you would be any good. So here you are!

I wish I could be here all the time, but I have my family, and officially I only work from 10.30 to 3.00 making up prescriptions, while he does other jobs and serves. Lately I have been here all the time the shop is open, and my husband has warned me he'll make me leave if I don't get back to less hours. So, Elsie, it is all going to depend on you. Jim is not going to get better as far as I can see. What the future holds for him, I don't know. It is the pieces of shrapnel he has in his head that are causing the problem. I think one is moving, and causing a lot of pain!"

"Poor old Jim!" said Elsie. "I knew he had been badly wounded, and has suffered ever since Bill and I used to see him after darts matches, but didn't realise he was getting worse. I'll do what I can, so you can throw me in at the deep end. I think I shall love it here, so let's get on!"

Joan looked at the clock. "It's time we opened again. Jim has gone out for a while. You look after any customers who come in. Call me if you need any help!"

Elsie said "Of course Joan, and thank you very much. I see the situation now, and will do all I can to help!"

"I knew you would Elsie, We'll make a good team together!"

And so it turned out. In the next few weeks, Elsie learned all the essential details of running the shop, and with Joan's guiding hand when she got stuck, the shop prospered. Jim came in as much as he could, but left more and more to her as she became more confident in her ability to handle the small problems. What was even more pleasing to him was how the number of customers was increasing. Joan commented to him about it. Some of his friends and acquaintances remarked how pleasant Elsie was in the shop. Also, Elsie had many friends in the town who were transferring their custom once they knew she was working behind the counter.

About three days after Elsie joined Shaw's, Betty came in. She had heard Elsie was now working there. Elsie was in the dispensary talking to Joan when she heard someone call loudly "Shop!"

Betty was standing by the counter. "Hallo, Betty" greeted Elsie, "How are you? Did you take the job at Klingers?"

"I'll say I did!" Mr Perkins liked me, and took me on for the day shift. I work every day except Saturday. I think he has taken a fancy to me. He keeps coming over to chat when he passes the shop floor. The other girls think so, and say he has loads of money!"

"What about your fiancé?" asked Elsie pointedly.

"Douglas? Haven't heard from him since he went to sea again. Don't expect to until he returns to port." She was indignant. "I'm not doing anything I shouldn't."

Elsie knew Betty. "I should hope not! Don't even think about it with Douglas waiting for you back here!"

"Of course I won't" responded Betty. "Now, can I have some Milk of Magnesia, please, I keep getting indigestion. I think it's the food they serve in Klingers's canteen. Not nearly as good as we made at the camp!"

She obviously didn't like what Elsie implied, and handing over the correct money, turned on her heel and left the shop in a bit of a huff!

At 5.30, Joan helped Elsie to close the shop, and put the takings in a bag ready for Jim when he came back. He arrived soon after six, and knocked on Elsie's front door.

"Sorry I'm late Elsie. How was your first day? I told Joan I might be late back, so she asked you to take the money upstairs with you. I hope you didn't mind."

"Of course not Jim." replied Elsie. "Only too pleased to help. Here it is." She handed the blue bag containing the days takings and float to him.

"Thanks," said Jim taking it from her. "Did anything happen of importance?"

"No, I don't think so, Jim. Betty came in and I'm afraid I may have offended her a bit!"

"That doesn't worry me," said Jim. "She is a real fly-by-night, that girl! Been out with the whole of Sidhurst, or so her reputation goes!"

Elsie was taken aback. "I didn't know she had a reputation? Is it common knowledge?"

Jim quickly shut up. "Oh well, perhaps it's just a rumour I've heard, and I'm being unkind. Forget what I said, I may have got it wrong!"

Elsie didn't comment, and Jim walked to the door. "Hope you hear from Brian soon. Have a good day tomorrow. Doing anything special?"

"No" answered Elsie. "Will be off to church in the morning, and after that have a lazy day. It's been quite a week one way or another. I think a rest will do me good, and there is still much to be cleared in the flat."

"Yes," said Jim. "There are fewer V1's coming over now, but still enough to do plenty of damage. I hear the RAF have found a way of tipping them so they go down without even having to fire at them, and the Ack Ack are doing very well. Perhaps they will soon stop them. Still quite a worry, aren't they."

"Yes, I suppose so." replied Elsie. "Well, good night Jim, see you on Monday."

"Goodnight Elsie"

Elsie heard his feet plod down the stairs to the shop. Well, that was that until Monday.

On Sundays it was usual, if she had nothing planned, to go to church. The nearest to her was St Johns, and she could see the steeple from her flat. It was the local parish church where she had been attending about once a month since Bill died. After he was killed, the vicar came round to see her, quite uninvited, and gave her help and support. At the time nothing could soften the pain of her loss, and he became a regular visitor. As time passed, she felt that she should go to church for no other reason than to repay what he had given her, and to understand more of his faith. Her family were not church people, and so her first visit had also been curiosity.

The vicar, Reverend Greenwood, was a lot older than her, but she liked him. There were no frills or camouflage in his words. He spoke what he meant, and did not embroider the facts. Bill was dead. He made sure Elsie knew it, and didn't push her to move on until he knew she was ready. Going to church on Sunday morning was the first sign, and Robert Greenwood saw it. He gave thanks to God his parishioner was returning to life out of the chasm into which she had descended.

To start with, she prayed to God for Bill to remain close to her. Then later for his happiness in his new life, but now she also prayed for him to allow her to move on and start a new life. He would want her to live on, and it would make him happy whatever he was doing now. In addition, he would want her to see Brian came to no harm, and always had a home to return to. Elsie was returning to normality, and with God's help would soon look outwards again.

The morning service was the one she enjoyed, and she had made friends with some of the regulars. Mrs McIver was always there and this Sunday, as she walked in, beckoned Elsie to sit next to her.

"Good morning Elsie, Not too busy to come to church. You look a lot happier these days!" She whispered quietly.

"Thank you Mrs McIver. Yes I am. How are you? Have you heard from Gordon again yet?"

"No, but expect to this week. What about Brian, any news?"

" No" replied Elsie. "I hope to have some on Monday. I am due a letter from him."

No more was said, as the choir procession appeared, and both ladies concentrated on their devotions.

After the service, they walked slowly out of the church, shaking hands with Rev. Greenwood at the door.

"Glad to see you here again Elsie, I hear you are working for Jim Shaw now. I wish you could get him to come sometimes. It would help him, I'm sure!"

"Thanks, if I get the chance I will, but I doubt he will listen to me!"

"I'm not so sure, he thinks a lot of you, you know!"

The ladies continued walking together out of the church and along the road.

"How do you like Shaw's?" asked Mrs McIver. "Finding your feet? I'm sure you will be a terrific help to Jim! We need an independent chemist in Sidhurst. Otherwise all we have is Boots, and they already think they rule the roost! You could make a big difference, I know!"

"I like it very much so far. Joan has helped me enormously, and made me feel at home."

She didn't mention Jim. Mrs McIver was far too ready to talk about relationships, and Elsie was not having it. She was interested in her son, however, so returned the conversation in that direction.

"I know Gordon was in the territorials before the war. Does he intend to stay in when it's over?" she asked Mrs McIver.

"I don't think so. Although he is a Sergeant Major, he would need to take a commission for him to do that. Not much future for a non-com, unless he decides to make it his career. Who knows what all the conscripted men will do. There could be a lot of competition to stay in, or may be not? Who knows? What about Brian?"

Elsie thought for a moment. "No, don't think he will want to be a regular. He went in to do his bit and to avenge his father. He has done well to get a commission, but he will not want to stay in. He is only nineteen, you know. How can he tell what he wants to do with his life at his age!"

Mrs McIver nodded in agreement. "They grow up very fast. Next time you see him you will find he is an adult with a mind of his own. That's what I found with Gordon, and he was only a Sergeant then, and Brian is already a lieutenant!"

Elsie was not so sure whether she liked the thought of Brian having a mind of his own. "We'll just have to wait and see when he comes home. One thing's for sure, He will take care of me, if he can. It was his solemn promise the day he joined up!"

Still Elsie had not got the information she wanted. "When did you say Gordon was coming?"

Mrs McIver looked at her. "I didn't. If I read correctly between the lines of his last letter, in about three weeks. Why?"

Elsie made quickly to reply innocently. "It is such a long time since I last saw him, and I remember him from when we went to school together. It would be lovely to renew our friendship."

"Yes, and I'm sure he would think the same." Mrs McIver thought Elsie would make a very suitable wife for Gordon. Neat, intelligent, well turned out, and very loyal. Just what he needed!

They reached the McIvers' house and Mrs McIver turned in towards the gate. "It's been a pleasure to chat on such a lovely morning, Elsie, and no doodle bugs! I'll tell Gordon you asked after him. Goodbye."

"Goodbye Mrs McIver, my best wishes to Tom." She wanted to make sure she mentioned her husband.

She walked back to her flat thinking about Gordon McIver. She wondered again what he was like. His father was tall and good looking. If Gordon was the same it would be a pleasant experience meeting him again.

On the way home, instead of going straight around the corner and on to St Marks' Parade, she went across the High Street, down Craybrooke Road, turned right along Rectory Lane to where the doodle bug had landed on Friday. All was quiet now, except for two Rescue men still working to clear up the mess. Three houses no longer existed. Where they had been was a heap of rubble. Who had lived there, she wondered? Surely she ought to remember. All the fronts were the same Victorian façade, semi-detached terraces. Then it came to her. At number 11 lived a dear old lady. Then, next to her a family of three small children with their mother. Their father was away in the Navy, and in the third lived an elderly couple. He was very nice, and often used to talk to her on her way to school, and later when she worked in the dairy.

"Hallo, Elsie!" said a voice interrupting her thoughts.

It was Mr Culley who owned the sweet shop at the end of St Mark's Parade. He did a roaring trade before the war, and she still bought her sweet ration from him.

"Hallo Stan! What a lovely day. How are you? D'you know what happened to the people in the houses?"

Mr Culley looked sad. "Two of the children were killed, also the older couple, but the old lady was in the cupboard under the stairs and rescued without a scratch. Sad about the children. The youngest lad is O.K., but still in hospital, and his Mother with him. They have put her in the next bed to him. Both will be O.K. Their father is expected home as soon as he gets back to Portsmouth."

Elsie remembered immediately. Betty had said that her fiancée was on the same boat. Not a happy return for him.

"What about you, Stan? Shop alright?"

"Patched up, just like Jim's. How's your flat?"

"The same. We were lucky by the look of these houses. Let's hope they will soon stop."

Mr Culley finished the conversation. "Sorry, Mrs Winter, must go. My lunch is early today. See you again soon!"

"Goodbye Mr Culley" said Elsie. I must make some lunch for myself, she thought. Then, I know, I'll pop into the Black Horse. I pass it on my way home, and see if I can get something to eat there. If I can, it will save my rations a bit. She was not sure if she would be successful. She hadn't booked, and restrictions meant they only served a few lunches each day. Anyway it was worth trying!

Rather than go straight into the Dining Room and try her luck, she went first into the Private Bar and walked up to the counter. She knew it was not seemly to go unescorted into the Saloon, although she much preferred it. "May I have glass of cider, please" she asked the barman.

"Of course" She waited while he opened a new bottle and poured out a glass for her.

"That will be four pence please, Madam" he requested as he passed the glass.

She gave him sixpence, waited for the change and walked to one of the easy chairs, sat down and sipped her drink. There was nobody else in the Bar.

"D'you think there is any chance of having some lunch here?" she asked him.

"Just a moment Madam. I'll go and find out." He left the Bar and went through to the Dining Room. Meanwhile Elsie sat up and realised she could see through to the Saloon Bar from her chair. Sitting up at the counter was a tall man and sitting next to him with her arm touching his as if by accident, was Betty! She looked again and the man turned a little and she was flabbergasted to see it was Mr Perkins from Klinger's! Gosh, she thought, Betty didn't waste much time! But what about Douglas, her Navy fiancé? At that minute the barman returned.

"Yes Madam, you are in luck. A couple who booked have not arrived, so if you care to come into the Dining Room as soon as you've finished your drink, they will serve you immediately."

"Thank you very much, just two minutes and I'll come straight in." replied Elsie.

Mr Perkins and Betty were still talking and looking straight into one another's eyes. Elsie decided she must make a protest. Finishing her drink, she got up and walked slowly through the connecting passage, passed the door to the Saloon, and on to the Dining Room. As she reached the door, she saw Mr Perkins and Betty facing her.

"Hallo Betty! Fancy seeing you here, and with Mr Perkins! How's Douglas? On leave shortly?"

Betty started to say something. "Can't stop now Betty. They're waiting to serve my lunch. See you soon. Bye"

She carried on to the Dining Room. The atmosphere she left behind you could cut with a knife She could still feel it coming through the door! Betty had some explaining to do!

The lunch was just about eatable. It was just a tiny piece of real beef, and two thin slices of the tinned variety. The vegetables were cabbage and two small boiled potatoes. She had jelly and imitation cream for sweet. It served it's purpose, and she left for home knowing she need not worry about food again until teatime. Meanwhile her thoughts were about what she had seen in the Saloon Bar. Mr Perkins must have almost asked her out at the interview!

Funny, she thought, there have been no doodle bugs today, not that I have noticed anyway! She walked along the High Street and it was a lovely warm Sunday afternoon. As she pattered happily along the road, two people passed the time of day before she was back at her flat and upstairs making a cup of tea in the kitchen. As the water boiled, she heard the now familiar sound again, and a V1 hurried over, it's engine going full blast. No worry there then!

After tea she went down to the little back garden, carried an easy chair out from the shop, and sat enjoying the afternoon sun in the sheltered grassy patch by the Anderson shelter. It was warm, and gradually she fell into a doze as the time passed. She was woken by the ringing telephone in her flat through the open window,. "Who's that!" she said to herself.

Rousing herself, she ran lightly up the iron staircase to answer. She might have guessed. It was Betty!

"Hallo, Elsie, Betty here, I must speak to you to explain."

"Hallo, Betty. No need. You were having a drink with Mr Perkins, weren't you?"

"Er, well, yes" responded Betty. "He just suggested we might have a drink as he was in Sidhurst on Sunday morning. That's all!" she sounded embarrassed.

"Yes, I understand no need to make excuses. What you do is up to you. How is Douglas, by the way?"

"Oh, he's alright, still at sea. It's no good Elsie, I know you disapprove. But there is no harm in having a quick one with Mr Perkins. He is so gorgeous, you know!"

Elsie had other ideas about the spivy Mr Perkins, but knew she had caught Betty out.

"No, I don't know Betty. What you do is no concern of mine. I'm sure he does not mean any harm, but do be careful. I must go and make some tea now. Bye!"

She put the phone back. Betty was incorrigible. Anything in trousers would do. He looked a slick sort who would take advantage of her, but then didn't they all? And didn't Betty ask for it? One day she would take a tumble, and it was no good coming to Elsie for help. She had warned her enough times in the years they had been friends. No wonder Jim's comment.!

****

Chapter 4

$\mathcal{O}$ver the next few weeks, Shaw's the Chemist occupied Elsie's life to the full. By the end of June she felt she had more or less mastered the products, identified the many customers, and settled happily into her new life. She was getting on well with Jim, and except for his moods when he had one of his headaches, she liked him very much. He was kind, fun to chat with, and her presence seemed to lighten up the dispensary on Tuesday and Thursdays when he was usually in the shop.

A letter from Brian arrived on the Monday after the embarrassing encounter with Betty, and he was well. There was little mention of what he was doing rather more about his concern for her. He had heard about he V1 attacks on London, and worried she was alright. She sat down and sent off a reassuring letter, also telling him about working with Jim.

She had met Betty since, and the episode was never mentioned. They had gone to the cinema a couple of times, and apart from saying that Douglas would be on leave for a week soon, the episode with Mr Perkins was forgotten, except that Joan mentioned she had seen Betty in Woolworths talking to a tall man in a dark pin stripe suit. That will be him, she thought to herself!

Early July brought a spell of particularly warm summer weather, and on the first Thursday, being early closing, all three sat in the back garden enjoying a cup of tea after closing, before they went their various ways home. Jim had planted a few flowers early in May, and now coming into flower, they made the little garden quite pretty. Elsie had suggested the idea of a small tea party on Wednesday, and had spent some time making a few scones, and had got out a jar of her own gooseberry jam – Brians's favourite. Elsie looked at Joan and Jim and thought how pleasant it was. Jim drank up his first cup of tea, and she noticed Joan too had an empty cup.

"Another cup, Jim?" she asked, "and how about you Joan, manage another?"

As she poured Jim's refill, she heard the all too familiar noise of a V1 in the distance, approaching. They all ignored it, and Elsie noticed it was getting nearer and the sound increasing. No one moved. Elsie finished filling Jim's cup, and began to put milk into Joan's while she held it out.

The doodle bug came on rapidly and then silence! With one movement they all looked up at it, and sat in silent fascination as it glided nearer, lower, nearer again, until it just cleared the line of elm trees. They held their breath waiting for what seemed inevitable disaster! By now they could see every detail, the stubby wings, the cigar shaped piece in front of the tail, and the lethal nose housing the bomb. As it came on they could hear the low hissing of the wind passing round it. Elsie sat mesmerised. With a violent jump Jim unfroze.

"Get down!" he shouted, pushing Elsie to the ground, with Joan almost on top of her. From the grass, she watched as the flying bomb seemed to lift a little, then glided on, right over the roof above her flat not clearing it by more than a few feet! As quickly as it came it had gone! They sat up waiting for the explosion that was certain to follow! For several seconds, not a sound, then 'woomf', it had hit somewhere near. Elsie ran up the stairs to her flat as the blast from the explosion rattled the covered windows, and watched as the now all too familiar fountain of black and grey smoke billowed above the shops the other side of the High Street. Jim was close behind.

"My God, that was a close one Elsie!" he looked shocked and pale. "Where d'you think it hit?"

"Just beyond Craybrooke, by the look of the smoke."

"Went further than I thought." said Jim. "Probably because the ground falls away after St Mark's Parade. It glided more than we expected before hitting. Come on we must see if they need any help!"

They both ran down the front stairs. "Keep an eye on the shop, Joan. We'll be back as soon as we can!"

They ran across the High Street, and round the corner to see where it had landed, but it was further away than they realised. In fact, it had gone as far as Priestlands Park Road, only a quarter of a mile from Sidhurst Station. Later Elsie was told that Arthur Seymour, a first would war veteran and a friend of Bill's, and his wife had been killed. Like Elsie, they had been sitting in their garden having tea. It must have landed on them. They never had a chance. It was on them, gliding quietly, and destroyed their lives. They never knew what hit them!

Jim and Elsie did not continue, and after pausing for breath for a minute or so, walked back feeling a little shocked, to rejoin Joan who was now in the shop. While telling her what had happened, they closed down again, and Joan went off home. Elsie and Jim sat for a further hour or more drinking a second pot of tea and recovering from the fright! As Jim said "It was a near thing!" Much nearer, and it would be them! A sobering thought. Elsie felt more uneasy than she had done since the V1's first came over. Please God, she thought, make them stop sending these terrible things over!

In fact, the Priestlands Park incident proved to be the last V1 to explode in Sidhurst. The new Tempest fighters could catch the V1's. They were flying alongside, and placing their own wings beneath the flying bomb's wing, lifting it and tipping the V1 over so it immediately spiralled down and crashed in the countryside well away from houses. As a result, very few were getting thought the defences. Just when Elsie was really becoming afraid, the menace was nearly over!

A few mornings later, Mrs McIver came into the shop. "Morning, Elsie, another lovely day by the look of it!" She was obviously in a good mood.

"Haven't come to buy anything, but to tell you that Gordon will be home within the week. I don't know exactly when, but he is already in England. He 'phoned me to say he was home, just landed apparently."

"That is marvellous news, Mrs McIver. I hope he will visit the shop.!" said Elsie.

"I'll make sure he does, my dear! If necessary I shall send him shopping for me and put Shaw's on the list! Now, you must call me Elizabeth. I already call you Elsie, and I enjoy our talks so much."

Elsie was very happy, and she really liked Mrs McIver. "Yes, I will, and thank you." She felt privileged. Not many people were allowed to address her by her Christian name!

"Now, I must go." said Elizabeth. "I have not got Tom's lunch yet, and he said he would be home today. I'll pop in again when I know the date Gordon will be home. Goodbye!"

Off she went leaving Elsie feeling a twinge of excitement, but why? What was so special about Gordon McIver? She hadn't looked at another man since before she was married and now, suddenly, this man, who she hardly knew was stirring her. How silly!

Jim came into the shop. "Hallo Elsie, all quiet so far?"

"Yes, only Mrs McIver, and she only wanted to chat for a few moments. Did you know Gordon is coming home almost immediately? She told me just now."

Jim of course had known Gordon since he was a lad, and as the son of one of Sidhurst's wealthier residents made it his business to cultivate the family.

"That is good news. He's been out in N. Africa since the beginning. I expect he is a very hard-bitten soldier by now. Sgt Major, isn't he?"

Elsie thought about how he might look. "Yes, he is apparently home for a while on a course, although Mrs McIver couldn't, or didn't, know what for. Maybe it is OCTU, he deserves it!"

"I doubt it" said the knowledgeable Jim. "Not often non-commissioned officers are made up, and when they are it is usually a field appointment because they have done something exceptional."

At that point the conversation ended as a customer came in the door, and started examining the soap display Elsie had completed that morning.

"Good morning," Elsie greeted her, "Can I help you? You know that soaps are now becoming more plentiful, do you?"

"No, I didn't." said the lady. "Have you any of the new scented types that are being advertised in the papers?"

"Only one brand so far" answered Elsie. "It's Mrs Jamieson, isn't it?"

"Yes, that's right." She looked pleased at being recognised. "I'll try a bar anyway. Good morning Mr Shaw." Jim had looked in from the dispensary.

"Nice morning, Mrs Jamieson. Good to see you again! Is Elsie looking after you alright?"

"Yes thanks" replied Mrs Jamieson. "She is always helpful. A real asset to Shaw's, she is!"

Elsie smiled. "That's very kind of you to say so!"

"Well you are. A real tonic it is to come here. See you again soon" She went out of the shop with her purchases in the bag handed to her by Elsie with her change.

Jim stayed and chatted for a minute..

"There is no doubt Elsie, you are bringing in more customers. People are getting to know you are here, and it's making a difference!"

Elsie was delighted. She felt life had a purpose again, and she enjoyed what she was doing.

A few days later she heard from Joan that Elizabeth McIver had come in and told her to tell Elsie she had heard from Gordon, and he would be home next week.

About ten days later, towards the end of July, Elsie had just drunk her morning coffee with Jim when the door bell tinkled, and a tall fair haired handsome man, about Elsie's age came up to the counter. He was broad, had a rich brown suntan, and Elsie couldn't help thinking how attractive he is. She felt herself going pink in the face as she said "Good morning."

"I've come for Mrs McIver's tonic." he said. "Oh, by the way, I'm Gordon, her son. She said to mention it to you, and ask if you would like to come to tea on Thursday."

Elsie felt her knees weakening. He was so attractive. She reached up to get the tonic from the shelf where made up prescriptions were kept. It was quite high, and she had to stand on tip toe to get it.

"Here, let me!" said Gordon McIver, and moving to her side, reached over her shoulder and took down the package. "Is this the one?" he asked.

He was standing right over her, so close it made her knees weak.

She managed to gasp "Thank you, that's the one." He gave it to her. Elsie recovered her composure as she put it in a bag for him.

"Thank your Mother very much. Yes, I would love to come to tea." she replied. "I'm Elsie, by the way. Your Mother said you would be coming home on leave soon. Tell her I'm looking forward to it. Did you say Thursday this week?" In her confusion she had already forgotten the day.

"Yes, that's right." He was looking at her, and smiling. "I shall really look forward to having tea together -'til Thursday then!"

Of course, once he had gone, she came to her senses. What on earth was she doing, a forty plus lady, accepting a date from a man she had not seen for over ten years. But he was rather gorgeous, and why not? It's time she started to mix again, and he was the son of a well known local family. She would talk to Bill about it tonight, and obtain his approval before finally accepting on Monday!

She began to recognise most customers by name as they entered the shop, but one youngish man had her puzzled. She asked Joan about him.

"Joan, I don't know if you've noticed, but we seem to be getting busier"

"Yes, I agree," answered Joan, "I am definitely getting more prescriptions to make up. Many are from new customers, and I even had one of Mr McIver's colleagues in last week, and I'm sure it's because you are in the shop, Elsie. Jim is a nice man, but I always felt he put customers off because of his appearance. As a result, we had our regulars, but very few new ones. Now, we are expanding, and getting our proper share. Long may it continue!"

"Joan," asked Elsie, "there is one thing I wanted to ask you about"

"What's that?" answered Joan, "I have noticed that sometimes a young man comes in, looks a bit taken aback when he sees me, buys a trivial item and goes out. Sometimes he returns a bit later and buys another. So why didn't he buy it the first time?"

Joan burst out laughing. "You ninny! What he hoped was that Jim would be behind the counter. He wanted to buy a French letter, but was too embarrassed to ask a lady assistant!"

Elsie blushed. "How silly of me! Why don't we place them near the door, and put the price large enough to be seen easily. Then they can help themselves, have the right money ready, hand it over and go!"

"Good idea" answered Joan. "And it will save embarrassment too! You'll have to get used to it. There are far more embarrassing products you'll be asked for!" She did not enlighten Elsie, who did not ask what they were. In her innocence, she realised she still had a bit to learn.

Two days later, Mrs McIver visited the shop to leave a prescription.

"Gordon was very taken with you, Elsie. I know it although he didn't say anything. What did you do?"

"Nothing Elizabeth, as far as I know. But I'm looking forward to seeing him a again on Thursday. He is a very attractive man"

Mrs McIver said nothing.. "I will send Gordon in tomorrow to collect the medicine." "Yes, I'm sure it will be ready. Jim will make it up this afternoon." replied Elsie.

"Thanks very much Elsie, see you Thursday, about four if that's suits you?"

"Yes, that will be fine, thank you."

Elizabeth McIver smiled and left the shop.

After the shop closed Elsie had nothing planned, and spent the evening making herself a proper supper. She had not had a decent meal for some time. Not since she started working in the shop. She was always making a quick snack, and rushing back downstairs to work. This lunchtime she went to the butcher and spent a whole week's ration on a small lamb joint. She soon had it prepared and in the oven, peeled a few potatoes, and a fresh cauliflower to go with it. A small pot of her own mint sauce completed her repast. While the oven did it's work, she sat down for a rest, prior to putting on the vegetables, and listened to the six o'clock news reporting the advances being made in France, and how well the RAF were dealing with the V1's. She realised there hadn't been one over for some time.

The telephone rang. It was Betty.

"Hallo, Elsie, how are you?"

"I'm fine Betty, how's the new job going?"

"Well at first it was boring, and I suppose it still is really, but I have a new boy friend.!"

Elsie was appalled, but not surprised after the pub encounter. Betty carried on.

"It's Ron Perkins, you know, the man who interviewed me and you saw in the Black Horse. Soon after I started, he began talking to me at work, and got me transferred to the day shift. He asked me to go out some time ago, but I refused. About a week later, he asked me again, and we went out together. I like him, and he certainly knows how to look after a girl. He says he is going to see I get a better job in Klingers when there is a vacancy in the office."

Elsie was disgusted, "What about Douglas, Betty? Forgotten him already? Have you written to him, and had a reply?"

"Oh, he's at sea still. I shan't hear from him until he's back at Portsmouth. Who knows, he may never come back. You know what the war is!"

Elsie could stand it no longer. "Betty, you are quite disgusting and extremely disloyal. You should be ashamed of yourself! Why on earth did you become engaged to Douglas if you weren't serious? What will happen when he comes home and expects you to marry him, because that is what he will be dreaming about!"

There was silence at the other end. Betty did not know how to reply and Elsie thought she had rung off.

"I'll have to write to him and tell him our engagement is off!" she replied, sheepishly.

"I'm absolutely sure you must!" said Elsie firmly."Even so you are being very unkind, but better that than keeping him dangling. I hope he gets the letter soon, and not after a long trip away when he gets back to England again. I feel every sorry for him, and you have been very casual about the whole relationship!"

Betty became annoyed. "Oh well, if that's how you feel, I won't talk to you about it again. See you some time."

Elsie heard the receiver put down and Betty had gone.

Elsie felt totally disgusted and it was only the smell of her dinner cooking that broke her ill temper with her friend. Poor Douglas! He might not be her idea of a husband, but Betty should have thought more about the whole thing before committing herself. Elsie knew it was far too quick at the time, and she had been proved right!

Still distressed for Donald's sake, she sat down and ate her dinner, to which she was looking forward. She could not get Betty's treachery out of her mind, until without warning, her brain turned to Gordon McIver. He really is an attractive man.! As she washed up the crocks, she found herself thinking about him and when they would next meet. It was tomorrow. He was coming to the shop again, but why not? She was free, not committed to anyone, and surely she had been in mourning long enough. She would consult with Bill tonight and see what he thought!

After she had cleared up, she went to bed to read, still thinking of Gordon. The more she thought of him the more her infatuation with him grew. She must see him again. For a while she tried to concentrate on Bill, but he seemed to be moving further away, and remote from the present time. Suddenly she knew he would not mind, and as she fell asleep her last thought was of him, and that he would not want to stand in her way if the right man came along. In the night she dreamed of him again, and he reached out to her, his face close to hers as it always used to be when they were in bed together. She asked for his permission to see Gordon, and he laughed. "I'll always be here, Elsie, but you have a life to live, mine is gone. Enjoy it while you can. It will make me happy to watch you and I'll make sure you pick the right one if you decide on a new husband!"

She woke in the morning with her mind freer than it had been for three years. Bill approved, and she would dress up for Gordon and see what happens!

As she got up, she laid out her best white dress with a lacy low neck top and found a slimming skirt to go with it. Under her clean white coat it would show just enough to interest him. Then she had a fit of conscience! "Was she being too forward?" Well it was a long time since she had set out to attract a man. She was out of date. So be it. If he was the wrong one, she would soon find out.

With all her preparations, she was late going down to the shop, and Jim was already sweeping the front in his customary manner.

"Good morning, Elsie! You look very smart today. Is there something special on?"

"No, Jim, I just felt like dressing up this morning. I hope you approve."

"Why yes, Elsie." he answered. "You always look neat and tidy, but I must say how young and pretty you look in that outfit!"

Elsie blushed with pleasure and embarrassment. She had not meant to impress Jim, but she obviously had, as he didn't usually comment on her appearance. She hastily donned her spare clean coat from the shop and when she came out to the front again, Jim was in the dispensary busy working on last evening's prescriptions.. Mrs McIver's was already on the shelf behind the counter. She settled down to wait Gordon McIver's appearance, collecting the medicine for his mother.

Just after eleven she was tidying up the top shelf when she heard a customer enter, and looking down saw it was him! As she went to jump down, he caught her hand to steady her. "Caught you, Elsie Winter! What were you up to on that top shelf again?"

Elsie felt her knees giving way as he held her hand and took her weight for the small jump to the floor. His gesture had been quite unnecessary, and deliberate, and she felt her face reddening again.

"Thank you Mr McIver. That was very kind of you, but quite needless. I am well used to clambering up and down from the shelves!"

"You never know what might happen, Elsie, and just look at you, pretty as a picture. I've just got to confirm our date. You will come out with me, won't you?"

Elsie was stricken with conscience again and almost refused, although why she couldn't think. As it was just what she was hoping for. He continued.

"I am only home for a few weeks at the most. Please help me to make the most of the short time I have at home. How about going up to London tonight to a show and some dinner? I can get tickets this afternoon. I think The Crazy Gang are on somewhere."

He had conquered her, and she began to laugh. "You don't give a girl much chance to refuse, do you! But yes, I would love to go. What time shall I be ready?"

Gordon stopped, amazed. "I never thought you'd say 'yes'. My luck is changing at last. Could you meet me outside the station at six thirty?. I have a lot to get through before then, otherwise I would have collected you from your flat."

"That will be lovely, Gordon. I will see you there. Now, don't forget the medicine for your Mother, or had you forgotten about it?! She teased him and he grinned.

"No, if I forgot, Mother would send me back again like a small boy. Still it would have given me a reason to talk to you again!" He was as cheeky as before and she liked him better all the time. He was so fresh and happy. His personality lifted her, and she felt twenty three again!

Holding the medicine, he left with a quick wave saying. "Six thirty, don't forget!" and went out closing the door. For a few moments she stood and tried to calm herself. It was the first time she had been out with a strange man for over twenty years, and her mind was in turmoil. "What should she wear? What would he expect if he took her to supper as he promised? As another customer came in it took her some seconds to realise the man was looking at her in an odd manner, as he said. "Are you serving, lady?"

"Oh yes." She answered. "Sorry, I was miles away!"

She found what he wanted and after he left was able concentrate on what she needed to do before she left for the station

The first thing to ensure was the time she had to leave to

give herself an hour at least to get ready. So when Jim came out of the dispensary she asked him

"Jim, I need to finish early tonight. Is that O.K.?"

"Of course, Elsie," he replied. "There is not a lot to do. I shall finish just after lunch, so we will shut on the dot, and we can both have an early evening."

"Thanks, Jim, I have a lot to do, and it will help."

Jim looked at her curiously. He had not seen her look so animated before, and he wondered why. He didn't ask, it was not his way.

He was as good as his word, and just after five announced to Elsie he had finished the dispensing, and might as well get off home, unless there was anything more to do that required his help. Elsie assured him there was not, and he just said. "Alright, then I'm off. See you in the morning. Goodnight, don't forget the blind before you go."

Elsie was left and waited impatiently for the half an hour until half past five so she could start preparing for her date with Gordon. At twenty past she could stand it no .longer, closed up, drew the blind, and locked the door. Sharp at half past she was upstairs making her preparations.

She was in such a dither it took her some minutes to collect her thoughts. Eventually she decided to have a bath, and while it was running, laid out what she would wear. Was it to be a dress? Blouse and skirt again, or a suit? She still had one from when Bill was alive, and had used her clothing coupons on everyday items. She decided on a dress. It would be hot in the theatre, and so she selected a short sleeve blue and white print, that was a favourite. Combining this with the best stockings she could find – she didn't have any of the new nylons, that were being talked about, she picked her only and best court shoes, and dusted them off. Underwear was a problem, and picking out a light cotton bra, knickers and a cotton slip to ensure she did not allow anything to show she shouldn't on a first date, went in and ran a cool bath.

At a quarter past six, she was dressed and ready, and examined herself minutely in the long mirror by her bed. She appeared neat and tidy, and younger than her years. Then without warning, a huge spasm of nerves hit her.

"What was she doing? About to go on a date with a man she hardly knew, and she a widow of over forty years! She must be out of her mind and knew what she must do!" Her courage had failed her, and she sat down in her armchair fully resigned to undress, and settle back for a quiet evening. At that instant, the front door bell rang.

"Who can that be? I'm not expecting anyone!"

"She tripped down the stairs, opened the door and asked curtly "Yes, what d'you want?"

"Hallo Elsie" said Gordon's voice, "Are your ready? I got through the chores earlier than I expected, so had time to come and collect you!"

Her manner changed abruptly/

"Oh it's you. I'm just about ready. Give me a minute while I collect my coat." She turned and ran back up the stairs, all doubts forgotten.

Gordon looked the perfect escort. He was wearing a blue blazer with a badge that Elsie did not recognise, had an immaculate pair of grey flannels, and light brown shoes. His tanned face set off a smart white shirt and tie. Elsie felt on air!

Taking her arm, he took her gently out through the door, that she pulled carefully shut, and together they walked along the pavement to the bus stop. Elsie had not done anything like this for years, and she felt nervous, but knew she was going to enjoy the evening and her handsome escort – Gordon!

Gordon had arranged the evening perfectly. Once at Charing Cross, he didn't make for the underground, but called a cab and they set off for the London Palladium. On the way up to town, Gordon remarked how well her dress suited her, and had been most charming, saying how pretty she looked and that he seemed much too old for her. She knew he must be several years older, but did not say anything, just enjoyed the compliments, and chatting with him. As they left the taxi his hand lightly held her waist for a second, and again she felt her knees weaken at his touch. "Please, Gordon, don't do that!" she thought, "Or I shall have difficulty walking!"

The theatre was only about half full, probably because of the doodle bugs, or so Gordon surmised, and he was probably correct. Those who were there were nearly all servicemen, many in uniform. She mentioned it to him, and wondered if he would have worn his, but he said very firmly "Plenty of time to wear that, but not on leave, I want to forget all about the war tonight!" He apologised there were no chocolates, and they soon found the seats he had booked in the dress circle. They sat down to enjoy the performance. Elsie had not been to a theatre of any sort since before Bill died, and she was soon laughing at the jokes, funny costumes and capers the performers were putting over. Gordon laughed occasionally, and as the show progressed, Elsie found herself almost in tears of laughter. Some of the jokes were decidedly 'blue' but this was no time to appear shocked, so she just laughed all the more! She could see Gordon was slowly unwinding, and starting to join in. As the second half began, she realised he was laughing at and with her, and it was she who was giving him pleasure. It was a compliment to her, and for the first time in many years, she felt relaxed and happy as she had always been in the years before the war.

The show finished, and just after ten, they sauntered out of the theatre and on down towards Charing Cross. When they reached Lyons Corner House, Gordon without asking, simply guided them to the left down the stairs and into the Brasserie, where she could hear an orchestra playing. A rather old and decrepit waiter met them. "Good evening Madam, Sir, table for two?" He led them over to a small table just to the side of the band. "Not this one" said Gordon "over there, please!"

The waiter found another table more to the side. "This will do fine." said Gordon, and they took their seats.

"I thought this would be better as we can talk." he said "Yes, that's true" replied Elsie. "D'you know I'm just starting to feel a little tired. I've had a lovely time!"

"Of course, you have been at work all day," said Gordon. "Why don't we just have a light snack, and then make for home. We ought to be able to catch a train before eleven."

"Thank you, Gordon, that would be ideal!"

They sat together and ate a small salad, followed by coffee. Elsie found herself listening to him relating some of his life, and past travels. He had spent time abroad and was very interesting, being a good storyteller. When Elsie asked about his wartime experiences, he said nothing. "I'm afraid I can't tell you about that!" he replied. "Still secret – maybe one day!"

Elsie dropped the subject. They finished their coffee in silence. Gordon paid the bill, and they walked up the stairs and along the Strand to the station. On the way Gordon held Elsie's arm, and continued as they sat on the platform waiting for the train to Sidhurst to arrive. Elsie did not object, and when he put his arm around her waist on the walk up from Sidhurst station to the High Street, she let it remain for a few minutes before tactfully pushing it away. Not too much the first evening!

When the reached Shaw's she said to him "Gordon, I have had a most wonderful evening, and enjoyed it more than I could have ever believed. Thank you very much indeed. I shall see you the day after tomorrow for tea at your house with your Mother. Until then, goodnight, and I hope we can meet again soon."

"Goodnight, Elsie" replied Gordon, and with a quick movement gathered her into his arms and kissed her firmly and with tenderness. She gasped with a mixture of feigned surprise and pleasure, and to his amazement kissed him back, with her arms round his neck, before letting him go and pushing him away. She opened her front door and said softly "Goodnight Gordon, until next time."

She shut the door behind her before he could see her knees were weak again, and she knew that if she had not escaped at that instant, she would have been back in his arms and whatever might befall!

She did not sleep very well. She had loved every moment of the evening and as for Gordon, her thoughts were overwhelming. She lay awake until nearly five o'clock before she found enough composure to settle down in a brief sleep until daylight.

In the morning she managed not to be late for the shop and although Jim had already opened, it was only five to nine when she joined him at the counter. He looked at her curiously as he wished her "Good morning" She wondered what had caused his look!

"You look happy this morning, Elsie,. Did you have a good evening?"

Without thinking she began to enthuse about the theatre and Gordon, pouring out details of the show, the meal, and how much she liked Gordon. In the middle of her flow she caught the look on Jim's face. He was not pleased, and she realised with embarrassment that she had done something wrong, but what?

Jim didn't reply and turned away from her to go into the dispensary. "Can't stop and chat" he said curtly. "I have too many prescriptions to make up this morning!" She knew it was a lie and he had deliberately cut her short, but why?" Somewhat subdued, she went to the counter and started to clean off the overnight dust from the polished counter surface until it was gleaming again.

It was not until several hours later that it occurred to her that Jim was jealous! How could she have been so unfeeling! Poor Jim. He probably never went out with a lady, and she had been, babbling on in front of him about the fantastic time she had with Gordon. No wonder he had beaten a hasty exit! Some time she must suggest to him to take her out somewhere. In the meantime however, Gordon was everything, and she could hardly wait until Thursday when she was going to tea at the McIver's house.

About ten o'clock, a V1 came over, quite low as usual, and she heard the engine falter, then stop! As she waited for the explosion she realised she had not heard one for ages. Had they stopped, or hadn't she heard them? She would ask Jim in their break. She hoped it was the former, as when one came over now, she experienced an uneasy feeling in her stomach. She guessed everyone did, although it was never mentioned. Typical of the English, she thought, and continued in that vein until the first customer came in. It was a man, a young serviceman in uniform on leave. He purchased a number of items and went out after paying her. She was reminded of Brian. She had not heard from him for over two weeks and felt guilty that she had forgotten him during the last two days. It was Gordon! He was taking her mind off everything!

There was nothing from Brian on Wednesday, but on Thursday morning, a lettercard came through her letterbox and she knew it was from him. Feeling a bit conscience stricken she opened it immediately and read it over her morning tea. He did not say a lot, only that he was very busy, and would write again when things settled down. She was not sure what to make of it, because his manner was not as usual, and he was obviously trying to tell her something. His final note said 'See you again when the campaign is finished!' This was not his usual signing off, and she wondered what he was trying to get passed the censor. Putting it down on the table, she finished her breakfast and went down to the shop for her morning. Thursday was early closing, and she was going out to tea! The letter was forgotten!

Just before closing time, Betty came in to ask if she would go with her to see the new film at the Regal in the afternoon. She obviously wanted to make up with Elsie, and tell her about her new boyfriend. She was buzzing with it, and Elsie wanted to tell her about her own date, but had to refuse because of her tea appointment with Mrs McIver. "Sorry, Betty" she replied to the invitation to the cinema." Mrs McIver has already asked me to tea this afternoon, so I can't make it today. What about tomorrow evening, would .that be O.K?"

Betty thought for a moment. "No, sorry, make it Saturday, if you can."

"Should be alright" replied Elsie. "Give me a call, or look in tomorrow!"

Betty agreed, and went out.

At ten to three Elsie set out along the High Street to Mrs McIver's house, some five minutes walk from the shop. She was excited and a bit nervous. Excited to see Gordon again, and nervous of Mrs McIver in her formidable home. As she knocked on the very elegant polished wood front door having walked down the longish drive, she was even more apprehensive. Mrs McIver's maid opened the door, and ushered her into a beautifully furnished drawing room, and on into the garden to a large immaculate lawn. On the way, she could not help noticing the damage to the walls and ceiling. The house must have caught the blast from the doodle bug that did the damage to her flat. Of course, the force would have come through the gap and caught the McIver's house. Mrs McIver had obviously concealed the worst of the scars with strategically positioned furniture, and a tapestry. Elsie felt sad to see such a lovely room marred by the damage.

Once in the garden, Mrs McIver rose to greet her. "Hallo, Elsie, I'm so pleased you could come. I did wonder with the shop being busy whether you might have to cancel. How's Jim? Is he O.K.?"

Elsie looked quickly about her. There was no sign of Gordon, and her heart sank. Where was he? Mrs McIver continued. "You haven't met my husband Tom, have you?" A tall, oldish looking man got up from his deckchair and came over to them, "Hallo, Elsie, you don't mind me calling you by your Christian name do you?" Elsie thought how like Gordon was to his father.

"Good afternoon Mr McIver, or should I have address you as 'Doctor' I have often seen you in the High Street but never knew you are a doctor!"

He laughed. "It seems I have created an impression, perhaps not quite the one I would have preferred with an attractive young lady!"

He appeared to be in his seventies, possibly ten years older than his wife, but extremely charming. It was obvious where Gordon got it from!

"You're just trying to flatter me Dr McIver" said Elsie blushing a little "Isn't Gordon here today? I did enjoy the evening we had together. It was nice of him to take me to the theatre."

Mrs McIver looked conspiratorial. "He is very fond of you from what he says. You know, all his friends have either gone away, are serving in the forces, or too busy to have time off. It is grand for him to have someone to enjoy his brief leave in Sidhurst. You know, he has a secret job, and we never know when he will come home even if it is only a short break. Now, my dear, sit next to me and we shall .have some tea while you tell us about yourself." Elsie sat in the deck chair proffered to her, and realised she was about to be examined by Mrs McIver as if she was a potential daughter-in-law.

Elsie decided to try and find out more about Gordon.

"Gordon seems to be very severe, perhaps as you might expect from a Sergeant Major!" Mrs McIver laughed. "Is that what he told you! He's having you on – why I can't think. Gordon is not a Sgt Major, he's an officer in the Intelligence Corps. This is just his role at the moment. I don't know what he does. It's very secret."

Elsie was stunned. No wonder he had been so charming, and in charge. She felt and looked shocked. Mrs McIver continued. "Perhaps I shouldn't have told you, but you must not let on that you know,. He'll only blame me, and he must have a reason. I'll have to trust you to keep it our secret until he tells you himself."

"Don't worry Elizabeth," replied Elsie. "It'll be easier for me to pretend not to know. Where is he by the way?"

"Had to go up to town urgently this morning. Didn't say why, but then he never does, and I don't ask." She looked a little irritated that he hadn't told her.

Elsie took a piece of bread and butter handed to her by the maid, and spread a little plum jam on to it with a pearl tea knife from the table next to her.

She said to Mrs McIver. "You have a lovely house and garden. Do you look after it yourselves? Is Mr McIver keen on gardening?"

"Does it all himself since he retired." answered Mrs McIver. "He was a chemical engineer, you know, not a medical doctor as most people think."

"Ah," answered Elsie, "Now I understand why I have never seen his name on a prescription."

This appeared to amuse Mrs McIver. "Why of course not," she said. "I don't think he could write a prescription to save his life! He designs and builds, or used to, chemical factories, processing plants, and oil refineries. The Government wanted him to carry on after war broke out, but his health has been poor, and although he didn't want to stop, Dr Hargreaves wouldn't have it. He has been retired for several; years, and busies himself 'digging for victory' in our vegetable patch over there." She motioned to what seemed a smallholding behind some bushes.

"You can have some early beans if you like." continued Mrs McIver.

The small talk continued. Elsie liked Elizabeth McIver, who was quite different to the impression she gave from her normal gruff greeting. After a time chatting, Elsie excused herself and bid them goodbye. It had been a pleasant relaxing afternoon. Pity Gordon wasn't there!

****

Chapter 5

*A*nother fine hot day ahead, thought Elsie as she woke up on Friday morning. Still feeling happy about her tea with Mrs McIver, together with being settled in the shop, she went down happily as soon as she heard Jim carrying out his morning ritual sweeping in front of his shop.

As she entered, Jim came forward to meet her.

"You have an admirer, Elsie!" he announced, and thrust a bouquet of flowers into her hand.

"These came for you yesterday afternoon, but had to be delivered this morning as we were closed"

Elsie took them in silence. She did not know what to say in reply because she knew how he had reacted to the mention of Gordon previously. "I suppose they are from Gordon?" he remarked questioningly.

"Yes" agreed Elsie. "They must be an apology for not being at his Mother's when I went there for tea yesterday. He said he would be, but had to go to London unexpectedly."

"Well, he obviously regrets not being there." continued Jim. "I hope you like his attentions. If he, or anyone else is ever a nuisance, just let me know and I will deal with them!"

"Oh no, Jim, I like Gordon and I'm sure he would never press himself on me to the extent he was a nuisance!"

Jim noticed the speed with which she had reacted, and knew she was attracted to him. Let's hope it doesn't become serious, he thought to himself. Elsie opened the small card that came with the flowers. It just said "Sorry I have to go to London. Can't do anything about it. See you tomorrow, Gordon."

She decided to let Jim down gently.

"Yes, it is just a brief note to say he missed me, and his apologies."

"He sounds a nice person." said Jim. "Yes, he is," replied Elsie. "I expect he will come into the shop again before long."

She thought Gordon would come in that morning, and waited impatiently for him to appear, but he didn't. It was not until she had finished for the day and was making tea that the 'phone rang. It was him!

"Is that you Elsie?" She knew his voice at once.

"Sorry I had to miss you yesterday. London took longer than I expected, and I didn't get back until the evening. I didn't think you would want to hear from me so late."

"Hallo, Gordon," she answered, "It was very kind of you to send some flowers. Your Mother and Father are very charming and it was a pleasure to meet them. I knew your Father before, but had never matched the person to the name. I enjoyed the afternoon very much, but it would have been even better if you had been there!"

"I hoped you would say that!" replied Gordon. "Now, how about meeting again? There is a new film at the Odeon, Eltham, tonight. If you get a move on we could just make the last performance. How about it? Are you game?"

Elsie knew she was! "That would be fun, Gordon. Shall I meet you at the bus stop outside at half past six?"

Gordon was delighted. "Sounds fine Elsie. See you later then, goodbye."

Elsie felt her excitement rising. This time he would see her home just about eleven o'clock, and she knew, if he asked, - well perhaps he wouldn't. Mustn't get ideas. Was she going too fast?

Elsie was no fool. She knew what could happen with Gordon. In fact she wanted it to. That is why as she was leaving the shop for her date with him, she quickly picked two French letters from the box and put them in her handbag!

The film at the Odeon was only mediocre. Half way through the main film, she felt his arms around her, and the thrill it produced was enough to make her feel quite ashamed, but she did not push his arm away. He made no further advances, and she sat happily soaking up his presence, the odour of a man close to her, just as Bill used to be in days past. It was so long since she had been out with a man - and what a man! Handsome, confident, and with an air of mystery about his work and rank!

In common with many of the audience, at the end of the performance, they both jumped up while the final credits were rolling, and made a beeline for the exit so as not to have to stand for the national anthem. They were able to get to the staircase, down to the foyer, and out into the warm still night with the sound of it in their ears. It was July, and they walked quietly along the High Street in the cooling air to the bus stop. They sat in silence among the few late night passengers for the fifteen minute ride back to Sidhurst. Elsie was in a kind of spell that she did not want to break, and somehow knew Gordon, also, was stuck for words. Neither could express the way they felt. Just before eleven the 21 bus pulled up outside the shop, and Gordon helped her off. Together they walked the few yards to her door. As they reached it and she felt in her bag for her key, Gordon took her arm again and swung her forcefully into his arms. Bending down as she looked up at his face, he kissed her and held her close. She could feel his hot body through her summer dress, and the urgency in his embrace. "Oh, Gordon!" was all she could say, and her senses reeled. Again he kissed her and with her arms round his neck, kissed him back with careless abandon, yet realising it was only her second date with him. She was being too forward - like Betty!

Again, and again he kissed her, and she felt his hands moving steadily from her back across her breast, and she knew what he wanted and could not resist him. She was so intoxicated. She felt herself gasp with a ripple of desire. The release of much pent up emotion. She wanted him, no matter the consequences, and all her inhibitions evaporated. Fumbling in her bag, she at last found the key, and opened the door. Quite deliberately Elsie let him kiss her once again as he held her, and drew him firmly through the door and shut it behind her with her free hand.

"Come on up, Gordon, darling," she breathed. "You don't have to go just yet if you want to stay!"

She felt a shiver pass through him, and knew he wanted her. Keeping his arm around her waist they walked together step by step up the stairs. Elsie knew what she was about to do, and had no regrets. She felt Bill would approve, and knew she loved Gordon already, even after such a little time. As they entered the small drawing room, her knees were weak, and he had to support her. Still kissing, she fell rather than sat on her large armchair.

"Would you like a drink, coffee or something?" she asked, trying to act normally.

"No, Elsie, I want nothing except you! D'you feel the same?"

Elsie did not answer. Instead, she took his hand and gently led him up the small flight of stairs to her bedroom. She felt Bill's presence, but he did not disagree. As they entered her bedroom, she placed her arm under his jacket, and gently opened it and put her arm tightly round his waist. She felt and heard him gasp, and responded by turning her back so his hands touched her breasts, and nipples, arousing an enormous surge of desire within her.

Carefully holding her by the shoulders, he lifted her quickly on to the bed. As he did so she knew her skirt was ruffled up, and then his hands were exploring her legs, thighs, and every past of her. As her underwear came off, she slid her hands along to his fly buttons, undoing each in turn and feeling him rising to her touch. She turned on her back and raised herself to meet him, feeling him shudder with desire and raising her own to inordinate levels. It was her beloved Bill! He was here, just as he always was, close, and taking her all the way, until they were passionless!

It was not Gordon, it was Bill she slept with that night, and in the morning, when Gordon came in with tea and biscuits, she looked up in surprise and felt ashamed. He must never know it was Bill she had finally given herself to, even if her body had been tricked into someone different!

"Good morning, Elsie darling" said Gordon handing her a cup of tea and a small plate of biscuits.

He slipped into the bed beside her, and she was embarrassed. What had she done! She knew she had done it deliberately, and it was not his fault. In fact as she sipped the tea, she knew she had enjoyed it, and felt more relaxed and happy than for a long time.

"No regrets, then Elsie! I'm sorry I lost my head. It's a long time since I met someone like you. I am certain I loved you the first time I saw you in the shop, and it has grown since I missed the tea party at home."

"Gordon," said Elsie, "all that matters is that we needed each other. If that leads to love, then so be it. Let's enjoy the present, and let the future take care of itself!"

"Thank goodness you can see it that way." responded Gordon. "Let's meet as often as we can until I have to go back off leave. Is that O.K. with you?" Gordon was dressing, and checked in the mirror to see he was respectable. He kissed her once again, and with tenderness. "I will try and see you this evening. It's Saturday, and we shall have the weekend together once you have finished your shop duties."

"You can come up to the flat at lunchtime for a snack together, if you like!" suggested Elsie.

"No, let's wait until this evening. "

"Agreed." said Elsie, as he went smartly down the stairs. Elsie heard the front door click shut. Thank goodness, she thought, Jim is not yet in the shop. What would he think if he knew?

She finished dressing and made up before going downstairs. She could not get Gordon out of her mind. Once surrendered, she wanted him more and more. It was as if a dam had burst, and broken her years of abstinence. Gordon had done it, but what now? She did not love him, not yet, anyway, and his leave couldn't last more than a week more. She would try to talk to Margaret about him. She is always a good sounding board! Suddenly an awful thought struck her like a thunderbolt. She had completely forgotten about the French letter! How could she be so stupid! They had taken no precaution whatsoever! What if she was pregnant! The thought of the scandal of such an event frightened her! Elsie knew that if the worst had happened, she could only blame herself, and she deserved it!

For nearly three weeks, she and Gordon went out together, dined in London, enjoyed long walks in the country on hot July days when she was not working in the shop, and held each other close when the last of the dreadful V1's passed over Sidhurst. Not that there were many now, but Elsie felt comforted and secure when Gordon was with her. She dreaded the nights when she was alone, and the odd one still rumbled over. She was still worried about being pregnant, and made sure that whenever they had sex together, they took precautions. The box in the shop would soon need replenishing!

It seemed only natural that he should spend the nights with her and soon they were living together as man and wife in the flat above the shop. She realised that by now Jim must know about the affair, as must most of the local people, but she didn't are1 Gordon was everything, and in between times, she had to work for her keep.

After four weeks, and still no news about when he had to go back, she began to have doubts. He was not now quite so ardent, and although they were still intimate, and he still professed his love for her, she felt he was becoming bored. She, also, was beginning to escape from the initial dreamy paradise!

One evening before Gordon called, she plucked up courage to 'phone Margaret .Her sister was delighted to hear from her and wondering why she had not called her for over three weeks! She was about to find out!

The operator put Elsie through.

"Hallo Margaret, it's Elsie here."

Margaret sounded a bit vexed. "Wondered what had happened to you1" she replied. "Twice I have telephoned, and got no reply. Have you been working at night, or what?"

Elsie took her courage in both hands.

"The reason why I haven't had time to speak to you is because I have been very tied up with Gordon who is home on leave." Before Margaret could ask who he was, she continued.

"You see, he is my new boy friend, or should I say man friend, who I have become very attached to." She used that phrase as it did not appear so shocking.

"Oh, I see" replied Margaret. "I guessed there was something going on. Who is Gordon, and how long have you known him?"

Once started, Elsie poured out the tale of the affair. Margaret was silent for a moment.

"I hope you know what you are doing, Elsie. He sounds a dream, but you're not being naughty with him, are you?"

"Yes, Margaret. I'm afraid Gordon and I are lovers. I just couldn't resist him, and we have spent every free moment together for several weeks, since he came home on leave. I have quite lost my head over him, but I'm beginning to wonder if I have gone too far too soon!"

Margaret tried to be kind. "So, are you getting engaged? Is that why you have called me, to break the news?"

"No, Margaret, I'm afraid it's not like that. We haven't even discussed a permanent relationship. I rather hope it will develop, but so far he has not mentioned anything in that direction!"

Margaret was appalled. "Then you are being used. He is having his way with you, and will leave as soon as he gets tired.

You must tackle it and ask his intentions immediately, and if necessary tell him to go! Otherwise you will be sorry. What ever possessed you to have such a wild fling, at your age, too!"

Elsie began to wonder herself. "I just fell for him when I saw him coming into the shop. He is so gorgeous and unmarried, and it has been such a long time since I had a little romance. I suppose I just got carried away, and didn't think of the consequences."

Margaret, older than Elsie, had similar experiences herself that Elsie did not know about, so supplied the answer.

"I think it's your age Elsie. You are in your mid-forties, and having a last fling, so to speak. You must find out how serious he is, and if not, finish the affair. That is all it is, and if you don't end it you'll be sorry!"

Elsie changed the subject. She had heard enough to realise her sister was probably right. She would ask Gordon when they next met, and at an appropriate time, his intentions regarding their future.

"How is Arthur?" she asked her sister. "Are you both well? Are you getting any of the doodle bugs your way?"

Margaret wanted to hear more about Gordon, but let the subject lapse until another time. "Arthur is fine, thanks Elsie. Working hard as usual. He gets no rest. Too many problems and not enough staff!"

Arthur was too old for military service, and escaped call up, but lost many of his staff. This placed the load on him as the Bank Manager.

"He has joined the Home Guard, and is out on an exercise of some sort nearly every weekend. Thoroughly enjoys himself if you ask me. It gets him away from work – and me, of course. Probably does him good. We had a V1 over here for the first time this week. Must be something to do with the place they re being launched. I think. He says it may get worse if they don't capture the coastal areas soon, as they are being despatched from near the Dutch border."

"Yes, you're probably right. We certainly are having less over here, now. Thought it was just the RAF and the ack - ack shooting them down. I hope you don't get any near you. It is very unpleasant!"

"So do I" continued Margaret. "London and your area are the run in, and seem to have had it the worst. Please God it will soon be over!"

"Amen to that," said Elsie "Talk to you again soon Margaret, goodbye." She rang off as she heard her doorbell ring, and knew it would be Gordon.

That evening she broached the subject with Gordon, but got little response.

"Have to wait and see how the war goes, and when it is likely to finish, Elsie." He said. "Anything could happen to me, so let's just enjoy what we have for the time, and worry about it then. I do love you, you know!" He put his arm round her. "You see, I couldn't think of an entanglement at the moment. I hope you understand. Now let's get off and have some dinner and forget all about it!"

Elsie was dismayed. It was quite a rebuff. He did not make any form of promise. She began to feel less loving towards him. She had given herself to him totally, and he had given little in return except wining and dining her. It wasn't right for a man to act in this way if he was truly in love. Margaret had been correct!

She began to see less of Gordon, who was having to go to London more often, and she started to think of other matters. One morning almost two weeks later, she thought about Brain from whom she had not heard for more than two weeks. Where was he? It is unlike him not to write regularly. She felt concerned as to what might have happened. The old stomach churning feeling arose again inside. Elsie was returning to normal.

That evening long after the shop closed, Gordon had not called her. She wondered why? Perhaps he was called away to London again. Next day she had just opened the shop when Mrs McIver came in. "Good morning, Elsie, how are you today?"

"Very well, thank you Elizabeth, What can I do for you?"

"I've come with a message from Gordon. He has gone away. In fact he has been posted suddenly, and left yesterday afternoon. I think from what he said he has gone abroad, although he could not tell me where, and was very vague about it. He said to say goodbye to you, and I have come to tell you." Elsie felt a huge sadness that she wouldn't see him today, and her face must have shown it because Mrs McIver immediately said.

"I know you have become very fond of each other, but there was nothing he could do. The posting was urgent and he left within half an hour of receiving a telegram. I'm sorry to bring you disappointing news. Were you expecting him today?"

"We had nothing planned, but he usually looked in during the day, and if we were both free, we sorted out something for the evening."

Mrs McIver turned to go out. "Well, Elsie, I've passed on his message. There is nothing I want this morning, so I will get on. It looks like another lovely day. Goodbye, my dear."

With that she went briskly out of the shop leaving Elsie to think about Gordon's rapid departure. No doubt he had to go urgently, but he could at least have telephoned. Did he really care? In her mind she began to let him go. He, and of course she, had their fun. That was all there was to it unless he got in touch again. No doubt there would be other ladies for him to enjoy! She blushed to herself as she realised it was really she who had seduced him. Or at least pressed herself on him. Gordon had enjoyed it, but what man wouldn't! She really had been a fool!

Jim must have heard the message because he came out from the dispensary and remarked.

"It looks as if it's going to be a lovely day again. Did I hear Mrs McIver say that Gordon has gone back to his unit?"

"Yes," replied Elsie. "Apparently he left yesterday evening. I shall miss him."

"Well, now perhaps we can get back to concentrating on work. At least I'm not sorry to see him go."

So Jim was jealous!

That day, and for quite a few more, Elsie missed Gordon. In her heart she was relieved. She had thought she loved him, but it had become obvious that his appeal was waning and after a while, as she became used to him not being there, saw that his departure had removed a huge worry from her mind. If he really cared he would write, as Brian did. If not, that was the end of it. If nothing more, he had removed the ghost of Bill that had been always in the background. She was free to live her life at last! At night she still feared the sound of the V1's coming over. The first night one flew over was the only time she badly missed him, and her stomach churned a little when the engine cut out. But she heard nothing more, and it must have glided on so far the explosion was put of hearing, or it was a dud. Which ever it was, the initial scare was gone, and she went back to sleep.

During her affair with Gordon, she heard nothing further from Betty. Two days after he went, her telephone rang in the evening. It was her.

"Hallo Betty," she answered. "How are you?"

"About time I caught you in, Elsie" said Betty, "You've been busy. I must have rung you six times or more in the last two weeks, and you've never been in. What have you been up to?"

Elsie was vague. "I have been busy, mostly in the shop. Lot's of overtime." She lied most innocently to ensure Betty found out nothing. "What about you, Betty? Still going out with the man from Klingers?"

"Yes, I have. He and I are getting engaged. That's why I'm calling. Would you like to come to our party on Saturday next?"

Elsie gasped with incredulity. "What about Douglas?" she asked. "I thought you were supposed to be engaged to him!"

"Not any longer. I wrote to him several weeks ago and told him. He never replied, so that is that. What more can I do?"

Elsie was horrified. She didn't even know if he had received her letter!

She felt she couldn't attend the party. It was not right. She had no special feeling for Douglas, but he was a decent chap. Betty's behaviour was disgusting, and she supposed, typical of her.

"I would like to come, Betty," she lied, "but I have a previous date next Saturday, and I will be going out as soon as I have finished in the shop. Please accept my wishes, and the best of luck this time. I hope you are not going to make a habit of this!" She couldn't resist a dig.

"Nearly all the girls at Klingers will be going. It will be a huge party. Are you sure you can't make it? I would love you to be there."

Elsie refused to be swayed. She was afraid she might say something at the party out of order.

"No, really I can't Betty. Have a lovely time, and tell me all about it, next week."

"How are you getting on at Shaw's?" Asked Betty.

"I'm thoroughly enjoying it. It's hard work, and Jim is a strict taskmaster, but I find returning to my old shop work plus learning about dispensing is something I like very much."

"That's good Elsie. I've been promoted at Klingers, and work in the offices now. My fiancé," and she giggled at the word. "is seeing I get any chance going that is within my abilities, so hope to progress even further."

Elsie wondered how long that would last once Ron Perkins had her tied to him.

"Take care Betty, you've not known him long yet!"

"You are an old spoil sport, Elsie. He is a very good man, and I love him. We're going to have a house the other side of town, near Jim's place."

"I didn't know you knew where Jim lives." said Elsie.

"Oh yes," replied Betty. "Used to go out with him a long time ago, didn't you know?" Elsie was even more amazed than ever with Betty. Was there no one she had not been out with!

"Look Betty, it's fun to talk, but I must go. I am in the middle of cooking supper. Give me a ring next week after your party. See you soon. Bye." She put the receiver down and pondered Betty's news. Surely not another disaster – it rather looked like it!

With Gordon out of the way she was able to concentrate on learning about the chemicals and materials used by Jim in the dispensary. He recommended a book from the library, and she spent many of the light August evenings sitting in the garden behind the shop reading up on the technical aspects and the sort of chemicals used in dispensing. Often immersed in her book, she found herself reading in the gloom and had to complete the chapter sitting up in bed. When she had difficulty understanding a particular detail, she would ask Jim or Joan to explain it the next morning. Jim was delighted at her interest, and she found Joan most helpful as she saw how Elsie was becoming involved in the medical side of a chemist's work.

It was about half past nine one evening and almost dark when she heard the front door bell ring, followed at once by a familiar 'rat tat'! It was Bill's knock! A sudden fear gripped her, and she ran down the stairs to answer. In the half light of the summer evening she was confronted face to face by a man in a military peaked hat and full uniform. Panic almost made her shut the door in his face. The shape of the head could only be Bill! She knew it from a lifetime together. Was she going mad?

"Who is it?" she faltered.

"Come on Mum, don't you know you own son!" Brian laughed at her from the doorway.

Instantly she threw her arms round him. "Brian, how wonderful!" She kissed him and hugged him all at the same time. He laughed again just as he always did when his Mother embarrassed him.

"Steady on, Mum." He was still laughing. "So this is where you live now. I thought I could remember when you said you were living over Uncle Jim's shop. How is the old devil, by the way?"

Elsie ushered him inside. "You didn't tell me you were coming!" she accused him. "Why didn't you let me know, and at least give me a bit of notice!"

"Don't nag Mum. Always the same! Can't do anything right! Shall I go down to the Black Horse if I'm in the way? What have you done? Got a man up there or something?" He teased her as he always did. Little did he know how near he was to the truth had he been a few weeks earlier.

"Stop your teasing" said Elsie "and come upstairs to the flat. Of course I'm ready for you. What d'you think I have been waiting all this time for. It must be three years since you went off just after your Dad was killed."

Brian became serious. "That was terrible Mum. Is the pain still as bad? I can never forget your face when that policeman called"

"Yes, of course it is, but not as sharp as it was. In the last few months I have been able to feel free from grieving. I'm just beginning to live a normal life again."

They reached the first floor and Elsie lead him into the living room as she switched on the light.

"Brian surveyed the room. "This is very cosy, Mum, and well furnished too. More than I thought you would have. Do you like it here?"

Elsie considered her answer. "It was very lonely at first, but once the canteen closed, and I started to work for Uncle Jim, I've been more settled. I like working in the shop, and Uncle Jim as you still call him, is very kind and helpful. I'm even learning to become a dispenser."

Brian turned to the immediate problem in his mind. "Now Mum, I have two weeks leave before I report again. Is it O.K. for me to stay here with you? Have you room for me?" He looked quite pathetic. "Why, of course you can son," answered Elsie. "I have a second room upstairs next to mine, and there is a single bed in it. It is always made up ready for just the day you return. It is yours, not only when you are on leave, but anytime when you are at home, even after the war. This is your home now, if you want it to be."

For the first time since he arrived, she looked at him in the full light. There was something different about his uniform. He was obviously older, looked more mature, handsome as ever, like his father. There was also a worldliness she had never seen before. He did not look well, tired and a bit thinner, and he had an air of authority that stood out. Then she saw it. He had three 'pips' on his uniform shoulder. Again she accused him.

"You never told me you had been promoted, Brian? When did this happen? What are you now, a Captain?"

"It happened just before I left Italy, Mum. I was involved in a little affair with some tanks, and our second in command was killed, so I had to take over. Soon after I was confirmed in his place and my new rank also, shortly after. Not sure if I like it yet!"

He did not mention he had been recommended for a Military Cross for bravery, but as yet no official announcement.

"There is something else, Mum. While I was waiting in the transit camp in Rome, I met a Sergeant in the A.T.S. She was coming home to England as well, and we have become friends. She has just lost her parents, killed in an air raid and I think her home has been destroyed. When I left her in London, she was on her way there. I'm afraid I took the liberty of asking her to call here if she needed any help. Is that O.K.?"

"I should be delighted to help if I can." replied Elsie instantly. "Does she know how to contact you?"

Brian said "I gave her the name of Shaw's, and said to telephone there if necessary. I rather think she might! Could she stay here if necessary?" He hastened to add before his mother could protest.

"I would go and stay at he Black Horse of course. There is nothing like that. I'm only getting to know her so far."

Elsie wanted to help, and so reacted positively to his request.

"Look, Brian, I will do all I can to help, but you must realise that I have my work these days and there will not be much spare time. There would be meals to get ready, and to be frank, a guest needs more attention than you would.. You know what I mean, don't you, but alright, let's wait and see if she calls, then we can decide."

Brian smiled gratefully. "I know it's a bit of a cheek, Mum, but I felt she needed someone to call if necessary. She said she had no other relatives."

Elsie turned to practical matters. "Have you come straight from the plane dear, and what about luggage, I don't see any!"

"I have arranged for what little I have to be sent over from Woolwich in the morning. I have this small bag." He held out a small shoulder bag that Elsie had not noticed. "This will see me through tonight."

Elsie walked through to the kitchen with Brian close behind. Together, they made a pot of tea, two pieces of cheese on toast, which used up practically all Elsie's ration for the week, and took them into the living room, where they sat with the plates on their laps.

"This is just like old times. Mum," said Brian "It seems ages since we sat in the room behind the dairy after supper. Now, tell me about Uncle Jim and everything else that's happened since Dad died."

Elsie related everything, except about Gordon. How she had come to live over the shop, and how kind Jim been to her.. Gordon was another matter and Brian did not need to know anything about that! For a while he did his best to listen, but she could see that his eyes were slowly closing from sheer fatigue. He was back home in Sidhurst, and as he relaxed, all the tiredness welled up, overtaking him.

Before he actually nodded off, Elsie broke off for a moment. "I think you have had enough for one day, Brian. I'll just pop up and make your bed while you have a drop of Dad's whisky that is still in the side board." She went over, took out the half bottle still there from the day before Bill died, and poured her son out a small glass. She turned to hand it to him, but he had leaned back in the chair and was fast asleep.

Quietly she took his hand to wake him. Sleepily, swallowing the drink at a gulp he said "That was marvellous, Mum." She guided him up the stairs to the small bedroom opposite hers. Without a word he walked in and shut the door just saying "Goodnight, Mum" and she heard him flop onto the bed.

After a few minutes she went in and he was lying fast asleep on the top of the bed with the eiderdown hardly ruffled. With infinite tenderness, she loosened the jacket of his uniform, pulled back the bed, and covered him with the eiderdown. He didn't stir, and tiptoeing out of the room as quietly as possible, she went back to her drawing room.

There would be a lot to talk about in the morning and she was soon in her own bed thanking the Lord for bringing him home. "Two weeks" she thought, "and Brian all to herself, or was he? What about the girl he had befriended? Tomorrow would reveal all!"

****

Chapter 6

*N*ext morning she woke early, but Brian was even earlier. Before she was properly awake, there was a quiet knock on her door and he came in with two steaming tea cups on the small tray.

"Hallo Mum, a very good morning to you. Did you hear the V1, or I assume that's what it was, go over in the night?"

"No, I didn't." replied Elsie. "We are so used to them now that we often don't realise there are still a few coming over – until one explodes near. Then we have a sudden reminder of how dangerous they are. I told you about the one that landed in Sidhurst, didn't I?"

Brian had seen all sorts of violent action, but found lying helpless in bed listening to one pass over, and unable to do anything about it, quite unnerving. Still he wasn't going to show it in front of his Mother, who obviously ignored them.

"Do you still get many, Mum?" he asked as they drank their tea together.

"Not as many as we used to. At first they were coming over continuously, and it was very frightening. But now – well I don't seem to hear them. Like last night. Didn't even know any had gone over! What do you think Brian? Will they finish soon?"

Brian thought for a moment. "I'm sure they can't go on for much longer, Mum. The invasion forces must be close to taking the launch sites. It can only be a matter of time, but they are finding it very difficult to make headway. The Germans are resisting fiercely all the way. Now, what is the order of the day? Is it your half day? When does Uncle Jim arrive, as I'm looking forward to seeing him again!"

He was obviously rested and full of get-up-and-go. Elsie sipped her tea while she worked out the answers to his questions one at a time. "Right, the order of the day is that I go down to the shop at nine. Jim arrives a bit earlier and sweeps the shop front. It's early closing day, so we shut prompt at one o'clock, and I have nothing fixed for this afternoon. Mind you, I shall need to do some shopping, otherwise you won't eat. By the way, have you brought any coupons with you?"

"Yes, of course." said Brian. "There's a whole pack in my coat. So we'll have the afternoon together. That's great!" Elise felt tired already at his energy and enthusiasm.

"Now Mum, while I get the breakfast for us. Get dressed and it'll be ready by the time you get down to the kitchen. I have already made a 'recce' and know where most things are – I found some bacon and eggs, and you seem to have enough bread. Can I use these?"

"Yes, sounds fine Brian. You carry on while I get up. Anything we use I'll replace this afternoon, if your coupons are enough."

He had only been home a few hours, and he was already taking charge. She enjoyed having a man about her flat again, and letting him give the orders, but thought. "I will have to tactfully point out I am not going to be run, even by my own son, and he will have to moderate his enthusiasm a little!"

Brian was a good as his word. When she came into the kitchen he had laid the table in the sitting room, just as they always did when he was at home in the dairy, had cooked their breakfasts, and was keeping them hot while he waited for her. At her usual pace, she steadily consumed the plateful he put in front of her. Before she had eaten half, Brian had wolfed down his cooked egg and bacon, three pieces of toast and marmalade, and was on his third cup of tea.

"Don't they feed you in the army?" she asked.

"Sometimes" he replied. "But there is never enough for me. I'm always hungry, although I did have an excellent dinner in the Mess at Woolwich before I set off for Sidhurst. I had virtually nothing before that after I left Rome, so I was pretty hungry, I can tell you!" He laughed, and it was Bill all over again. So like his Father it was uncanny!

Brian looked at his watch and Elsie noticed it was a good quality timepiece. He was very much the young officer, and she felt very proud to think he was her son. If only Bill could see him now!

"Do you mind if I go down and see Uncle Jim, Mum? He asked

Elsie wanted to introduce him to Jim herself, so stopped him. "Before you do that, and anyway I'll come down with you. Jim is very busy when he first opens the shop. He won't welcome you if you go down before I do, as he will not be able to devote his attention to you if a customer comes in.!" It sounded plausible, Elsie hoped. "Perhaps you could nip down to Plant's and get a newspaper for me. I normally have the Express. There is some money on the mantelpiece."

"Of course," responded Brian. "Don't insult me Mum. You don't think I would let you pay for a paper. I'm not short of cash, so just forget about it." He turned to go out and she heard him call "Back in a minute!" as he went down the stairs and out of the front door. As his case had not arrived, he was still wearing his uniform and Elsie wondered if any of her friends would see him. He looked so smart and handsome in it!

He must have had a chat with people he met in the newsagent because it was nearly a quarter to nine when he returned. As he ran up the stairs two at a time, she heard Jim arriving, unlocking the shop door, and going in.

"Thanks Brian!" she said as he handed her paper. "I heard Jim arrive just as you came in. Let him settle for a minute and we'll go down and surprise him!"

Brian helped her wash up the breakfast things and they went down to the shop. With Brian behind her, she went in.

Jim glanced up and "Good morning Elsie" then stopped in surprise as he saw Brian. At the sight of the uniform he quickly stood up and gave a smart salute. "Sorry sir, didn't see you there!" He gave a huge grin and came over and shook the young officer's hand. Brian took it and threw his arms around him, giving him a huge hug.

"How are you, you old devil!" he replied, raising his hand to return Jim's salute. "Not only are you wasting time as usual in the shop making up potions, but you've also got my Mother at it! Are you well?"

He could see that in fact Jim wasn't. He was drawn and older than he remembered him three years ago with his Father, but didn't comment.

"Not too bad" answered Jim. "Now, what's this I see? Captain Winter, is it! Don't expect you want to talk to an old veteran, do you?"

Beside Brian, Elsie thought Jim looked an old man, both weary and scarred.

"Now, Uncle, there are lots of things I want to know, and more to tell you. When can you leave this dusty old shop for a minute and have a chat? Why don't you leave it to my Mother and come up to her flat for a drink later?"

Jim looked at Elsie, who nodded in agreement. It would do Jim good, she thought, to chat to Brian about the war and his experiences. He couldn't have had a man to man chat for a long time.

"Right, that's agreed then." said Jim. "Now young fellow I must get on if we are to meet later. Off you go and let your Mother and me get on with the shop. Customers will be in shortly and we're not even open! By the way, you don't call me 'Uncle' It's Jim from now on, and mighty glad I am to see you home safe and sound!"

"See you later then Jim." said Brian, "and Mum, I'll have coffee ready for you before I see Jim if that's O.K." He was taking charge again! He went out and back upstairs leaving Elsie and Jim to open the shop.

"He looks very well, Elsie." said Jim after he had left. "But a bit tired. It must be tough in Italy. He looks thrilled to be home. Do you know how much leave he's got?"

"Two weeks, he told me, but I don't know what or where he is going after. He'll tell me in his own time if he can. I hope it isn't straight back into action again. He's done enough for one war already, I think!"

"Two weeks will do him a power of good. Have you planned anything yet" asked Jim.

"No we haven't" replied Elsie. "Haven't had time. He only got home late yesterday evening. Oh, and while I remember, you may get a telephone call from a young lady Brian met on his way home. Don't know her name, but if she does ring, she will ask for Brian, so you will recognise her. I think Brian is a bit taken with her, although he didn't actually say as much. Anyway forget it until she calls."

"He didn't waste much time!" grinned Jim. "Good luck to him. Let's hope she's nice!"

Their first customer of the day opened the door, and prevented further discussion.

Because it was early closing day, they were busy. Joan came in as usual, and of course, heard all the news about Brian's homecoming. She and Jim settled down to clear the prescriptions by lunchtime and all else was forgotten. At eleven Jim went up to keep his appointment with Brian and when he came down he immediately went over to Elsie.

"Brian has asked me if I would be kind enough to let you have some time off while he is on leave, and I have agreed. Unfortunately I can't let you have every day, but would it be alright if you have the days Joan is here. It will give you a chance to spend some time with him, and from what he has told me, he certainly deserves it. I have already cleared it with Joan and she has offered to do full days for the next two weeks while Brian is home."

"Thanks very much, Jim, you are kind. It would be lovely. I don't know what Brian has in mind to do, but I'll try and keep up with him!"

"That's agreed then." said Jim "Now Brian has gone off to do your shopping and will be back, he thought, about twelve. Finish what you are doing by then, and off you go. I don't want to see you again until Monday. Joan and I will handle things and on Monday morning we'll see how things are."

"Are you sure?" questioned Elsie.

"Yes, I am" he replied. "Have a happy weekend together, and look in first thing on Monday. Now no more discussion, the decision is made!"

Elsie completed setting out one of the cupboards she had been dusting and went to thank Joan for standing in for her. As she entered the dispensary the telephone rang. It was Betty.

Joan passed the receiver to her. "Hallo, Betty, Is there something wrong?" Betty did not usually telephone the shop as she knew it irritated Elsie to be called at work.

"Elsie, thank God I've got you. I'm in terrible trouble!" "Why, what's the matter?" answered Elsie.

"I've had a telephone call from Douglas' Mother. He is landing at Portsmouth on Monday, and coming home on leave. He has received my letter, and is angry. He wants to talk to me as soon as he gets home. I haven't dared tell Ron. What shall I do?"

Elsie told her in no uncertain manner.

"You must see him, and try and explain. He will be bitterly disappointed. How long has he known? When did he get your letter?"

"Apparently he got it when his ship called in at Gibraltar on the way home, and he cabled his parents immediately. That is the first time he knew! I'm terrified of meeting him. He has a bad temper when he is upset."

"Look, Betty, you must face him and try and explain. Once

it's done, he will be free to spend his leave how he wants, instead of with you, which he no doubt looked forward to. At the very least he will be disappointed, but you must meet him. It's only fair."

Betty seemed to calm down a little. "Yes, I know you're right, Elsie, you always are. Thank you and see you again soon."

"If you need to talk again, Betty, call me at the flat, or come and have some tea with us – oh, by the way, Brian is home on leave. So you could meet him if you come."

"Alright, I'll try. Good bye and thanks for your advice" Elsie returned the receiver to Joan who put it back in place. "That sounded a bit of a problem?" she enquired interestedly to Elsie.

"Yes, it looks as if it could be an unpleasant interview for Betty. Not that she doesn't deserve it. She has treated Douglas very badly. She was, after all, engaged to him and wearing his ring. I hope it works out O.K."

She went to leave the dispensary. "Sorry Joan, with the call I forgot to thank you for helping out and letting me have some days off. It is most kind. I hope I can do the same for you when you need it."

"Thank you Elsie, don't worry, I'll see Jim is O.K I wish he looked better 'though. He worries me when he looks so tired and pale. Enjoy your weekend with Brian. Now get off with you!"

She went behind the shop and took off her white coat before going upstairs. As she passed the dispensary again, she heard the telephone once more. Joan answered. "Shaw's Chemists, Joan speaking" A pause, then "Just a minute, I'll try and find Mrs Winter for you."

"Elsie, are you still there? Oh yes, good. There's someone asking for you."

Elsie took the receiver again! "Elsie Winter here"

"Could I speak to Brian Winter, please."

"He's not here at the moment. I'm his Mother, can I help?"

"Oh, hallo Mrs Winter," said a girl's voice. "Brian said to telephone if he could help at all. I wanted to see if I could take up his offer. I would like to come to Sidhurst today. I have nowhere to stay for my leave. We have been bombed out by a V1, and he said there is a good hotel he could recommend for my week's leave. Can you let me have directions how to get to Sidhurst after I get off the train from Charing Cross?"

Elsie made a quick decision. She sounded polite, pleasant and rather pathetic. Brian had recommended her and that was enough for Elsie.

"Brian has already told me you might need some help. You can stay here if you wish. Come to Shaw's the Chemist in the High Street. Knock on the door of the flat next to the shop entrance. It is early closing day so the shop will not be open this afternoon. Brian and I will be upstairs in the flat above the shop. Come in time for tea and we can discus the best thing for you to do."

"Thank you so much, Mrs Winter," she replied and Elsie could hear the relief in her voice. "By the way, my name is Jane Parlour. I should get there as far as I can tell about half past four. Is that alright?"

"Yes, of course. Come as soon as you wish. I'll tell Brian you're coming when he comes in from shopping. We'll see you this afternoon, then. Goodbye, and don't worry. We'll sort something out for you."

"You sound very kind Mrs Winter. Brian said you were. Goodbye "

Elsie out down the receiver and paused for reflection. Brian was home and chaos was taking over, as usual with her son!

It was just after three in the afternoon when Staff Sergeant Jane Parlour found a corner seat in the train on Platform 5 at Charing Cross Station. Although there were only a few minutes before departure, the train was almost empty. The rush hour did not start until nearer five o'clock, and she had found an empty compartment. She sat quietly waiting for the train to pull out and thinking about her last twenty four hours. It seemed hardy a moment since she had walked up the road to the home she knew so well and to the shock of seeing the utter destruction that greeted her as she neared the place where her house had been. All that was left was a large open space. The V1 had totally destroyed her home, her parent's house, and those either side. In all, three had been completely destroyed, and those neighbouring suffered severe damage, now being patched up by a swarm of repair teams.

In the four days it had taken for her to receive the news, get compassionate leave, and travel from Rome, the bodies of her Father and Mother had been recovered from the wreckage and taken to the local mortuary where they still lay, the site cleared , and now all she had left was an open space and her memories. Although the area was well known to her, when she reached the place where her home had stood, she descended to the depth of despair and shock as her loss struck home.

One of her neighbours saw her standing aghast at the scene and ran from her house. Putting her arms around Jane she supported her knees that had become strangely weak.

"I knew you'd come Jane. What have they told you? Do you know what happened?"

Jane steadied her emotion. She had not been home for over a year since she left for Italy.

She answered with a tired and weary voice.

"Hallo, Mrs Walker. Yes, I have been told most of what happened, and I know my Mother and Father are in the mortuary. Has anything been arranged about a funeral?"

Mrs Walker looked very severe, yet with great sympathy at Jane as she said

"I hope you won't be offended, Jane but we, that is the Phillips and ourselves, had to make a decision. We did not know if you have any relatives, and we could not get in touch with you, so we arranged for the funeral to be this afternoon at three o'clock."

Jane held herself steady, but did not let go of Mrs Walker's arm.

"Thank you Mrs Walker. You did the right thing. I did wonder if they would have already been buried when I arrived, but I was lucky to get a lift on a plane returning from Rome, so got here in time, it appears. I shall, of course, go and see the undertakers immediately and approve the arrangements."

Mrs Walker was most relieved that Jane had readily accepted the decisions that had been taken. She seemed well composed, and observed with interest the three stripes on Jane's arms.

"Come over to the house Jane, and please use our 'phone . In the meantime I will make us some coffee. I'm sure you could do with one and a quiet sit down for a few minutes. Would you like something to eat while we talk? Please ask me anything you want to know, and I'll try and fill in the details."

Jane thought she was being very kind.

She sat in Mrs Walker's front room for a while and tried to collect her thoughts. She felt no emotion, or grief, yet. All she could think about was the funeral, and afterwards. As the hot coffee and biscuits produced my Mrs Walker sank in she felt a wave of tiredness and despair flood over her. What now? Her parents were dead. She would have to return to her unit in a few days time when her week's compassionate leave expired, and where was she to stay in the meantime? At a hotel?

Her thoughts moved to the past and to her life since leaving home to join the A.T.S.

It was her Italian Mother who had enabled her to become fluent in the language that had taken her to Rome. Her mother often talked about her early years in the city. At first she had wanted to join the Nursing Yeomanry, but at interview, her accent was not sufficiently fluent for the demanding work in an enemy territory, so they suggested she could work as an interpreter once Italy had been occupied by the allied forces. She had not been able to volunteer for the A.T.S. until she was 17 years old, and disappointed at being refused a chance to join the F.A.N.Y., she had accepted a post in the R.T.O in Rome.

After training and a further eighteen months in which she showed her intelligence and ability to organise, she was promoted to Sergeant – Staff Sergeant, and felt proud of the work she was doing in liaising with the Rome authorities.

She had met Brian Winter in the R.T .office when both were trying to get transport back to England. She liked the handsome young artillery Captain at once, and he had been instrumental in getting herself on the same flight back to Northolt. As an officer he was able to exert more pressure, and staff in the R.T.O. listened to him. He realised her mind was in turmoil when he found out the reason for her return home, and supported her as best he could on the flight. Sitting on adjacent seats in the Dakota, she found herself sharing experiences as they chatted. She was attracted to him even at this time, and when he asked her to call him if she needed a place to stay, or any help, she knew, if necessary, she would take up his offer.

So it was when Mrs Walker asked her about her plans, she said
"I have a friend who will look after me until I have to return to Italy, Mrs Walker, but thanks very much for the offer. If you will allow me to stay with you tonight after the funeral, I will get off to see him as soon as I have completed matters here."
Mrs Walker felt very sorry and sad for this organised young lady, who had not so long ago been the 'little girl next door'. She was only too pleased to give her a bed for the night. It was the very least she could do in the most tragic circumstances.

It had been on the plane that her grief had first surfaced. After being quite calm and composed until they took off, she had, after a few minutes and without warning fallen on Brian's shoulder and sobbed piteously. Brian was very affected, and together they clung closely for nearly half an hour before she felt better. Since then an icy calm had taken over and in perfect control she dealt with everything that arose with the same efficiency that had earned her quick promotion in her job.

The funeral was a very sad affair. Mostly neighbours, because the family had no relatives in England still living, and some ARP Wardens and Rescue Workers. The next morning she visited the undertakers, collected the account, agreed the sum to pay and said goodbye to the local people who knew her and she had met again at the service. Just before lunch, she telephoned Shaw's the Chemist as Brian had suggested, had a snack at the W.V.S. canteen, and set off to Charing Cross.

When she got on at Charing Cross the carriage was empty, but at London Bridge two soldiers not in uniform jumped in. They both looked approvingly at the trim ATS Sergeant with the unusual shoulder flashes opposite them, but did not attempt to speak to her, as her expression said very clearly 'Keep off the grass!" They were even more taken aback when they saw the Sergeant was sitting with her eyes closed and tears streaming from them. They wondered what they should do. A torrent of grief, self-pity and emotion had flooded over Jane as her thoughts moved violently over the past week. One of the men said quietly

"Is there anything I can do to help, Sergeant? Pardon me for asking, but you look so sad. I felt I must see if there is anything we can do." Jane came back to the present with a jerk.

"No, thank you for asking. I'm afraid there is nothing anyone can do. I'm best just left to myself." The soldier sank back with relief.

"We won't disturb you Sergeant, Ma'am. If there is anything just say."

The carriage returned to silence and twenty minutes later she felt the train slowing down and saw the 'Sidhurst' sign appear on the platform fence.

She stood up. One of the men reached for her small case on the rack and helped her down on to the platform. The door swung shut with a bang, and she was almost alone on the station. Being early afternoon the train was empty, and she was one of three who handed in her ticket to the collector on the barrier. She walked slowly down the station approach to the road below. She had no idea where Shaw's was, so asked a woman for directions.

"You could walk it, but it is almost a mile to the High Street. I think you'd be better to take the 241 bus and get off at the Black Horse. Shaw's is a bit further down on the other side of the road."

"Thank you very much." answered Jane and walked across the pavement to the bus stop where 241 was posted. A bus came almost immediately and in a few minutes she alighted outside the Black Horse. Crossing the road she walked quickly to where she could see Shaw's sign above a single fronted shop on a wide parade. She rang the bell on the front door of the flat next to the shop, and waited.

Elsie did not know when to expect the young lady her son had asked to visit, but she felt she must give her a real welcome if what Brian had told her about her parent's death was true. She had just about prepared herself, cleaned up, sent Brian off to get himself a room somewhere, when she heard the front door bell go. She went carefully down and opened the door to see a smallish young lady dressed in a extremely smart uniform, Sergeant's stripes on her sleeves, and with well groomed hair in the fashionable 'page boy' style of the modern young woman. Elsie also noticed her face was heavily stained with dried up tears. They did not suit her!

"Hallo, my dear. You must be Jane!"

"Yes, that's right, I'm Jane Parlour. You must be Mrs Winter, Brian's Mother."

Elise smiled warmly at her. "Yes, that's right. I'm so pleased to meet you. Now come inside. You must be tired after the journey, and I will have some tea for us in a jiffy. Come in, come in!" She led the way upstairs with Jane behind her, talking as they went.

"Yes, I am a bit tired, but no matter. I'm delighted to be here. Without Brian's suggestion, I would have nowhere to go for my leave, but I don't want to be a burden, and can go off to the hotel Brian mentioned."

Elsie already liked the polite courtesy of this young lady who was certainly no older than Brian. How well composed and confident they are today, she thought. Not a stunning looker, but fair enough and with lovely dark hair. She could see why Brian was attracted to her being fair. Dressed in civvies she would look even better.

"Come on up. Brian is out, but will be back in a few minutes. Now, make yourself at home. This is the living room, the bathroom is next door and that's the kitchen. Now, you are going to stay with us aren't you?" Jane could feel the genuine warmth in Elsie's voice and tears started to run down her face again at her kindness to a stranger.

"Yes, please Mrs Winter, if it is not presuming too much. I know you work in the Chemist and are busy, so I will help as much as I can while I'm here. Now are you sure it is alright for me to stay?"

"I wouldn't have asked if I hadn't meant it" said Elsie. "Now, I have tea ready, and as soon as Brian comes in we'll start. Sit here while I make the tea. Afterwards, I'll show you your room. Put your case by the kitchen door for the time being."

For the next few minutes they chatted about nothing in particular with Elsie trying to make friends with this obviously sad young lady. Fortunately, Brian came running up the stairs and she saw Jane's face brighten as she recognised him in the doorway.

"Hallo, Brian" she said simply. "Oh, it is good to see you again. Your Mother has been absolutely charming and so kind to me, and I'm feeling at home already. I hope I'm not a burden to you. You must have lots of plans for your leave and here I am making a nuisance of myself!"

Brain grinned at her, as he always did when he met someone he liked.

"Look, let's get one thing straight. I wouldn't have asked you, if I didn't want you to telephone, and if Mother had not agreed. Anyway, what do you think I could find to do for two weeks?"

He looked at his Mother with a cheeky smile. "You know she would be bored to death in a day or two, and is just waiting for the day I go back!"

This was too much for Elsie. "There are times, Brian when I really hate your teasing. If there is any more of it I shall turn you out on your ear, and have Jane to myself! She is much more polite than you'll ever be!"

Brain held up his hands in mock surrender, and changed the subject.

"Mum, I have managed to get some digs at the Black Horse for a few days. So, Jane, you will have no problem in staying here with Mum. I hope you can. There are so many things we can do. Go to town, walk in the hills, or what ever you like. Do you play tennis?"

"Jane for the first time, smiled. And Elsie, for the first time saw a radiance break through. "I play, but extremely badly. If I can get some shoes, we could have a game. I hope you're not brilliant at it!"

Brian had got her alive, so now he asked the inevitable question. "How did you find things when you got home? As bad as you feared?"

"Quite honestly Brian, it's been terrible, and I still haven't been able to bring myself to talk about it. The funeral was this morning, and after it was over all I could think about was telephoning Shaw's as you said. Once I spoke to your Mother I finished up the business with the undertaker and caught the first train to Sidhurst, and here I am!"

Brian listened carefully until, she finished. "Did you find out what happened?"

"Yes, but there was nothing to do. The neighbours and authorities had organised everything, not realising I would be home so soon. There is nothing left now. Both my parents are dead, and having no other relatives, I shall go back to Rome as soon as my leave is over. There's nothing for me here. I have to decide what to do with the possessions, clothes, and everything that were saved by the rescue teams. At present they are in the council store, but I shall have to decide what to do with them before I go back. Anyway, I shall need some clothes, if there are any fit to wear. I could not face it before I came here."

Elsie interrupted her from carrying on as she could see she was becoming upset again.

"I don't believe there is nothing here for you, for a moment. What about your school or family friends? Have you none? I'm sure they would love to hear from you, if not now, later when you have more time."

Jane looked uncertain. "You are probably right, Mrs Winter, but at the moment I can't think too far ahead. I just want to try and get some sleep and see how I feel tomorrow."

Brian joined the conversation. "We quite understand, Jane, you must be very tired. Lets just finish our tea, and as it's' such a lovely evening, I will walk you round Sidhurst and show you the High Street and the best bits. Then we can turn in early. I am tired out as well after so much travelling. I have to sort myself out at the Black Horse, and you can settle in with Mother. As for your clothes and your possessions, we can go over tomorrow, or when you feel up to it. Forget it all for the present."

Jane was becoming too tired to either object or argue. "Sounds fine to me." she replied. "Now let me help Mrs Winter wash up and we'll set off. A walk will do me good, I think."

"No need to help me today Jane," said Elsie. "Off you go with Brian. Leave it to me. Come back by eight at the latest, and we'll have a quick drink before bed. You can unpack what you need for the night then."

With that she got up and ushered them to the stairs. "See you later. Have a good time."

Jane and Brian went down the stairs and she heard the door close.

As she thought about the bereaved young girl, Elsie sensed that Jane was replying automatically to the activities going on around her. She wanted to help both Jane and Brian. It was obvious she was at home with him, almost as if they had known one another in a different time. She was reminded of her and Bill in the days when they had first found each other. Was history repeating itself in totally different circumstance?

Jane and Brian walked slowly along the High Street and turned left at the Police Station and continued on to the local Park – Sidhurst Park. For a while neither spoke, but finally Jane took hold of his arm and began to unburden herself. Tired, dead tired, she still could not relax and tell him the pain within her. It was as if she was in another world, the present far away. They turned the corner at the end of the park walk and could hear the sound of another V1 in the distance. The first I've heard, she thought,. Brian heard it too, but said nothing, just put his arm gently round her waist as if to protect her. They continued as it droned off into the distance on its way to London, hearing no explosion. Perhaps it was a dud, thought Jane, slowly releasing Brian's arm. Time for that when she felt better!

By the time they had walked what Brian called 'the outer circuit', through the park, round Mrs McIver's road and back to the shop it was gone eight. Together they walked up to the flat. Jane was yawning long before, and knew she needed to sleep, but could she? She hoped Mrs Winter's bed was comfortable.

Elsie had prepared some biscuits and cups of cocoa for them all.

"Now Jane, "she said. "I saw you yawning as you came in. Tale this with you to your room, drink it in bed and get off to sleep as quickly as you can. There is time for everything in the morning. I will bring you in some tea about eight if you aren't awake. Is that O.K.?"

Jane sighed with relief and tiredness. "I'm not going to argue Mrs Winter. Good night Brian. I hope your pub bed is O.K., and I'll see you in the morning."

She began to walk towards the stairs to the spare room. Elsie touched her arm and said. "Jane, please call me Elsie. I know I'm Brian's mother, but you're a Sergeant with an important job,

and an adult. You must call me Elsie from now on. I would be so
pleased if you would. You should find all you need in the little
bathroom. If not please call me. I'm sure I can find anything you
haven't brought."

"Thank you Elsie" she replied. "Eight o'clock would be fine.
Goodnight."

Brian and his mother went back to the drawing room and
chatted for a while. Elsie would have liked to ask Brian more
about Jane, but did not dare in case she heard. They sat for a
while chatting then Brian stood up.

"Mum, I hope you don't mind, but I'm absolutely tired out.
Can I say goodnight and see you in the morning. Can I come in
for breakfast, and what time do you think?"

"Please don't be later than half past eight, dear. I have to be
downstairs at nine, so try and make it by then if you can."

Brian moved towards the door, then turned, came back and
kissed his Mother. "Thank you for what you are doing for Jane,
Mum. She needs a lot of help at the moment."

"I know Brian. Don't you think I know what she is going
through?"

"Sorry Mum, I forgot for a minute. Goodnight, and sleep
well."

He walked slowly down the stairs and was gone. Elsie sat
alone with her thoughts for the night. She went quietly up the
stairs and listened. From the spare room came the sound of
steady breathing. Jane was already asleep, exhausted with all the
grief, exertion, and trying to keep her head in strange company.
Hopefully she would have a peaceful night. Elsie undressed
quickly and got into bed. Plenty to think about, she began to
mull over the events of the last few days, but before she could
do more than wonder about Jane, and what her son had told her,
she went fast asleep.

She was woken by the sound of the birds singing outside
her window and realised it must be after six as the sun was
already streaming into her bedroom.. Something had woken

her, but what was it? Not another V1 she hoped. She listened again. It was the sound of quiet weeping coming from the spare room. She knew, of course, it was Jane. She wondered what to do. Should she go in and comfort her, or leave her alone with her grief in private. She waited for nearly a quarter of an hour and decided the best thing she could do would be to make some tea. She slipped on her dressing gown, went down to the kitchen and made a pot of tea with two cups on a tray and biscuits. She took them all back upstairs, gave a little rat-tat quietly on the spare bedroom door and went in. Jane was lying facing the window away from her and she sensed rather than saw the rears running down her face while enormous muffled sobs came from her, her shoulders heaving. Elise's heart melted. Poor girl! What a terrible experience for her, and so young. She can't be more than nineteen!

Moving over to the bed, Jane heard and turned to face her. She held out the tray.

"I heard you stirring Jane, so thought we might both have an early morning cup of tea." She sat down on the edge of the bed, noticing Jane had been sleeping in her underwear. She obviously had not brought any pyjamas with her. She sat up trying to hide her tears.

"That was kind Mrs W – Elsie. I was feeling very low. A cup of tea is very welcome. Come and sit with me." Elsie poured the milk, put in two spoons of sugar, although Jane did not take any the previous afternoon, and handed put the cup to her having put two digestive biscuits in the saucer.

"Did you sleep well? You look more rested." That was a lie. Jane looked awful!

"Not too badly, Thanks, but I have had a bad few minutes since I woke."

"Yes, "said Elsie "I heard, but don't worry. It has to come out and the sooner the better. So you can get back to normality. Now, let's talk if you feel like it."

Elsie made herself comfortable on the bed and listened as Jane told her the whole sad episode. All the while, rears rolled steadily down her cheeks. Elsie let her go on in spite of her emotion. The relief, as she gradually relaxed was plain to see, and finally she stopped, her reservoir of grief spent for the time being, and sat back to see what Elsie would say.

Elsie did not attempt to sympathise. That was not what the young woman needed. So she asked about her plans.

"Now you have got it all out, what will you do? I suppose it's back to the job in Rome until the war is over. But what after that? Did you have a job before you joined up?"

"No," replied Jane. "I joined up straight from school as soon as I was seventeen and a half. I will have to see what my experience in the ATS is worth, and maybe try for a demob grant. There are a number available, I understand, you can apply for."

Elsie liked the businesslike manner with which she tackled the question.

"I'm sure there will be something to your liking, Jane. You are intelligent, quick and have an excellent service record as far as I can see. Now, I'd better get down to the kitchen and get us some breakfast. Brian will be coming in shortly like a starving lion. Can I leave you to sort yourself out here, and come down as soon as you are ready? We can always talk again. I'm always here. Oh, and one thing I meant to have asked you before. Do you have any clothes with you besides what you came in?"

Jane obviously hadn't from her expression. "No, I'm afraid I don't. The army have given me some coupons, and I hope I can find some things in the High Street when I go shopping. I am not going to stay in uniform, that's for sure!"

Elsie thought for a moment. "Look, Jane, I know they may seem old fashioned to you, but if you want to see if any of my things are of help, it might do temporarily so you don't have to buy the first clothes you see. What d'you think?"

"I think you are very kind," said Jane "but I can manage in uniform for shopping, and change as soon as I get back here."

"Well, the offer's there if you want it." She went back to the kitchen in time to hear Brian's knock on the door anxious for his breakfast!

Elsie found three eggs – one each, lightly boiled them, and soon they sat down to plenty of cornflakes, and an egg each.

"What shall we do today, Jane" said Brian. "That is after you've been shopping?"

"Why not get out in the country for a while." suggested Elsie "It's a lovely morning. It will do you both good."

"Would you like to do that Jane?" said Brian "There are some lovely paths along the Darenth Valley, and we could get the bus to Farningham, and walk along the river. First, though, you must meet Uncle Jim. He was a great friend of my Father, and I never miss keeping him up to date on what's going on. He was in the last war, and badly hurt, but he has a heart of gold, and Mum is very fond of him."

Jane was quick to agree. She hadn't given the day much thought other than she must buy some clothes. "That sounds fine. Let's go down and see Uncle Jim as soon as we have helped Elsie with the chores, and then we can get out together. I'm not sure you will like shopping for women's clothes, but you'll have to bear it until I can get into civvies again. I must also get over to Croydon as soon as possible. I will telephone and make an appointment for tomorrow to arrange to collect the belongings they are holding for me. Is that alright Brian?"

Brian considered the idea. "Yes, sounds fine. I think I may be able to get a van if we talk nicely to Uncle Jim. That is, if he has any petrol coupons left! What shall we do with the things you are collecting? Perhaps he can help there too!"

Elsie looked at the clock.

"Just look at the time, it's ten to nine. I have to go down in a minute. You get on, and I'll see you after shopping, and we'll have some elevenses together."

"Leave the washing up and beds to me, Mrs – sorry, Elsie" said Jane. "You go down to the shop and we'll come down to meet Uncle Jim when we've finished here."

Jim was even more surprised than the previous morning when not only Brian, now dressed in mufti, but also a very smart and attractive ATS Sergeant came in with him before he started his day. Brian wanted him to hear all about Jane, how he had helped her, and was obviously keen to find out what Jim thought. It as not until they had gone, and Jim had promised to contact one of the Wardens who had a small van and some petrol, that Elsie and he could discuss the new arrival.

"She seems a very nice young lady" remarked Jim "It looks as if Brian has found himself an intelligent well organised girl. She has obviously taken a very great liking to your Brian. What d'you think?"

"I like her very much already" answered Elsie. "I think they will have a happy leave together. She has to return before Brian, but unless they fall out this week, I think it will not be the last time I shall see her!"

Jim agreed. "I don't believe I have met such a strong personality in a young lady for a long time. In some ways she reminds me of when I first came to see Bill and yourself at the dairy. How old were you then? Thirty, perhaps?"

"But they are so much mature for their ages today, Jim. It must be the effect of the war. It makes them grow up so fast, and my goodness, she certainly has had her share of misfortune."

"Very nice girl indeed." said Jim "Now. Elsie there is a lot to do today, particularly if I am going to find a van for Brian and – what did you say her name was – oh yes, I remember, Jane. I expect you will want to finish early as well, so let's get down to it!"

Together they set about completing the work from the previous day and were ready to open a little late just after nine thirty. Joan arrived soon after and the daily routine had begun.

The young people returned after about two hours with a huge parcel of clothes, and Jane retired to the flat to change. Brian went with her to make coffee for them all, and came down shortly after to announce 'Coffee is served!" Joan insisted she and Jim both went up for a few minutes, and Jane now looked far younger, almost still a schoolgirl to Elsie's eyes. Jim was obviously very smitten with her, and Brian could hardly keep his eyes off her. She really was very attractive, not beautiful, but alert, bright, and becoming much happier in her manner and appearance. Elsie hoped the afternoon in the country would be a success!

Jim was as good as his word, and one of the Wardens came round with a Rescue lorry, and parked it outside. Brian could now drive, and the two set off for Croydon early next day. When they returned in the afternoon, they had completed the sad job. Elsie could hardly believe how much they had achieved, until Brain and Jane told her how much the people round her home, and the Council staff helped. They had agreed to hold the large items in a local store at a tiny rent, well within Jane's means, and the belongings she wanted were in the van. She had changed, pleased the loathsome job had been completed, and for the first time came up to the flat with a smile and a laugh at Brian who was playing the fool with some of her things.

Later when Jane and Elsie were sitting in the drawing room after Brian had gone off for the night to the Black Horse, Elsie learned the reason for Brian's return to England. She was surprised to find out from Jane he had been highly praised by his C.O. after an attack on his Troop of guns by German tanks. Jane had seen the citation, just after she met him, and although it was confidential, had read it, The first rounds fired at the battery killed the captain in command, and without proper orders the guns were disorganised. Brian the command post officer had taken the initiative. Taking personal command of the nearest 25 pounder, whose No 1 had been wounded, directed the crew to attack the nearest tank coming through their line. The second round disabled the first tank, but the layer was killed, and Brian took his place, engaged the tanks still advancing, disabled another, while the rest of the troop followed his example. This forced the remainder to stop, and finally retreat from the intense fire put up by the battery. By the time a senior officer came, the engagement was over. Brian was immediately promoted acting captain, and later recommended for a Military Cross, now unofficially confirmed.

The action coincided with his posting to England for 'special duties'. Jane did not know what they were, and all Brain had told her was that he was attending a course in Oxford which would take about six weeks or more, but he would not be returning to Italy as far as she knew. Elsie did not know whether to be delighted or concerned. Brian had never been a boy to avoid a fight, but it worried her. Why had he been called back? Was it for some special mission? She hoped and prayed not!

Occasionally during the rest of the week Jane was with them, her grief surfaced although she tried her best to hide it. What she said to Brian when they were alone together, Elsie didn't know, but it was very obvious he was becoming very fond of her. She did not think it had developed into a love affair, but from his expression as he saw her off at the end of her leave at Sidhurst station, he would miss her very much indeed.

After Jane departed, she attempted to ask him about the citation, but all he got was that he had simply done what was needed at the time. He was posted, he said, to somewhere near Oxford for a special course and would be able to get home occasionally, he thought. After that he would be posted again but did not know where. Elsie saw she was not getting any more information, so decided to simply enjoy his leave, and spend as much time as she could with him away from the shop, if Jim would let her. The following morning she spoke to Joan and made her a promise. If Joan would work extra time while Brian was home, she would do the same for her when she needed they same favour. She presented the idea to Jim then following day, and after a little thought, he agreed. Brian was at home for another six days and she would spend it with him.

She found Brian without Jane, soon returned to his youthful

ways, but with some major differences. He was more serious for a start, and one afternoon he old her how he saw his future after the war. He would go back to university, get his degree, and take up a career in engineering. He had it all mapped out and she listened with interest.

"Brian" she said one afternoon. "You know I will be happy to support you in every way I can. Your father never managed to qualify, and he would already be very proud of you. You can stay here after you come out of the Army if you wish, until you find a place to settle. What about Jane? Have you any ideas about her?" It was a leading question, and she was surprised at his reply.

"No, not really, Jane is very nice, good fun, and I like her. However, she is not in a right state of mind to do anything serious, and I am not sure if she is right, even if she was." Elsie didn't expect such a mature view.

"I shall see her if and when I can, and we'll see how things work out. Now Mum, what about some tea, I'm starving!" He always was. At least that hadn't changed!

In between times he told her much about life in Italy, and the suffering of people caught up in the war. His insight was alarming to Elsie. It seemed as if nothing happened that he did not remember in detail, and its effect on the surroundings, and circumstances. The ten days flew by. Together they went walking in the hills above Eynsford, a place he had always loved to visit when he was young. They picnicked on the steep scarp slope above the Weald. He talked a lot about his Father, and many times they were close to tears as the years of his growing up were recalled.

"Brian" she laughed, "You are so like your Father. It is as if he is here again!" He responded by laughing back, exactly in the way Bill would have done. "And why not Mum, unless you had a fling with the milkman! If I were not like Dad I would be very sad!"

Later that afternoon they went back down the hill to a little teashop in the valley, a favourite place before the war at the end of rambles through the hills. They sat down to a plate of cakes and a huge pot of tea. In the past there were more exotic fancy cream cakes, but now they were just plain, but they enjoyed them as much. At five o'clock they caught the train back to St Mary Cray and the 51 bus on to Sidhurst. It was a very tired but happy Mother and son, who trudged up the stairs to the flat on St Mark's Parade.

Another morning, Brian surprised her by coming into the shop with two tickets for a London show. He had it all planned. They caught the train up to London about six, had tea at Lyons Corner House and went on to the Dominion Theatre. An amusing comedy was playing and Brian had been fortunate to get two cancellations. After the show he took his Mother to a little restaurant behind Liberty's for supper. It was a long time since she had been escorted to an evening meal by a handsome young man, and she could sense the heads turning. "They must think she is cradle snatching, going out with such a young man." she thought, but didn't care, and sat with her son in attendance letting some of the girls at the next table envy her. After they had eaten, he turned to her and said.

"Mum, would you like to dance?"

Elsie replied incredulously "I didn't know you could dance Brian, Where did you learn?"

"Ah" said Brian "that would be telling. You know they teach you many things in the Army!"

"Surely they don't include dancing?" rejoined Elsie. "I thought it was all about officer qualities!"

Brian laughed out loud, catching the eye of the young ladies nearby, who were dancing with one another.

"Only teasing Mum. I learned at some dances I went to after school when I was supposed to be staying late to play rugger!"

"Oh, did you!" said his Mother "And what other things did you get up to when you were supposed to be staying late?"

"I'm not telling you that!" he laughed again, and whisked her around the floor in a practised waltz.

"I think I've had enough for a few minutes." puffed Elsie. "Let me sit down for a break and get my breath. It's a long time since I did this!"

Brian took her back to her chair. "Mum, while you rest, would you mind if I asked one of those girls over there to dance?"

Elsie smiled to herself. He had done his duty and she thought he had not missed the admiring glances from the next table. He got up and walked briskly across to them. She did not hear what they said but there was a quick laugh and one of them stood up and let herself be twirled off in his arms. Brian was certainly not the shy youth she saw off to join the army three years ago!

Together they sat talking a few minutes before the last train left Charing Cross, and climbed aboard almost as the guard blew his whistle. The carriage was quite full of late night revellers, and Elsie found herself listening to the young people discussing their lives and mishaps. They were all servicemen and women on leave, out to make the most of the brief interlude in their service lives. One girl fascinated Elsie. She was in the WAAF, and had obviously one or two more to drink than was good for her. Amid much shushing from her companions, she insisted in telling all around about her work in her camp in Suffolk., where she was a radar operator. She could not have been much more than eighteen and from what she said obviously had a responsible job guiding bombers to and from their target. After a minute or two she was told very firmly by her companions to 'Shut up' who realised she should not be shooting off her mouth about her work. She went to sleep in her companion's arms and snored all the way to Mottingham where they got off. As the door swung shut she heard the dreaded sound of a V1 coming over. No one seemed to hear it but her. The door swung shut again and the sound died away as the train moved off and the next stop was Sidhurst. They managed to catch a late bus home. Brian was staying in the flat now and they sat talking about the evening's events, before retiring for the night. Elsie slept better than she had done for a long time. Her beloved son was home, and all was right with the world!

In what seemed no more than an instance, Brian was dressed in his uniform, looking happy to have some extra items from his Mother to take with him to Oxford. She went with him to the station although he protested there was no need, and waved him off from the station. Feeling sad, she decided to walk back to the flat. It seemed lonely and deserted, so she sat and had a late cup of tea in her sitting room. It was back to the shop tomorrow and her brief happy interlude was over. Later, before she turned off the light, she said a lengthy prayer for her son's safe future, then snuggled down to sleep.

****

Chapter 7

$\mathcal{T}$he next week passed uneventfully. On the following Monday morning, Elsie went to retrieve her post to find a lettercard addressed to her with unfamiliar writing. Wondering who it was, as it was certainly from someone in the forces, she opened it immediately. It started 'Dear Mrs Winter, I hope you don't mind my writing to you, but I know you are a friend of Betty Manners to whom I am, or was, engaged. She does not reply to my telephone calls since I reached Portsmouth last week, and as I am coming home for a few days leave at the weekend, I wanted to ask if you would be kind enough to contact her and tell her I shall be home on Friday, and want to see her.' It went on for a few more lines to a polite finish and was signed 'Yours sincerely, Douglas Armstrong.'

There was just time to catch Betty before she went down to the shop, so she immediately called her number.

"Hallo Betty, Elsie here. Sorry to call so early, but I have received in the post today, a letter from Doug He asks me to tell you he is coming on leave this week, and will be home on Friday. He wants to see you! I thought you told him last leave."

There was a cry of vexation and trepidation from the other end.

"No he didn't get leave. Elsie, I've written to him, and told him it's over. Why does he want to see me?"

"Well, it's none of my business. I'm just passing on his message as he asked me to, but I expect he wants an explanation and to find out why you left him!"

"Well, I'm shall make a point of being out! My Mother can talk to him. I'll go off and stay with Ron for the weekend, or until he goes back to sea!"

"I think the very least you could do is to see him and tell him to his face that you are engaged to someone else. Poor man, he will have been counting on spending his leave with you until he received your letter when he got to Portsmouth. It is too late to reply to him before Friday. You'll have to do whatever you think fit."

"I know what to do – keep out of his way! Thanks for telling me Elsie. Bye."

Elsie had a feeling this was not the last she would hear of Douglas and his leave.

All the week she worked hard in the shop helping Jim and making up the time she owed Joan, who took most of the week off. She was over sixty, and in normal circumstances would have retired, but the war stopped it as there was no chance of Jim getting someone new in the present labour shortage.

The shop trade had increased again, due to Elsie's presence, Jim said, and she was kept extremely busy as he had to deal with the prescriptions which were also increasing in leaps and bounds. Both Brian and Jane telephoned during the week. It seemed Jane had not returned to Rome, and was still in England. How else could she have been able to telephone! No doubt Elsie would find out in due time!

On Thursday, Brain 'phoned and said they, he and Jane, would like to come home for the weekend as they had 48 hour passes. Well organised thought Elsie! They met in London and went out before coming on to Sidhurst. The friendship was developing, and Jane told her she had succeeded in getting a compassionate posting to the War Office, and was not returning to Italy. Elsie guessed it was really to stay near Brian on his course. They were both very happy when they sat down to one of Elsie's breakfasts on the Saturday morning. Later that evening, Jane deliberately gave Brian a reason to go out, and as soon as he went, spoke to Elsie.

"Can I speak to you frankly, Elsie?"

"Yes, of course you can, my dear"

"I have to tell you that Brian and I are thinking of getting engaged. I know it's very quick, but we may have so little time, and we want to make every moment count."

Elsie was taken aback. "But you've only known one another a few weeks. How do you know you're right for each other?"

"We knew immediately we met in Rome. We both love one another, and we're both so sure!"

Elsie felt nothing would stop this determined young lady having her way. She liked her very much, but it was so soon! How could they know? She and Bill had been courting for six months before anything was sure, but then, she had been sure from the day she met him! Perhaps it was the same with them! She thought of how she would see Jane as a daughter-in-law. It was a new experience and she was uncertain whether to be pleased or not!

"Look, Jane," she said. "Only you and Brian can know for sure, but if you're both absolutely certain, I would not dream of standing in your way."

"I knew you would think that way, Elsie." continued Jane. "It was only that Brian was so worried you might not be happy about it. I said I would talk to you first, and pave the way."

Elsie looked hard at her. "You are very pleasant, but you know what you want and are not afraid to go for it, are you? Alright, I'll give you both my blessing, but if you ever let him down, you will have me to reckon with!"

Jane sighed. "There is not the slightest chance of that. He is the one for me, and I know he thinks the same. We are very happy, and now you have approved, we shall go and buy a ring to make it official, this afternoon."

At that moment she heard Brian coming up the stairs, and was ready for him.

"Now, Brian," she said in mock anger. "What's all this Jane is telling me about you two?" She pretended to look very severe, but gave a suspicion of a wink to Jane.

"Mum," he cried out. "I thought you would be pleased, and liked Jane. We have been so wound up with each other, but I'm sorry we haven't told you how we were feeling about one another before!"

Elsie hit back. "Well, I haven't a clue, and I'm not sure what to say."

"Oh, Mum" continued Brian. "You must have seen we are very fond of each other!"

Elsie had one more sally to make. "It's far too early! Why, you've only known each other for a week or two. Bill and I were friends for six months before we got engaged."

He started to get embarrassed, while Jane said nothing. Elsie suddenly laughed out loud!

"Brian, Jane has told me how much you love one another. Of course I'm delighted for you both. Now, off you go and get the ring, and I will have a celebration tea ready for you when you return. Now, don't you think you had better tell your Uncle Jim. He will be furious if he's not the first to know!"

Brain relaxed and smiled. "Thank you very much, Mum. You are a tease. You really had me worried for a moment, then!"

"Serves you right for taking me for granted. My congratulations to you both, and if you ever let Jane down, young man, I will get the cane to you as once I threatened when you were at school!"

"O.K., Mum. I would deserve it. if I ever did." With that he turned to Jane.

"Come on, darling, let's be off to Woolwich. There's a good jeweller there. I saw it when I went into the town from the barracks last week. It'll be far better than anything in dreary old Sidhurst."

"Off you go, then," said Elsie. "Now, be careful what you

buy. If you can find a second hand ring it'll be better value than a new one, but that's just me. Get what Jane likes and will be happy with."

"Thanks for the suggestion, Elsie "said Jane. "See you at tea time. Come on Brian, we haven't got all day!" and they were off, running down the stairs like two happy children, leaving an amazed Elsie alone in the flat.

When the young people returned form Woolwich, Jane was already wearing a neat, small diamond and sapphire ring. Elsie had gone down to the shop to talk to Jim before the shop opened. She told him, in confidence the earlier happenings, and he promised to be suitably surprised when they told him their news. Like Elsie, he thought it far too quick, but had to agree that in these days, hazardous for young people in the forces, they had to take their chances. If they were both sure, why not!

As soon as they returned they went down immediately to 'Uncle Jim', and he congratulated them heartily. He was grateful Elsie had pre-warned him and was able to appear shocked but happy for them. Time indeed was short, for they had to be back in their units the next day. Jane was working on a staff supplies job at the War Office, and Brian was at a base near Oxford. Jane let it slip he was on a special training course, and it was keeping him very fit, but then clammed up as she saw Elsie's enquiring reaction.

About ten to one, Jane and Brian were out somewhere, and Elsie was busy in the shop when a very smart heavily built sailor in uniform came in to the shop, and walked directly up to Elsie. She recognised Douglas Armstrong!

"Did you get my letter?" he barked at her.

"Why yes, it's Doug isn't it? I passed your message on to Betty, but haven't seen her since."

Douglas quizzed her. "Any idea where she might be? Her and her spivvy boyfriend?"

"Sorry Douglas, I have no idea. Isn't she at home?"

Douglas appeared in a very bad mood. "No, and her Mother won't tell me where she is. Gone out with her fancy man? Wait 'til I see them! You definitely haven't any idea where they are?"

"No, as I said, I haven't seen her for some time. I telephoned your message to her on Monday when I got your letter. All she said was she had told you." She didn't add what Betty had said about keeping clear of him.

"Well, you're not much help. I'll have to look for her. I want a few words with that tart before I go back to sea!" he spat the word 'tart', and looked thunderous. "Thanks for passing the message."

He went out, and Elsie knew he was looking for trouble, and hoped he didn't find it!

That was the end of the matter as far as Elsie was concerned, and the next news came from Jim. Jane and Brian had gone back on Sunday night, and Elsie went down to the shop as usual on Monday morning. Jim came in as normal, but with some news of Saturday night.

"Elsie "he said. "Have you heard about Douglas in the Station Hotel?"

"No," replied Elsie "why?"

"From what I've been told, Ron Perkins and Betty Manners were in there having a quiet drink about nine o'clock when Doug Armstrong came in very much the worse for wear. I expect you know he was a navy boxing champion before the war. Well, he saw Betty and Ron together, and went up to them and ordered Betty to come with him. She refused, and Ron Perkins tried to prevent Doug from grabbing Betty's arm. Douglas drew back his right arm and with one punch, hit him so hard he fell on the floor, knocked out cold! Doug grabbed Betty and made off with her."

Elsie thought of Douglas' mood when he came into the shop, and thought how he would be after knocking back a few! "What happened then, Jim?"

"I don't know. Ron Perkins finished up at the First Aid Post, which is how I came to know via the Wardens. It is all over the town. No one has seen either of them since. I think Ron is O.K now, but he was lucky his jaw wasn't broken."

Elsie waited to hear from Betty. She knew that at the first opportunity she would be in contact with her as she always did when she was in a pickle! The day passed, but she heard nothing, and forgot about the incident. On Friday morning, Mrs McIver came in to the shop.

"Wondered if you would like to come over for tea on Sunday, Elsie, that is unless your son and his fiancé are coming home. Oh, and by the way. You knew Betty Manners didn't you?"

"Yes, quite well, why? Is she in trouble again?"

"More than that! My husband said that the police have found her body under some bushes in the Park. She has been strangled apparently!"

"What!"" said Elsie," Betty Manners! Are you sure? She and I have been friends for years. I know she has always been a bit flighty, but when did it happen? How terrible!" She couldn't believe what she was hearing!

Then she thought of Douglas. "Has anyone said how it happened or who did it?" she asked Elizabeth.

"Not so far, although they are looking for Douglas Armstrong. He was the last to see her apparently. Did you know him?" Elsie thought about it and decided to keep her mouth shut. Elizabeth McIver was obviously looking for scandal, and Elsie was not going to be the one to supply it!

"No, I may have met him once, but that's all. Now, Elizabeth, what can I get you?"

"Just a repeat of my usual medicine, please Elsie. Can you have it ready today, please, if possible?"

"Elsie knew Jim always kept a bottle of her medicine in the dispensary.

"Certainly, Elizabeth, I'll see it is ready for you this afternoon. About half past four alright?"

"Yes, that will be fine, thank you Elsie. See you later, bye."

After she'd gone, Elsie stood in horror at what she had heard.

Was it really true? Was Betty dead? She hadn't telephoned as she thought she would after the Douglas episode. Another customer came in and her attention was diverted until Jim came in from the back. She told Jim what she had heard

Jim didn't know, so could add nothing. The day continued, and she still could not believe it was true!

On Saturday, she was in the shop as usual, when two tallish severe looking men in dark suits came in. They asked for the proprietor, and Elsie called Jim from the dispensary. After a brief word, he motioned to Elsie to come over to them. "This is Elsie Winter, officers" The taller of the two, and obviously the senior, addressed Elsie. "I am Detective Inspector Stewart, and this is Sergeant Crowther. We are investigating the death of Miss Betty Manners, and I believe you were a friend of hers."

"Yes, I've known Betty for some years. What can I help you with?" So it was true! Betty is really dead!

The Inspector looked at Jim. "Could we use your office at the back for a few minutes, sir, if it would not inconvenience you. If not we shall have to ask Mrs Winter to come down to the station and give a statement. If we can interview her here, it will not deprive you of her services for so long." Jim readily gave his consent, and the three moved into the little room that Elsie used as a shelter from the V1's.

She told them all she knew about Betty, together with what Jim had told her. They asked to see the letter, and she went up to the flat praying she had not thrown it away. Luckily she hadn't. It was still on the back of the kitchen dresser. Picking it up, she took it to the officers.

"Do you know who did it yet?" she asked when she had told them all she knew.

"Can't comment I'm afraid, Mrs Winter, but I can tell you that we have sent a message to Mr Armstrong's ship, which sailed on Monday, and is now on the way to the Far East."

With a curt thank you to Jim, the officers went out. So it was Douglas they suspected. He must have had a show down with Betty, and turned nasty, then gone back to his ship and

sailed the same night, before they caught up with him. What a disaster! She couldn't help but feel that Betty had brought it on herself. Always the flirt and with no morals, she had numerous man friends, and any man could have her. Now she had got her desserts, but she did not deserve to be murdered! What about Douglas, poor man! Thought he had a fiancée at home, and then letting his temper getting the better of him. Now he will be a wanted man for ever!

She and Jim discussed every scrap of news. The Kentish Times had a huge news report. 'Local girl murdered!' it said, and went on to show a picture of the park where Betty had been found. There was hardly a customer who did not talk to Elsie about it, and it was generally agreed throughout the town, that Douglas Armstrong was the culprit. Jim was not so sure.

"I just don't believe it!" he said to Elsie a few days later. "He must know he would be the obvious suspect. I know he went back to his ship and he knew it was sailing on the Sunday night tide, but even so – if he did do it, he must have had a mad temper to go to the length of killing her just for revenge!"

"Perhaps he thought if I can't have her, no one else will either!" answered Elsie.

So they left it to be resolved, and Elsie went to the funeral two weeks later when the body was released for burial. Most of the Klinger's staff attended. Betty's parents were the chief mourners, and Ron Perkins, still with a very bruised but healing face, was close behind. Elsie slipped in to one of the pews at the back and said her prayers for Betty, who was later buried in the local cemetery near the Girls High School.

After it was over, Sidhurst slowly returned to normal, and waited for Douglas to return from the sea!

Jane and Brian had several weekend passes at Sidhurst, and, of course, heard all about the murder. Brian knew Betty, but didn't have much sympathy. "Always was a tart, as Douglas said," he commented. "Probably got what she deserved, If Doug hadn't done it, someone else would have one day. She went after every boy in the class when we were at school. I didn't like her. Thought a bit too much of herself, and always did. I'm sorry she's dead, but won't lose any sleep!"

That was the final word about Betty.

After two weekends, Brian came home for a third and announced to his Mother he had been posted to France. He could not say where, but it was, he said, some sort of liaison position attached to an armoured brigade. Jane explained to Elsie that although she did not know exactly, it was probably as an adviser, or observation officer, to the Tank Regiment with who he would be travelling. On his final leave, he was wearing his Military Cross ribbon and Jim took him and Jane out to lunch as a measure of his pride in the young officer's award. Elsie begged to be excused. She thought Brian and Jane, now a couple, should be on their own with Jim.

That afternoon, before they went back, while they were having a last cup of tea together, she asked Brian what they had talked about. Brian was evasive apart from the medal details, and Elsie wondered why.

"Did Jim mention my work in the shop, Brian? She asked.

"Yes, he said you are doing very well and hopes you will soon be able to dispense as well as serve customers. He did also say how much the business has increased since you started working with him."

"That was kind." said Elsie "Did he talk of anything else?"

"What do you mean, Mum?" asked Brian.

"Well, I wondered if he mentioned his health and me in any way."

Brian recognised his Mother was fishing for something "What are you hinting about, Mum?"

"Well, I wondered if he mentioned a friend of mine, Gordon?"

"No, I can't say he did." answered Brian. "Why, is there something special about this Gordon I should know about?"

Elsie hastily stopped. If Jim had said nothing, he had a reason. Perhaps he was just being loyal to her. She replied vaguely to Brian. "Oh, he got annoyed over something that happened in the shop with Gordon McIver, and I wondered if he had taken it seriously. That's all!"

"No. Mum. His name wasn't mentioned."

"Oh good," finished Elsie, "then I can forget it!"

Jane and Brian departed back to the War Office and France respectively. Elsie felt alone in the flat. It seemed very quiet and her life slow after all that had happened. Jane now treated her like her adopted Mother. She hoped she had helped to replace the loss of her parents. For the time being, she found happiness with Brian, and he more than anyone was helping her through her grief. Of course, it was always there underneath, and she noticed just occasionally the grief surface on her face.

She and Jim now worked closely together. Jim's health was imperceptibly deteriorating. Although he appeared well enough, she knew he was taking more aspirins for his headaches. He was leaving more in the shop to her and Joan. Some mornings he did not appear until late, whereas normally he arrived early and carried out the ritual sweeping of the front. Now, Elsie was performing the task and she could not make up her mind whether it was because she was there, or he was being forced to take life more easily. She raised the subject with him one morning.

"Jim, I notice you seem to have lost your appetite for the shop lately, is there anything wrong?"

He didn't answer without thinking as she could see. "I think it is the number of prescriptions. We are so much busier, thanks to you. I have to spend more time on the accounts and ordering, most of which I do at home as you know. I must admit I get more tired than I used to. Why? Have you noticed a difference?"

Elsie answered tactfully. "No, I haven't, I had forgotten how much work the extra business must make. If I can help at all, please tell me."

"No, Elsie. You are doing well enough as it is. Leave something for poor old Jim to do!"

No more was said, but Elsie knew he was not as fit as he had been, and wondered if there was anything else which he was not about to reveal. She returned to her daily routine and forgot about her fear for him.

The dreaded V1's had one last card to play. Hardly any at all came over, but the odd one that appeared was often damaged, and in consequence could be quite unpredictable in behaviour. One afternoon soon after their talk, she heard one approaching. The customers ignored it, and she carried on serving. The sound became louder, then almost disappeared, then louder again. Jim also heard it in the dispensary, and went outside to have a look. He quickly ran back into the shop. "Elsie, get in the back room now! There is a doodle bug circling the town, and it could come down anywhere, even on us. Please stay in the back room until it's gone!"

Elsie moved speedily to follow his instructions and peeped at him from the inner room. Jim continued to watch from the shop door. He suddenly shouted

"My God, it's coming straight down! Stay where you are!" The engine roared as it fell, and Elsie ducked down below the dispensary desk for safety, and waited for the 'Bang' Almost at once she heard it explode, but not the huge bang she expected. Why not? What had happened? Jim, who had come in the shop to get more protection, went running out and just as quickly returned.

"It's fallen almost opposite Boot's" he shouted to Elsie. "Look after the shop until I get back!" He disappeared out of the door and she heard him running along the High Street towards Boots. Someone passing the shop shouted "It's fallen on the High Street. I can hear the Ambulances coming!" and ran on. Elsie wanted to dash out as well, but had to stay as instructed to hold the shop. Medicines and First Aid might be needed, and she went over and checked the amounts of bandages and plaster in the cupboard. She wondered about Boots. Was it damaged, and how many casualties?

She waited and worried for Sidhurst. All this time and it had to be one of the last that hit our High Street!

Ten minutes later, Jim came walking back.

"Elsie, fantastic! It didn't explode. Well, it did partly, but only where it hit the road. The bomb must have been a dud or something. Most of the doodle bug is still there, lying on the pavement with part in Boots, and the remainder on the road outside. The police cordoned off the area as soon as they arrived, and are waiting for the Bomb Disposal team to come!" He paused to get his breath back.

"It hit smack in the middle of the road, and skidded into Boots window. The shop is pretty badly damaged, but there were only light casualties. Better get ready for a rush for First Aid in a minute. What a piece of luck! If it had exploded normally, half the High Street would have been destroyed, and Lord knows how many casualties among the shoppers!"

Elsie stood waiting for people to come in. Sure enough, in the next hour and a half they were very busy as lightly cut and bruised Sidhurst people came in and patched themselves up rather than go to the First Aid Post. They had enough stock to meet all the requests, and Jim told her. "Don't worry about charging for sticking plaster, we can afford to help. It will repay us in the end!"

After two hours the rush was over, and Jim reflected on the demise, if only temporary, of Boots their main competitor in Sidhurst.

"I think I had better ring Joan, and warn her we shall .be very busy now for several weeks. I hope she will come in full time until they are back in business. Otherwise it will be hard to cope!"

About a quarter to six, she went up to the flat to make some tea and something to eat. It had been a long day! Jim, once the emergency was over, became excited with the prospect of getting most of Boot's business for a while, and kept thinking of all the things he needed to do. Getting more supplies, more assistance, and if so who? Finally, he seemed satisfied they could manage without extra help provided Joan came in permanently for a while. Elsie was feeling very weary, and after clearing away the tea things sat down for a few minutes to try and relax after all the excitement. She put on the six o'clock news just in time to hear the announcer say --- in Sidhurst' So now it had been reported on the national news of Sidhurst's remarkable escape.

Within the minute, the phone rang. It was Margaret. She had been listening to the news!

"Elsie, are you all right? I just heard about the High Street. Was it near Shaw's?"

Elsie laughed. "Don't worry Margaret. It fell outside Boots. I'm fine. Not even a window broken. For some reason it didn't explode, just made a mess of their shop window and counters apparently. I haven't seen it yet but Jim has, and he told me." She related the story to her sister.

"Phew, Elsie, you were lucky. And I thought they were all gone. Just goes to show. You never know for sure. I imagine you'll be very busy now. How's Jim? O.K.? and Gordon? Do you hear from him at all?"

"No," replied Elsie, "Haven't heard from him since he went back. I haven't told you Brian has become engaged. I should have 'phoned you earlier and told you, but I've been so busy, and forgot. Her name is Jane Parlour, and they met in Rome and came home to England on the same plane. She stayed here for a week. I like her very much. There's quite a story that I must tell you when I have more time. They seem totally obsessed with each other which is as it should be. Oh, and another thing, Brian has been awarded the Military Cross just before he came home to England. He was wearing the ribbon when he put his uniform back on after his leave, He is a captain now."

"My goodness, Elsie, it's been all action since we last spoke. You must tell me everything!"

"Yes, I will Margaret, but not now. I'm so tired. I must get some rest. I'll call you as soon as things settle down and we'll have a long chat. Better go now. Thanks for ringing and love to Arthur."

She put back the 'phone and it rang again. This time it was Jane. She too had heard the news and wanted to check she was alright. She confirmed the details as she had just done with Margaret, and Jane was gone.

She was very pleased Jane had taken the trouble to 'phone her. She liked her more each time they made contact.

Later that evening, she strolled down the High Street to see the damage for herself. The late summer sun was quite low in the evening sky as she walked to the centre of the High Street. From a distance it appeared much as it always did, but as she got nearer, she saw there were minor dents in the shop fronts and windows were broken. Dawsons, the shop where she sometimes bought shoes, had lost all it's windows and glass still lay in the road. Nearer she noticed the road covered in fine dust that stuck to the tarmac surface. The road was badly scarred and Boots front knocked in. Bits of debris were spread about the area and a Warden was guarding the area against looters. A few spectators stood gazing sadly at the mess, but Elsie could see it was nothing like as bad as she would have anticipated. Clearly it was a minor incident in comparison with the usual V1 site. The Warden was one of Bill's old colleagues, and recognised her immediately.

"Hallo, Elsie, come to look at the damage?"

"Yes," replied Elsie. "What exactly happened? Where did it hit?"

The Warden pointed to the centre of the road at the white line. "See that small hole in the surface. That's where it actually hit the ground and then slid along the road. It hit the lamppost as it skidded which took off the wing. The rest of the body crashed through Boots window and is still lying there."

Elsie looked into what was left of Boots, and saw a dull grey cylinder surrounded in debris, and part of what looked like a grey sail propping up the counter.

"I suppose that's also part of it?" she asked the Warden

"Yes, that's right. It's the other wing, or what's left of it. The Bomb Disposal Squad have checked it's quite safe, and we're waiting for the Salvage team to remove the rest. Apparently the detonating system had been sabotaged. That's why it didn't go off! Lucky, weren't we!"

Elsie agreed wholeheartedly, and thanked the Warden.

"Don't see you around much these days Elsie." He remarked as they walked back from the remnants of Boots.

"I work at Shaw's now, you know." she said.

"I didn't know that!" he replied. "I must tell the missus, and she'll come to you for all our medicines in future. Not that we shall have much choice by the look of Boots!" he chuckled to himself for some reason that Elsie could not quite understand.

"I hope you do." she continued. "It would be lovely to see your wife again. How is she by the way?"

Elsie did not know his wife, but he didn't know.

"She's fine at present. Had a turn with 'er legs a few months ago, but all recovered now."

Elsie decide not pursue what was wrong with 'his missus' legs' and saying goodbye, made her way back to her flat.

The warden got it right when he said they had been lucky. It could have been a disaster!

It was nearly dark when she reached her flat, reminding her September was approaching. Perhaps autumn would be early this year, and she wondered how warm her bomb damaged flat would be in the cold weather. All the next week the three were busier in the shop than they had ever been in the time Elsie had known. Because Boots was out of action, everyone had to use Shaw's, or shop outside the town. Many customers appeared whom Elsie had known over many years, and were delighted to see her again. Apart from what they needed, most enjoyed a chat over old times with her at the same time.

One Saturday a few weeks later it was obvious they were all feeling the pressure. Elsie felt she must broach Jim on the subject of getting more help. He was looking extremely weary, his headaches returning longer and more painful. He needed rest. The extra business combined with the need to keep constantly in touch with re-ordering supplies and paying invoices, and keeping the books, was taxing him hard. She approached him on the subject in the afternoon.

"Jim, we will have to take on another person for the shop if it's carries on like this."

Jim stopped what he was doing and thought for a moment.

"Yes, Elsie, I agree. You know, since you came we have grown considerably, and now it's very busy indeed. I shall have to leave the shop to you, and concentrate, with Joan, on dispensing and bookwork. Both are increasing. I have never known so many invoices to check and pay. Not that it's a bad thing, mind. Let's put our heads together for a few minutes later this evening. Why don't you come round to my house and we can have a bite to eat and discuss some ideas in peace and quiet?"

Elsie was taken aback. She had never seen Jim's house, let alone been asked to supper. Often she had passed it when out walking. It was beyond the Police Station and almost outside the main area of houses, in a very select area. She was both curious and flattered by the invitation, and accepted at once.

"Thank you very much, Jim, I should love to. Can I get us something to eat when I arrive?"

"No, no, Elsie, Mrs Daly will do that. Come just before half past seven, and we can have a drink first"

With that he picked up the 'phone before Elsie could reply.

"Is that you, Irene? Look, I have invited Mrs Winter for supper. Is that O.K.? Can you manage enough for three? I don't want you to sacrifice yours!"

Elise didn't hear her reply but it must have been agreement because he said "Yes, I'm happy about that. Have a good weekend!" He put back the telephone and said to Elsie. "That's sorted. See you just before seven thirty."

"Yes, thank you very much Jim, 'I'm looking forward to it."

Joan went early, so Elsie and Jim shut the shop just before six. Else went up to her flat. What should she wear? She was a bit worried. While wanting to look as if she dressed for supper, it was important that she didn't overdo things, particularly not to give him ideas. She liked him, and he was very kind, but knew if she encouraged him he might make advances. He had always fancied her, she knew that, but poor man, she could not bring herself to warm to him in a more intimate way because of his injured face. It could never be hidden and put off every woman. She was no exception. She settled for a trim outfit with no glamour that she wore for going out, but in no way special. In fact she had few clothes anyway, the war had seen to that. What she did have must last until better days returned.

She was rarely late for anything if she could avoid it, and it was just before the half hour when she walked down the little path between two well stocked flower beds, to Jim's front door. He obviously loved his garden. The paved path was weed free and the beds still a riot of colour, although it was September. Mostly petunias, dahlias and fuchsias made a lovely display and she stopped to admire the colours before she knocked on the door. He opened it at once.

"Ah, there you are, Elsie, right on time. Supper is all ready, so come in and have a quick one before we sit down."

Elsie refused politely "No, thank you very much, Jim. I need to keep my wits about me for our discussion. If you have some squash I'd like some?"

He quickly fetched a glass from the kitchen and filled it with water and topped it up from a small bottle of squash by a decanter next to the dining table. "I hope orange is alright?"

He handed her the glass. "Thanks Jim, I was quite thirsty after the walk and it's still quite warm out."

"Now, Elsie, you sit here." and he pulled out a chair at the table for her. As soon as she was seated he went to the other side, and removed some cloths that Elsie could now see covered a cold supper. Irene had obviously taken a lot of trouble to prepare a delicious cold meat salad with jelly and blancmange to follow.

"This looks excellent Jim. You have a real gem in Mrs Daly, don't you."

"Couldn't do without her. She runs the house perfectly."

Elsie began to look about her for the first time. The little square dwelling that from the outside looked rough and ready, was, in fact, a well balanced house, deceptively larger than at first appearance. It was furnished in typical bachelor manner. Jim was not an artistic man, and everything in the house was masculine. It was spotlessly clean, but whether that was down to Mrs Daly, or Jim's influence she could not tell. Not at all the way she would have arranged it, but ideal for someone in Jim's position.

Jim noticed her looking around

"Would you like to see round the house after supper Elsie?"

"Yes, Jim, I would, if we have time. Don't you think we should talk about the shop first. That's what I have come for, and it is important."

""Yes, I know," replied Jim. "Right, when you have finished we'll leave the washing up 'til later and adjourn to the drawing room for our discussion. I have some decisions to tell you about."

Elsie continued to finish her meal She realised she had not been invited to Jim's just to approve the idea of extra staff, and wondered what was coming.

After they finished their sweet, he ushered her into the back room saying "This is the drawing room. What do you think?"

Elsie looked at the room in surprise. There was a comfortable three piece suite. In the corner was Jim's desk where he worked when at home. It was large and commodious, and big enough to take all his papers together with a wooden set of filing drawers adjacent to it. There were table lamps in strategic places round the room, and there was no central light as in most fashionable drawing rooms of the time. It was almost dark outside, and the effect was warm, cosy and very homely. She wondered who planned it. Could it be Jim himself? If so, he was not quite the person she always thought!

"Come and sit down, Elsie. I think the easy chair is the most comfortable. If I need any papers I will get them from the desk." He took out a piece of paper on which she could see a list of items. He had obviously been thinking about the meeting for some time.

"Right then, let's start. Firstly I have some news to tell you. Whether you'll think it's bad or not, I'm not sure, but anyway here it is!" and he continued.

"You know I have been getting more headaches for some time now, don't you?"

"Yes," she agreed, "I have noticed, and spoke to you because of it, you remember."

"Let me finish" he said testily. "Last week, when you thought I was having a headache, I took the day off and went to London to see a specialist to check if anything is wrong. I felt a change is taking place. After he examined me he had some X rays done. It seems a small piece of shrapnel that I always knew was still there in my head, is moving. In fact it has already travelled quite a way. Every time it moves, I get a bout of headaches."

Elsie started to say something but he held up his hand to silence her.

"The good news is that the consultant can do something about it. Now is not quite the ideal time, apparently, but it will come soon. He will remove the shrapnel, and if successful, I shall have much improved health. With the treatment of wounded in this war, the techniques and surgery are so much improved and he is confident it will go well."

Elsie again started to say something but again he stopped her.

"One problem arises, though. It will mean a long spell in hospital. After they have operated and removed the metal, I shall have to lie perfectly still for as long as it takes the wound to heal, to prevent damage to my brain. This could be anytime from a few days to many months. If I don't have the operation to remove it, I will continue to deteriorate and eventually become paralysed, or even die, so I must do it!"

He paused to gather his composure. Elsie answered immediately.

"Of course you must have it Jim. It is the best possible news. We can look after the shop while you are away and if we get another person, I can take over most of the tasks you normally carry out until you return."

Jim smiled. "I knew you'd say that. Elsie, but it's not as easy as you think. Have you ever worked in accounts?"

"No, I haven't, but it can't be too difficult to learn what is required." she responded.

"Well, we must talk about that." said Jim. "Now, let's start by engaging an extra assistant in the shop. Any ideas? Of course, it must be someone we can trust and you and Joan are happy to work with. A lot is going to depend on you once I am laid up"

Elsie thought for a while. "Give me a few days to think about a likely person. I have several friends and acquaintances who may be able to recommend someone suitable. I'll sound them out and see what is available."

"Good," said Jim. "If I can leave that to you for the time being, we'll turn to you."

Elsie wondered what he was about to say.

"Your effect on the shop, or should I say business, has been remarkable. Sales are up, more customers are coming through the door every day and I hear nothing but good about you. Now, however, just when your influence is increasing, I may have to divert you to more back room work away from the counter. You are really, apart from good old Joan, the only person I can trust to deal with the confidential parts of the business. So, in the next few weeks you will spend more time with me, both in the shop, and at home, learning the parts of the work you don't know in preparation for the day I go into hospital, so you can run the whole caboodle on your own. You will .have a new assistant in the shop who will have to be trained quickly and be both honest and reliable to back you up."

Elsie thought she could see a problem. "What about the prescriptions and dispensing? I can't do them yet. Joan will not be able to cope on her own, particularly if we get busier."

"Yes, I can see the difficulty already." grinned Jim, "but I think we can overcome it. I will make you Manager of the business, and we can hire pharmacists on a short term contract from the Institute to fill the gap. They will report to you as Manager. If they are unsatisfactory, you will have the authority to replace them. They will handle the dispensing, and until you are familiar with the work, Joan can check it when she is in. Now, Elsie, or should I say Mrs Winter, Manageress, will you accept the position?" and he smiled impishly.

"Of course I will, Jim. You know that. It's what I need. With Brian gradually moving away to Jane, it will give me something to work for, and enjoy. I'm sure it will be difficult sometimes, but if I can learn, in a few months, it will become easier." She was dizzy with the thought of her rise to managing the shop.

"Oh," said Jim, "One thing I forgot. From the start of next week, I shall pay you as manager and am doubling your wages. You will be paid monthly If you are short in the next few weeks, draw some money from the till on account"

Elsie started to feel embarrassed. "But you don't even know if I can do it yet!"

"Well, let's say it's a reward for what you have done already. I have no doubt at all you can manage the business excellently, probably better than me. Certainly better than I can manage in my present state of health! Now, there may be questions to ask on Monday morning after you have thought about it, so get off home, and have a quiet day tomorrow On Monday we can start the move forward, as long as I don't get one of my damned heads!"

She started to get up, but Jim began again.

"Elsie, so sorry, I forgot to ask. How's Brian? Have you heard from him since he went back?"

"Well, not directly. He hasn't written to me, but I think Jane has spoken to him. She told me he is France, but no idea where.

She keeps me in touch. Being at the War Office, she can speak to him occasionally and she rings me with any news she can pass on."

Jim smiled. "I do like Brian. He is a bright young man, and seems to have found an equally confident young lady, by the look of Jane. Straightforward, very obviously grief-stricken, she still very much in control of herself. If they don't fight too much, they'll be a formidable team after the war is over!"

Elsie looked at the fine carriage clock on the mantelpiece and Jim saw her.

"Right, Elsie, that's enough for one night. Off you go, and see you on Monday." He escorted her to the door, said "Goodnight" and watched her walk briskly down the path and along the road towards her flat. It was quite dark, not even a chink of light in the blackout, and no moon. Elsie had to almost feel her way back to the flat, but she was not concerned. Her mind was full of the plans Jim had put to her. She would handle it, she knew she could. Just wait and see!

Her brain continued to debate the programme and responsibilities she would assume on Monday. For several hours she tossed and turned in her bed and it was well after midnight before she fell into a deep sleep. Sunday was a fine morning and when she woke the sun was already in her room. It was later than she intended and she rushed to catch up for the lost time. The flat must be cleaned and her washing completed. There would be little time on Monday to do it, and after a light breakfast she set about the tasks. Normally she would have listened to the news, but in her haste didn't bother to turn the wireless on. Just after eleven, the 'phone rang.

"Hallo, Elsie, how are you?"

"I'm fine Jane, just trying to sort out the flat."

Jane went straight to the point of her call. "Have you listened to the news this morning?"

"No, I haven't" replied Elsie, "Have I missed something?"

Jane couldn't contain herself

"Our airborne forces have landed in Holland and are advancing on the Rhine. I'm sure Brian must be there somewhere. I haven't heard from him for some days and knew something was up, as he contacts me nearly every day if he can. Don't know much more yet but it will be all in the news soon. It is a huge landing apparently."

She sounded really excited, but all Elsie could think of was Brian's safety.

"Thanks for telling me, Jane. Are you alright?"

"Yes, I'm fine. Run off my feet, we're so busy. I hardly have time to grab a meal until off duty. Must go Elsie, will let you know if I hear anything about Brian and what he's doing. Bye"

The 'phone went click, and Jane had gone.

Elsie immediately switched on her radio to listen to the news, but there was little to be added, apart from the announcement that our troops were advancing to a place called Arnhem. There was no more, so she switched off and went back to her cleaning. The remainder of Sunday passed quickly. Finishing the work about half past two, she made some soup and sat for an hour reading her paper and enjoying a few slices of bread and marg'. Her butter ration had all been eaten earlier in the week!

On Monday everyone was talking about the landing in Holland. The news both on the wireless and in the papers was full of it. Jim greeted her with "What do you think of the news from Holland? What a surprise! It'll mean our troops get across the Rhine. Someone seems to have planned a marvellous coup. Bet it was Monty! Trust him to get cracking!"

Elsie agreed, but could not help keep up with Jim's enthusiasm. She knew Brian would be involved somewhere, Jim sensed her concern.

"I'm sure Brian will be alright. Don't think the artillery will be in the front line. Only airborne forces at the moment. Just be happy, Elsie, it will finish the war sooner."

Elsie wondered if he was just trying to ease her mind.

Probably just making an inspired guess and not necessarily correct. But it helped to stay her worry about her son, and she felt reassured for the time being.

Customers came steadily into the shop and she forgot all about the war, concentrating on serving their needs. Joan had a bad cold and did not appear, so Jim was hard put to make up the prescriptions. She helped as much as she could under his direction in the dispensary for the first time when the shop was quiet. Together they worked well, and at the end of the morning she knew they had kept up with the demand, and Jim was happy. He hadn't time to show her any of the details he promised, but at least they had coped without Joan.

After lunch the door opened, and one of the few salesmen not called up to the forces, entered the shop.. Jim always spent time with them, particularly this man, Mr Cheeseman. He often had special offers and bargains of one sort or another. Also, he told Jim about new products coming into the market. So far, Elsie had not spoken more than a 'good morning' and passed him on to Jim, but felt there was something nasty about the way he looked at her while talking to Jim, He was also familiar, more so than other salesmen who visited, and he made her feel demeaned and insulted.

As he came in she recognised his corpulent frame at once and greeted him

"Good morning, Mr Cheeseman. Jim is very short-handed this morning, but I will find out if he can see you. Just a moment, please." She hoped Jim would turn him away, but he didn't. Instead he came out quickly to greet him, and asked Elsie if she would be kind enough to make a cup of coffee. Mr Cheeseman accepted Jim's offer immediately and came over to Elsie.

"Two sugars, my dear, if I may?" Elsie backed away from him a little. "I am sure I can manage that Mr Cheeseman. I'll put the kettle on. It won't take a minute." She went quickly to the rear of the shop. In a few minutes she re-appeared with a cup of hot coffee with sugar and took it over to where he was in deep discussion with Jim.

"Thank you very much, my dear" he responded as she handed him the cup. At the same moment he slyly put his arm around her waist and gave her a squeeze. Elsie drew back in distaste. "Please don't do that again!" She shook with annoyance at his cheek.

He looked at Jim, who was till talking and said, "Your assistant is a pretty young thing, isn't she Jim!" Jim suddenly came to life.

"Do you mean Elsie?" he said "Why yes, of course. I should think she gets some looks in the shop!" Elsie found her face turning crimson. Jim laughed. "Don't Eric, you are embarrassing her!" Then he tactfully diverted the conversation. "Elsie, would you be kind enough to find the last invoice we had from Eversley's? I need to check some figures with Eric."

Elsie withdrew to the dispensary and took as long as she dared before passing the document to Jim. "Is this the one you want?" Jim took it and after looking at it said

"Elsie, would you carry on completing the prescriptions still to be finished, please? The customers will be in for them soon."

Elsie looked at him thankfully. "Of course, Jim, I'll get on with them immediately." She returned to the dispensary and stayed there until Eric Cheeseman departed.

Once the door had closed on him she came out to Jim who was still putting the orders they had been discussing in the file. "You don't like, him, do you Elsie?" he smiled at her.

"What a loathsome man," she replied. "You know he squeezed my waist when I handed him the coffee!"

"Yes, I saw that" said Jim "That's why I sent you in the back. I saw your reaction. You mustn't get upset by that sort of man. Salesmen have all the cheek in the world, but I don't think Eric has any harm in him."

"He'll not get the chance to do any!" responded Elsie hotly. "I hate the way he thinks he's God's gift to ladies. I wouldn't touch him with a bargepole!"

Jim studied Elsie as he continued. "What would you touch with a bargepole, Elsie? Me, for instance?" She saw him waiting to see how she would take the remark. He had never so much as made a comment before and she stopped to think of how she should reply, and decided to avoid a direct answer as tactfully as she could.

"Oh, Jim, how could I reply to a question like that! We are working colleagues, and I like you very much, but Bill is still uppermost in my mind. This was strictly not true and she knew it, but hoped Jim would leave the matter. "That's nice of you, Elsie I'm glad to help you. Bill was a good friend, and I can understand what he means to you, and still does."

By Thursday the Allied forces had cleared a town named Nijmegen and were advancing to meet the airborne men still in Arnhem. Everyone in the town was praying they would reach the beleaguered men. The Germans were providing strong resistance and although the announcers were confident of success, Elsie sensed the advance was losing impetus. Jim said so too. The week went by slowly and still the troops had not been relieved. He told her that in his view, airborne troops were lightly equipped, and if they didn't reach them soon, our forces might have to retreat.

****

Chapter 8

*Y*oung Bruce MacKintosh, now nearly fourteen, took the red Post Office bicycle from the front room of the terraced house where he lived with his Aunty Mary at the end of Blackhorse Road, and lifted it carefully to the front door. It was heavy for the slim under nourished lad, and he had to rest for a moment or two before he turned the Yale lock, opened the door and carefully placed it outside. The bicycle was his pride and joy. When he dressed for work in the special uniform for his job, he felt he was the most important worker in Sidhurst. Bruce was the Sidhurst telegram boy, and in his element as he set off each morning from his aunt's house, He was an out and out Cockney, and moved to Blackhorse Road when his mother and father were killed in 1941. The even smaller house in the East End, had been bombed during one of the intense night raids. He was sound asleep in the Anderson Shelter in the garden, when it suffered a direct hit from a small bomb. Both his parents were killed immediately, and he was found by the rescue workers sound asleep, and totally unharmed.

He was moved to his Aunt Mary in Sidhurst, and for a time missed his Mother particularly, but his Aunt was kind and treated him well. Now he had left school and had a job. He had taken his place in Sidhurst, and for the first time for two years enjoyed his life.

Soon he was pedalling along the High Street to the Post Office, to pick up the early batch of telegrams for first delivery. Being Wednesday, the usual large pile was waiting for him. As he sorted those marked 'priority' into delivery order, for his round, the Postmaster said to him. "Now Bruce, I'm sorry to say you can see this morning many are casualty telegrams. Please be sure to deliver these first, and remember, don't wait for a reply. Just hand them in to the name on the front in person if you can, and leave." He always said this, but Bruce liked those that didn't require an answer because he could get round with them quickly, and be back for a cup of tea with the postmen after they completed the early delivery.

He decided, as it was a fine dry morning, to complete the outer areas first, so it was almost exactly eleven o'clock before he reached the High Street. He handed in one in Church Road, and saw the next was for Flat 8a St Mark's Parade. Standing his bicycle against the kerb, he walked briskly to the front door on which 8a was painted in white letters, and knocked. He waited, but no answer. Instead a man came out of Shaw's The Chemist, and asked him what he wanted. "I have a telegram to deliver to Mrs Elsie Winter." he replied. "but there's no one in ."

"Mrs Winter works in the shop. She's inside, let me have it and I'll give it to her."

"Thanks" said Bruce. "Please see she gets it." and ran back to his bicycle and pedalled off to his next call.

Jim looked aghast at the small yellow telegram envelope. He guessed the contents, and now he had to give it to Elsie!

He walked slowly into the shop wondering what to do for the best. There was no way he could soften the blow he knew was coming. She had to know, and right now. Elsie was making coffee for them at the back of the shop, and it gave him a few seconds to prepare himself. At that moment Elsie came out from the back with two cups of hot coffee.

"Elsie" said Jim, "Would you put the cups down and come

over to the counter, please? I'm afraid I may have some dreadful news for you." With that, he handed her the yellow telegram, and watched as her hands fumbled in trepidation as she opened it in terrified haste.

Elsie looked at the printed words in front of her. All she read was "Deeply regret to inform you of a report --- Captain B. M. Winter M.C. 41st Regiment Royal Artillery was killed in action -----'. She read no more. A huge blackness welled up in front of her eyes. She stumbled to Jim with the most grievous cry he had ever heard, and fainted in his arms. Shocked himself, he carefully carried her into the little room she used in the V1 raids and laid her on the bed. He grabbed some smelling salts from the dispensary, and was about to place them under her nose when he thought "Why? She seems alright. Why bring her round to this?" so he left her where she lay, and picked up the telegram from the floor. Sure enough her son, her beloved Brian had been killed in action near Arnhem. Elsie was alone in the world!

He heard her moan from the little room and ran back to find her strangely normal. "Are you alright Elsie?" he asked not knowing what else to say. "Why, of course Jim. Now, as soon as we have finished coffee we must get back to completing the prescriptions. Then I will go upstairs and get some lunch ready. What about you? Would you like to join me today?"

It was as if the telegram didn't arrive. Shock had blotted out the whole incident from her mind. How long this state would exist he had no idea,. It was not like this when her husband Bill had been killed, and he was at a loss to know how to deal with her. He knew, of course, eventually she would come round, and his heart dropped at the thought of the intense grief to come. Best humour her for the time being and await developments.

Elsie carried on absolutely normally. To all appearances she was unchanged. At twelve, she announced she would go and get some lunch. "Are you going to join me Jim?" reminding him of her earlier invitation.

"Yes, Elsie, I would love to. Will you give me a call when it is ready?"

"Yes Jim, come up when you shut for lunch. It'll be ready then." She left what she was doing and went quietly out of the shop and up the stairs to her flat. Jim let her go. She could break any time, and he knew he must be there for her when she did. When there was a break, he telephoned her doctor, and was fortunate to catch him in his surgery. He explained the news, and her reaction. "Best to leave her until she unfreezes, Jim," he said. "But when she does, ring me immediately as I must call and if necessary give her something to make her sleep. Please don't leave her alone at the moment."

Jim went up to lunch as invited, and found everything as usual. Elsie had prepared lunch for them both and to all intents was quite normal. Jim, however, noticed a bright pink patch on each cheek. Small, but significant, and he knew she was being subjected to enormous grief stress, too much for her brain to acknowledge, and bear. He dreaded the future when she 'awoke'. He deliberately forced himself in spite of her protestations to help with the washing up. After a short rest sitting in the drawing room, they went back to the shop together and got on serving the afternoon customers and the work they generated. The afternoon proceeded as usual until just before three o'clock. Jim, keeping an eye on Elsie from the dispensary, saw Mrs McIver enter the shop. Hastily putting down the prescription he was working on, he moved fast to head her off before she spoke to Elsie, but too late.

"Hallo, Elsie!" greeted Elizabeth McIver. "How are you today? Have you heard from Brian lately?"

Jim heard her but could not prevent what happened next. Elsie looked at her white faced and with a strange ghostly expression. "He's been killed in action, Mrs McIver. I've just heard. I hope you don't mind, but will you excuse me please!" She turned on her heel, fled into the little room, and threw herself on the bed. Enormous sobs and gasps of pain came from her.

She writhed in the agony of her shock and grief surfacing for the first time. Mrs McIver went to go after her. Jim intercepted her. "Leave her Mrs McIver. She received the telegram this morning. Leave us alone if you would, please!" Elizabeth McIver said "Oh, how terrible, I'll go at once. Please tell me if I can help in any way!" She fled from the shop, and left Jim with Elsie.

The awful reality of Brian's death hit her with all it's terrible force. She knew it was her fault! The torrid affair with Gordon was the cause. God was wreaking his punishment. He had taken Brian, and she had only herself to blame. When Jim came in to see her, having closed the shop, and locked the door, she was distraught and seemed not even to recognise him. He went to her and tenderly put his arms around her heaving shoulders, but nothing he did seemed to help, so remembering what the doctor had told him, went quietly back into the shop and telephoned him.

"May I speak to Dr Hargreaves, please?" he asked the receptionist. "It's Jim Shaw." He heard her call to him. "Mr Shaw to speak to you, Doctor." He came to the 'phone at once. "Hallo, Jim, is it Mrs Winter? Can I help?"

"Yes, Doctor Hargreaves, the shock has hit her. She is nearly distraught with grief, and I would be grateful if you could come as soon as you can. She needs your help."

"Yes Jim, thanks for calling me. I'll be there in about twenty minutes."

"She's still in the shop, Doctor. I'll keep her here under my care until you come. The shop is closed, so give a loud knock on the door, please."

"Right, Jim, I'll see you shortly."

He replaced the telephone and went back to Elsie. She was no better. Although the intense sobbing had gone, she had assumed a sort of half consciousness. When she was not laying semi-awake, she was blaming herself for Brian's death, saying over and over, it was her fault and could he ever forgive her. Jim made her swallow two aspirins and told her to try and sleep, but whether she heard or understood him was doubtful. After a while she quietened down and not long after he heard the knock on the shop door. It was Dr Hargreaves.

"How is she now, Jim?"

"I have given her a couple of aspirins, and she seems to be a little quieter, but half the time she's somewhere miles away. She blames herself for her son's death!"

"It is her only son who has been killed, isn't it?" asked Doctor Hargreaves.

"Yes, that's right." replied Jim. "You remember, I'm sure, she lost her husband, Bill, about three years ago. She has no one now, except her sister in Gravesend."

Dr Hargreaves thought for a minute or so. "I think it would be a good idea if she went to stay with her for a week or so. She needs the company of someone who knows her and with whom she can talk when she's ready. Can you contact her?"

At that moment Elsie stirred in the little room, and called "Who is it, Jim?"

"It's Dr Hargreaves, Elsie. He has come to see you"

The doctor entered the little room and saw Elsie struggling to get up, her face running with tears and a chalk white face. She fought back her emotion to face him.

"Hallo, Dr Hargreaves, thank you for coming to see me –"He held up his hand to stop her carrying on.

"Now Mrs Winter, I am asking Jim to prepare a draught to help you sleep tonight. I know it will be hard, but rest is essential once you can. Is there anything you want to tell me?"

Elsie looked at him, tears running down her face again. "It's my fault, Doctor. Please shut the door and I'll explain."

Amid sobbing, gasping for air, and crying, she related the happenings with Gordon, finishing with "You see now. It's God's punishment on me for behaving so sinfully!"

Doctor Hargreaves was silent for a few minutes, and then counselled her.

"Elsie, please forgive me, but that is nonsense. Bill has been dead for three years now. You are a widow, and perfectly free to have any sort of relationship you choose with any man you wish. Brian's death is quite simply, terrible as it may be, due to the War. God is not angry with you. In fact he grieves with you. Ask for his help and he will give you strength. Now, drink this, lie down again and try to rest. I will help Jim to get you up to your flat. You can ponder what I have told you there. Now, up you get. Take my arm and we will go upstairs."

Elsie rose dutifully and between Jim and the Doctor walked unsteadily up to her flat. When she reached the door she said "I'll be alright now" and went in shutting the door firmly behind her. Jim and the Doctor took the hint and went back to the shop.

Like an automaton Elsie went to the kitchen and made a pot of tea, took it into the drawing room and sat down. For a while she did nothing, her mind a blank, not even thinking about Brian, and what had happened. Then, a horrible thought struck her. Does Jane know? How could she get in touch with her? She knew she was at the War Office, but no idea where. What a terrible thing for her, poor girl! First her parents, now her fiancé! Her sadness knew no bounds. She must talk to Jane! She must get Jim's help.

Meanwhile, Dr Hargreaves gone, Jim was trying to find out how he could get in touch with Elsie's sister. After about half an hour he realised the only way was to return to Elsie and ask her. He could also see how she was. He nervously knocked on her door and waited. She came to the door quicker than he expected. The thought of Jane had given her something important to do.

"Jim, I'm feeling better. I must telephone Jane and tell her what has happened. How can I reach her?"

Jim considered the question. "I don't know, Elsie. Her telephone number must be confidential. I am sure she will know almost at once if she doesn't know already. What about your sister? Shouldn't you tell her?"

Elsie was more concerned about Jane, so he said. "Would you like me to tell her? I could telephone her from the shop, if you let me have the number."

"It's Gravesend 2116, her name is Margaret. Could you tell her and say I'll speak to her myself later."

"Of course, leave it to me. I'll go down and call her now." Jim went to the shop, still closed, and called the operator for the Gravesend number A woman's voice answered the 'phone. "Is that Margaret, Elsie's sister?" he enquired. "Yes, who is that?"

"I'm don't believe we have ever spoken. My name is Jim Shaw the proprietor of the chemist where Elsie works." Before he could continue Margaret interrupted. "What's happened? Is she alright? You haven't had another bomb, have you?"

"No," said Jim. "Nothing like that, but it's just as serious. I'm afraid Elsie received news this morning that Brian has been killed in action, at Arnhem, I think. The telegram was delivered about half past eleven. She asked me to tell you she is alright, and will ring you later."

"How awful, I must speak to her" said Margaret in a shocked voice. "How terrible. She must be devastated. Let me think. How can I help?"

"Her doctor, Dr Hargreaves suggested that as soon as she is able, she should get away for a few days , preferably to someone she knows . I must confess, I thought of you. Is it possible you can help?"

Margaret, still shocked, reacted swiftly. "She must come here for as long as she wants. I'll get the first train tomorrow and be there by ten. She can refuse my invitation to my face if she wants, but there is no one or nowhere better for her in my opinion."

"Thank you, - er Margaret, sorry I don't know your surname. I know what she will say if I tell her you are coming. If you are happy to take the chance, just arrive and I will take you up to her flat. That way she will have little opportunity to reject your invitation. I think it is just what she needs for a week or two, and I can manage without her here for a few weeks at least. See you tomorrow, then, and thank you very much." He put down the 'phone, and breathed a sigh of relief. Much as he wanted to help Elsie, he knew her sister would do it so much better.

As shock was replaced with grief and loss, Elsie sat dazed with the horror and enormity of the news she had received, only a few hours ago. Imperceptibly an enormous void grew within her, plus a tremendous sense of loneliness. Alright, Brian had not been at home for over three years, but in spirit he was always with her. His well-being had occupied every waking minute of her life since Bill had gone. Now Brian had joined him. She wondered if they are together and what Bill said to him when they met. Bill would appear completely normal, without a trace of surprise as he always did when something unexpected occurred. Probably just say "Hallo, son! I didn't expect you here so soon. Come and sit down and tell me what happened. Are you alright? Need a cup of tea, or something?" Then Bill would have asked about her. "Seen your Mother lately?" Elsie wondered what Brian would say. Would he know about Gordon, and if so would he tell Bill about her affair? The guilt flooded over her again. Would he tell Bill it was his Mother's fault? She hoped not!

She felt in her pocket and there were still a few pills left that Jim had given her. Better take two more. She obediently poured another cup of tea, now almost cold, and used it to swallow down the tablets. The telephone bell rang. Ah, that's Margaret. Jim said he would speak to her, but it wasn't

"Is that Elsie?" said a young woman's voice.

"Jane!" replied Elsie recognising her voice immediately. "I knew you would call." Then the awful thought struck her again. Supposing Jane hadn't heard the terrible news about Brian? But she had.

"Elsie, I saw the list of casualties with Brian's name on it. I'm so terribly sorry. When did you hear?"

"About half past eleven, I think, Jane." Elsie thought how typical of Jane to ask about her first and not mention her own feelings. She must be heartbroken.

"Never mind about me, my dear. What about you? Are you alright?. It must have come as an awful; shock!"

Jane voice faltered. "Well yes, of course it was! But you see, I know what Brian was doing as he had spoken to me a couple of times from France and I knew he was involved in the Arnhem push, although I did not know to what extent. So you see, it was not entirely unexpected. Never the less, I am still trying to cope with the shock of knowing he is gone!"

"Sorry to ask, Jane, but have you any details of what happened?"

Jane didn't know the details, but knew what to reply. "No, Elsie, it was very sudden from what I have been told, but that's all. I expect I shall find out more in a few days."

"Jane, when you next get some leave, you will come and see me, won't you?" She sounded pitiful to Jane at the other end.

"Of course I will, Elsie. You know that. I will telephone as soon as I have a chance to come to Sidhurst. We shall not lose touch I promise you. Where else could I find a better adopted Mum? You forget I am all alone like you now!"

Elsie felt suddenly ashamed. Here she was feeling sorry for herself, when Jane had lost her parents and her fiancé all in a few weeks and was in a worse plight. She must take care of Jane if she would let her. She was the girl Brian was to spend his life with, and she would need all the help she could get.

"I am waiting for the day we can meet again, Jane. In the meantime, telephone anytime you want to talk. I shall be delighted to hear your voice."

"Thanks very much Elsie, must go now. I am wanted back in the Ops Room. Goodbye, call you again soon!" and she was gone, but already Elsie had a mission. Jane needed someone and she was the best person to fill that role. She felt a little better.

As she finished talking to Jane, a wave of tiredness came over her. She had forgotten the aspirins and draught she had taken. Now they were taking effect, overpowering the terrible loneliness and ache in her stomach that had filled her whole body.

"I think I'll go to bed and try to sleep. Nothing can be done 'til tomorrow now." She quickly undressed, got into bed and lay down. For a while her loss and loneliness pervaded everything and she felt the fears well up again, but did not try to control them. Still softly weeping, she lay still and looked out of the window. It was a dark evening, no sound of aircraft, and she thought about her life with Bill – Oh God – Brian! Her tears welled again and memories flooding back intermingled with them in her mind. Still crying in her brain, she slid into unconsciousness without knowing, and from there into sleep. Her draught and aspirin induced slumber grew deeper as they took affect, and her tears dried slowly as she slept.

****

Elsie's older sister, Margaret, woke early the following morning. She wanted to get to her sister in Sidhurst as soon as she possibly could. Although she would never have admitted it, she had wanted Elsie to visit her and Arthur, her husband, in their house in Gravesend for some time.. Previously, Elsie has always refused, or made some excuse not to accept he invitation. Now she was troubled by the reception Arthur had given her to her suggestion the previous evening, that Elsie should stay with them for a while. Her husband was Manager of the local Barclays Bank in Gravesend. It was very short of staff due to men taken for the forces, and had to rely on older or extremely young and inexperienced juniors under conscription age. For the first time in banking, head office had asked him to recruit ladies for the vacancies. Always an irritable man, the pressures of the job was becoming almost too much for him, and his temper reflected it!

When Margaret had said, perhaps a little unwisely after Jim had telephoned, she had asked Elsie to stay with them for a while, he immediately lost his temper, and point blank refused to have her. Margaret was equally adamant, and it resulted in the first serious row for some years. Seeing she was becoming very angry at his lack of sympathy for her sister, he decided to accept the visit. Margaret knew he was upset, but thought him extremely selfish. With no children, they had suffered virtually nothing compared with her sister. Whereas normally she would have given way and accepted his refusal, for once she held firm. She had forced him to accept Elsie, and hoped her sister would not suffer as a result when she arrived.

Next morning she gave Arthur a special breakfast before he left for the bank, using most of their week's ration of bacon. It would cost her dearly to get more under the counter from her grocer, but she needed to bribe Arthur so he was reasonable when he came home to find her sister with them. First dashing round giving the house a quick clear up, she caught the earliest bus possible to Gravesend Station. The trains ran once every hour, and by sheer luck, the first one to arrive came into the station ten minutes late when she thought she had missed it! Even better, it was a Dartford Loop Line train that went through Sidhurst and on to Charing Cross. She had expected to have to change at Dartford to pick it up, but now she would be at Sidhurst in three quarters of an hour.

At Sidhurst, she got out, leaving her seat to a smart business man, who was delighted at not having to stand all the way to Charing Cross as he normally did. It was a bright warm morning, and she walked to the bus stop wondering what she would find at Shaw's when she arrived.

Jim was performing his ritual of sweeping the shop front. As he watched the people passing for the bus and saying good morning to many he knew, he saw a tall, quite attractive lady coming towards him. He knew who it was. Margaret looked just like her sister, but older, more dignified, and expensively dressed. She came up to him and said "Good morning,. You must be Mr Shaw? I'm Elsie's sister, Margaret Bushell."

"Yes, good morning," replied Jim, "I'm Jim Shaw. Please call me Jim. You are earlier than I expected. Come into the shop for a minute or two. I don't know if your sister is up and about yet."

Margaret followed him in and listened attentively while he told her about Elsie's condition.

As soon as she heard of the plight of her sister, Margaret could not wait to get upstairs and see her. Jim took the precaution of preparing Elsie, by telephoning the flat to say her sister was here. He had planned it anyway but didn't have any idea what sort of night she had, so thought it prudent to give Elsie warning of Margaret's arrival.

"Hallo, Elsie," he said over the 'phone. "It's Jim here. How are you this morning? Are you up yet? I have your sister down here asking about you. Are you O.K to receive her, and can she come up?"

"Hallo, Jim. Yes, I am up. I'll come down and let her in, and I'll make us some coffee."

Jim replaced the receiver. "It's alright; she's up and sounds quite as usual. She'll be down in a moment and let you in. See you later I expect, and many thanks for coming so quickly. I think you will find she needs you."

Margaret went outside to the front door of 8a. Almost immediately she heard Elise's footsteps on the stairs and the door opened. Margaret was aghast at her sister's appearance. Elsie had not bothered to make herself up and her face was a white mask. Her eyes red with crying, tears moistened her cheeks under her eyes. She looked deathly pale and bent, and her whole visage had fallen in, giving her the appearance of an old woman. At the sight of her sister her face brightened a little.

"How good of you to come, Margaret – come in, come in.!" Margaret stepped inside the door and Elsie threw her arms around her.

"Oh Margaret, thanks for coming. I don't think I could go on for long without someone with me. Jim is doing his best, but he has no idea how desolate I feel. It's my entire fault, you know. I am being punished for Gordon. I should never have loved him and behaved so badly. Now God has taken Brian as well as Bill, and I am alone. What ever will become of me?"

Margaret let her ramble on until she had exhausted her breath. Once she began to settle down, she said firmly.

"I have come to take you back with me to stay with us at Gravesend. Arthur is at work all day and we can be together while you sort everything out. I have nothing to do and we can spend as much time as you want together until you are ready to get back to life again. I know you don't think so at present, but this dreadful pain will eventually pass. Bill and Brian will be a wonderful memory that you will always have. I have no children, you know, and how I would have liked some. I shall never have the memories you have. At least you will always keep those wonderful days with Bill and Brian for ever. Now, come on, let's get you ready together and we'll leave for Gravesend. Can I help you pack what you need?"

Elsie meekly followed her lead. She didn't much care either way, but knew Margaret was taking charge as she always did being her older sister. She was in no state to argue and said.

"Thank you Margaret, my dear,. I must go down to speak to Jim as he will be without my help in the shop. Please make us both some tea while I put some clothes in a case, and we'll go." She left her sister, went up to the bedroom, and packed a few clothes. She had no idea what she was packing, and hoped she had chosen the right things. Finished, she went down to Margaret in the kitchen and drank the coffee she had made. After drinking up, she went to Jim in the shop, leaving Margaret tidying up upstairs.

"Jim," she announced in a worried tone. "Margaret has asked me to stay with her for a while, but I said I could not go unless you are able to manage without me in the shop. Do you mind? I think it will do me good!"

Jim was pleased. It would relieve him of looking after her. In her present state she could not possibly serve in the shop, and he was going to find it hard to run it without her. He had nearly been in tears himself when he saw her appearance and knew she would find it extremely hard if customers were continually aggravating her grief.

"Don't worry at all, Elsie. I know Joan will help out. I am feeling fine at the moment, so you can get away immediately. As long as I don't lose you permanently, don't have any concerns about it. I'll see you when you feel ready to get back to work again. Now, off you go with Margaret!" he dismissed her with a wave of his hand and went back to the dispensary. He would miss her more than he liked to admit, but knew if he showed it she would not go.

By the time everything was tidied up to Margaret's satisfaction it was 12 o'clock. Elsie would not have worried. The flat could take care of itself until she felt ready to tackle it, but Margaret made sure all was shipshape for when Elsie returned. Jim called a taxi to take them to the station, and they caught the 12.30 train. Getting away from the flat and shop helped Elsie to feel better and although at first she just sat looking dully at the countryside slipping passed, by the time they alighted at Gravesend, she was feeling well enough to chat to her sister a little.

Once they left the train, Margaret said "I didn't have time to get anything prepared for lunch, Elsie, Shall we get something to eat in the town before we go to our house?"

Elsie didn't care one way or the other. "Just as you wish Margaret, but all I want is another cup of tea or coffee. Nothing to eat."

There was a small café near the station that was passably clean and cosy. Margaret had eaten there in the past, and headed for it. It was almost empty, and they found a seat in the window.

"I'm hungry." she said to her sister. "Won't you eat something? I'm going to have liver and bacon. I've been here before and it's very tasty." Elsie said nothing and sat vacantly staring out of the window.

"Come on Elsie! You must have something. If you can't manage a meal, have some buttered toast and a pot of tea? We can share one between us."

Elsie looked round at her. "Yes, alright. I think I might eat some toast."

When the waitress came over, she looked sideways at Elsie. Margaret caught her eye and gave her a look to prevent her asking anything. She gave the order and the girl hurried away to get it.

Quite without warning, Elsie said "Do you know Margaret, I've always wanted to see your house. In all these years, I have never had the opportunity to visit you and Arthur. It takes something as bad as this to make me come."

Margaret was amazed. The terrible dullness was disappearing, or was it just a fleeting glimpse of the old Elsie. She didn't attempt to start a dialogue. "It is lovely to have you, if only for a few days, Elsie. It's so long since we had a good chat."

"Yes, I agree, but not yet. Give me a day or so, and we will talk, I'm not ready at the moment."

"Fine, Elsie I understand, I leave it in your hands until you are ready."

In her mind Elsie was recalling the time three years ago when she lost Bill, and the pattern the enormous loss took. It had happened again, and she knew what to expect from her mind and body. Bill would help her to overcome her latest disastrous loss, and already she recognised how her feelings were moving. Rest, that was what she needed, and plenty of minor gossip to keep her from dwelling on her loss. She remembered how it was before. This may be different, but she would come through it, just as last time, even although she thought she never would. She clung on to that memory, and knew she must try slowly to come to terms with what had happened. She needed to get back to work to help Jim during his operation and for all he had done for her.

She stood up. "Finished, Margaret. Come on let's pay and get off to your house!"

Her sister also got up, they went to the counter and paid the bill and left the café to hail a taxi to get them to No 44 St Andrews Drive, where Arthur and Margaret lived.

44 St Andrews Drive was a detached house, to a quality

and size befitting a bank manager. The taxi took them down a short but imposing drive to the front door. The house was a commodious three bedroom detached dwelling, built, probably, Elsie thought, in the early 1900's. There was a fair sized front garden, and Elsie could see already, there was a large well stocked garden behind the house and garage, which stood adjoining the main building. It was clear Arthur had done well for himself! Margaret took her into a sizeable hall, and straight up the stairs to a landing off which were three bedrooms. "That one is ours" said her sister pointing at the first. "I will show you yours while you are with us. It is the larger of our two guest rooms, and overlooks the Thames in the distance. The hills you see are Essex." It was a much larger room than Elsie had at Sidhurst, and the view across to Essex was over the trees at the side of the house, and very pretty. She couldn't help but feel a little jealous!

"Is this alright for you Elsie?" she asked. "It's lovely, and you have a fine house. I shall soon get to love it here, I'm sure." Replied her sister.

"Alright, I'll give you a few minutes to unpack and have some tea ready for us in the garden. I think it's still warm enough to sit outside. Come down as soon as you like. Oh, the bathroom is at the end of the landing. You can't miss it." She went out and closed the door leaving Elsie to sort herself out.

She had rarely seen a better house. It reminded her a lot of Elizabeth McIver's house in Sidhurst. When she went to the bathroom, she found the fittings to be the best, and modern. There was even a shower!

With hardly anything to unpack, she soon went down to join Margaret in the garden.

The sisters sat for a while outside until it tuned chilly. Margaret led her back to their drawing room, and Elsie began to tell her about some of the events of the last few months. Margaret was wise enough to let her choose the subject, and Elsie told her first about Betty, and didn't mention Brian or his death, although it was what her sister really wanted to hear. Margaret was getting anxious about the reception her sister would get from Arthur when he came home at five. He had never warmed to Elsie, and it was the main reason why she had not pressed Elsie to visit in the past. Now she needed their help, and he must show some sympathy, or she would be very angry indeed.

At his usual time, she heard his key in the front door. He came in and went straight to Margaret and kissed her. The turning to Elsie, he said.

"Hallo, Elsie. I'm so sorry to hear your news. Margaret only just had time to tell me before I left for work. Please do accept my sympathy. If we can help in any way while you are with us, it is the least we can do."

Elsie was so surprised by his welcome that she immediately burst into tears and with them running down her face, shook his hand in greeting. Arthur couldn't do anything, so simply put his arm round her shoulder while she sobbed into his coat. It was the first time she had met anyone since her loss, and she realised as did Margaret, at her outburst, she would need plenty of help and rest before she could return to Sidhurst and to work.

The next two weeks passed in relaxation and quiet. The sisters took advantage of the fine autumn weather and went walking in the chalk hills in the nearby countryside. Margaret thought Elsie was beginning to come to terms with her loss, but at the beginning of the third week of her stay, a parcel was delivered addressed to Elsie. She opened it wondering who could know where she was, and assumed Jim has forwarded some post from her flat. But it was't. The parcel was from Jane, and enclosed most of Brian's personal effects sent on by the War Office. Included were some letters, his fountain pen, watch, and many personal items. Elsie glanced at them and returned them quickly to the box before closing it again. It was too early to look at them properly and she knew better than to try. Just the sight of them was enough to send her into sobs again. Once she saw what the parcel contained, Margaret went out and left her to face the task alone.

The letter from Jane she read immediately. She liked Jane and knew what the task of posting the contents, and writing about Brian must have cost her. The letter was to the point and informative. Pulling the big easy chair into the light by the drawing room window to read it, she saw Jane had written it while on duty.

'My dear Elsie,

The day before yesterday I received these personal effects from Brian's unit, and a letter from his Commanding Officer, Colonel Bruce. It was addressed to me instead of you, for which I must apologise, because I enquired for details. They sent it to me instead of you, I think because I am at the War Office. Even thought I am only a Sergeant. I have received more information than is usual on these unhappy occasions.

As you know, Brian was with the Armoured Brigade who set off from the Maas River to fight their way along the road to relieve the airborne boys at Arnhem. He was the Artillery Liaison officer attached to the armoured column. The plan was that he would organise any artillery support needed, and direct the guns to the targets from the front of the column as it advanced into Holland. He was travelling in an armoured car for protection, about half way back from the leading tanks.

All went well the first day. They advanced without meeting much resistance and stayed the night in Njimegen. On the 23rd, the column began to meet strong fire from anti-tank guns, and just after mid morning, an anti tank unit ambushed the leading tanks, letting the leaders pass their camouflaged, well dug in, guns. As soon as the attack came, the C.O asked for aircraft and artillery support, and Brian's armoured car took him forward to a better position from where he could direct the fire on to the German position. A bitter fight ensued and the excellent defensive position of the Germans made it extremely difficult to neutralise the fire.

Brian needed to get to a place where he could get a better view of the German position, and he followed behind two tanks on to a low hill between the road and the German position. As he pulled forward, an anti tank shell hit the tank in front of his car, and bounced off on to his vehicle, hitting it and killing the two men inside, one of which was Brian. He died instantly.

When the attack was put down, the bodies were taken to the rear to rest until the unit reached a little town just short of Arnhem. Brian was buried in the cemetery close to the town alongside the airborne casualties.

A soon as I have the address where he is buried, I will write and tell you, also any more information that I can find out. When I can get a weekend pass, I will come to Sidhurst if you want me to.

I know this letter will pain you, but thought you would want to have as much detail of Brian's passing as you could. If I have acted wrongly, please accept my apologies. I have done it in what I hope are your best interests.

My kindest regards and love ----- Jane.

Elsie sat looking at the letter for a long time, reading it over and over again. Her mind interrogated the information trying to visualise the moments up to Brian's death. It did not appear that he suffered at all. His death must have been very quick.

It was almost dark when she stirred and went to the kitchen and joined Margaret.

"You guessed what the letter was about, I suppose, Margaret?"

Margaret looked at her but saw no sign of tears. "Yes, I'm afraid I did Elsie. You hadn't mentioned you had received any letters about Brian's death, so I knew you would receive one sooner or later. Did it tell you much?"

"Yes, I think so. You see, the letter was from Jane. She is a Sergeant working at the War Office and has access to information not normally common knowledge. I think she has heard from his C.O. If so, I may yet find out more when I see her. Would it be alright if she came here when she has a weekend pass? Please Margaret, would you mind?"

What could her sister say? She knew it would not please Arthur but to refuse would be churlish to say the least. Anyway she was interested to hear all the details herself.

"Of course, Elsie, write immediately, or 'phone if you can. She will have the other room."

Elsie came to life. "You are kind Margaret. May I borrow some writing paper and get a note to her in the post today? She has put her address at the top. Now, are you absolutely sure it will be alright with Arthur?" Elsie did not want a change of heart later. She had experience of Margaret and her husband before!

"Well, just to be certain, I'll ask Arthur this evening and you can post the letter in the morning."

When asked, Arthur did agree, although not as graciously as he did before she arrived. So it was settled, and the letter went off next morning to Jane.

During her weeks in Gravesend, the sisters had seen a notice while in the town, announcing a séance meeting to be held by a 'well known' medium, Irene Haskell. More for something to amuse Elsie than because she had any interest, Margaret mentioned it to Elsie, and suggested it would make an entertaining afternoon if the weather was poor. Surprisingly, Elsie jumped at the idea, and so Margaret booked two tickets for the meeting. Later she wondered if she had done the right thing with Elsie in her present state of grief, but it was done, and Elsie seemed keen to go, so said no more.

On the Wednesday, they caught the bus into Gravesend, and found two seats towards the rear of the small hall just off the shopping area behind the church. While they waited patiently for Irene Haskell to appear, Elsie noticed there were only about twenty people in the audience. Neither had any idea what Irene Haskell was like, and hoped the afternoon wouldn't be a bore. Elsie didn't know why she wanted to go. She was not a bit interested in spiritualism, and had never attended a similar meeting in her life. What had possessed her to come?

Irene Haskell was puzzled. Early in her life she had shown an ability to forecast events to come and studied with Madame Alcarti a well known medium from Wrotham. Once she decided to hold her own meetings, her limitations were quickly exposed to her, if not to her clients, and she had resorted to subterfuge in order to give generalised messages to her customers. As she peeped through the curtain at the side of the small stage she saw two ladies sitting towards the back she had not seen before. What puzzled her was why they had come. They were not the usual old biddies who came for comfort or reassurance about those who had passed on. There was something different. Irene always went out and introduced herself to her audience. It was really an excuse to find out anything she could that would give her a link she could use in the séance. Irene was really a fraud, and she knew it! Often she felt ashamed at how she cheated her clients, but she was a shrewd observer, and many derived much comfort from what she told them about their departed loved ones. Information, in fact, they already knew and had told her without knowing.

In her early days, she had occasionally connected with those passed over, and the sensation she had experienced had been extraordinary. An experience she remembered and cherished, and always hoped would be repeated.

Stepping briskly out from her hiding place, she moved among her clients shaking hands with the regulars and chatting to any from whom she hoped to glean a few useful snippets of information. Quite deliberately, she went to the two newcomers, and introduced herself.

"I'm Irene Haskell. I don't think I have had the pleasure of seeing you hear before, have I?"

Margaret answered. "No, I'm Margaret, and this is my sister Elsie."

"Is there any particular reason why you have come to the meeting today?" she asked them both.

Neither seemed to want to reply, then Margaret responded vaguely. "Well, we wanted to pass an hour or two, and we saw the notice of the meeting, and thought we would see what spiritualism was about."

Irene Haskell was no longer puzzled. She could forget them and carry on with her usual agenda and clients. She said "I hope you enjoy it." and returned to the front and addressed the audience.

"Now ladies and gentlemen, shall we begin. If you would like to sit round me in a circle, and then may we have complete silence, please." As the audience moved to sit in a circle round her, the lights were dimmed, and she sat facing them and took up her 'trance' position. She relaxed, and put herself into her receptive state, although it didn't usually get any signal. All was quiet, and they watched her. After a suitable interval, Irene slumped a little in her chair, and assuming her trance voice, said "Is there anybody there?" She did not expect any result and she prepared her mind to do some false messages for her regulars.

She called for two well known members, and passed on some general details from her memory of each, and sat in her pose again. A strange sensation entered her head. It was like the time many years ago when she had really made contact, but this was different. It was stronger, it was urgent, and a message formed itself in her brain. This was exciting; she was in contact with something!

Then the message became clear and she spoke the words given to her.

"I wish to give a message!" She had spoken the words without thinking!

"Who is it for?" her mind asked.

"It is for my Mother." Again she had spoken out loud inadvertently. "Who is your Mother?" she asked.

"My Mother is with you. Her name is Autumn." That was wrong she felt and asked again.

"Are you sure, no one here is of that name."

Her voice said "No, It's Winter, Elsie Winter. Please give her this message."

This time she asked out loud in a man's voice. "Is there an Elsie Winter here?"

Elsie and Margaret sat up in astonishment. She could not know their names as they had not given them.

"I'm Elsie Winter" said Elsie. "Who is it and what do they want?"

"This is a message from Brian. Tell .her I am very happy, have met Dad, and don't worry. I will send her a white rose. I can't stay now. Goodbye!"

Irene felt the presence disappear. Elsie sat flabbergasted, and Margaret couldn't' believe what she had just heard.

"Elsie, that could only have been Brian. He's sent you a message."

Elsie was more sceptical. How ever did she find out I had a son named Brian, and that he was dead? It must be a trick, that's the explanation. How nasty of Mrs Haskell to do that to me knowing I have just lost my son."

The meeting didn't continue for long, and Elsie made a point of accosting Irene Haskell as soon as the meeting broke up.

"What do you mean by quoting my son, like that. How did you find out I had lost him recently?" She was angry, and wanted to know how and why she had done it.

"Irene answered her in kind. "I didn't. I swear I have never met you before and didn't even know your name was Winter, only 'Elsie' as you introduced yourselves. Is the message relevant?"

"I don't know, I'll just have to wait and see. How can he send me a rose. He's dead and buried at Arnhem!"

Irene Haskell was equally baffled, but knew she had been in contact with the spirit world. She said nothing, but was elated. At last, she had received a genuine message, and it was not a fraud. Why now? Then it occurred to her to ask Elsie a final question.

"How long is it since your son died, Mrs Winter?"

"Only a few weeks ago. He was killed in action at Arnhem."

Then Irene Haskell knew. Brian was still on his way to the other side, and that's why he had to go. It was obviously important for him to get the message to his Mother, and her visit to the séance had been timely. She bid her audience farewell, and went to the back to ponder her success, and note down the details in full.

Margaret and Elsie went out into the main road and into a nearby teashop and sat over a cup of tea discussing the meeting. Elsie felt strangely comforted. Perhaps Brian had sent a message, and that was why she accepted the suggestion by Margaret to go to the meeting. They returned to Margaret's house, still talking about it. Three days later a letter came from Jane, by which time they had forgotten all about it. She was coming the next weekend, and hoped it was alright. Elsie, rather stupidly had forgotten to put her sister's 'phone number on the letter, but Margaret didn't seem to mind when she announced the news. Arthur, however, did not look pleased. He liked his life planned in advance. Still, there was nothing he could do abut it, and he grumbled until Margaret put a good supper in front of him that she prepared specially, anticipating trouble when she broke the news of Jane's coming.

Unfortunately worse was to follow.. For some reason, perhaps delayed bad temper, Arthur decided on the Thursday evening that he was not going to welcome Jane the following day, and announced she could not stay. This was without any previous warning to his wife, who was most embarrassed. Elsie could see there was really more to it than that. Arthur was trying to get her to go home, and leave them to their own devices. In short, he had had enough of Elsie who in his mind was taking the attention away from him! To further aggravate the situation, on Friday morning there was an unexpected telephone call for Elsie. When she answered, Joan's voice greeted her.

"Hallo Elsie, how are you getting on? Rested, I hope."

Elsie knew her enquiry was not the real reason for the call.

"I'm feeling much better, thank you Joan. My sister has been very kind, and also I have had news from Jane which has helped me a lot. Is all well at Sidhurst?"

Joan paused. "Well Elsie that's why I'm phoning. The shop is fine and busy, but I'm afraid Jim is not at all well. His headaches have suddenly got far worse, and he is permanently at home and on sedatives from the doctor. He is waiting to hear from his specialist. I thought you ought to know. When do you think you will be coming home? I can manage for a while, but could do with you in the shop!"

Elsie was taken aback by the news, and knew immediately what she must do.

"I'll leave immediately, Joan. Have you had any calls from Jane? "

"Yes, she telephoned for you a few days ago, and left her number if you called me."

"Could I ask you to do something immediately for me, Joan? Telephone Jane and tell her I shall be back at the flat on Saturday morning, and she should come to Sidhurst at the weekend. Is that O.K.?"

"Yes, of course I will, Elsie. When can I expect you?"

"I'll be back in the shop on Saturday morning, or even Friday depending what time I can leave my sister's. Give my best wishes to Jim, and tell him not to worry. Can you manage 'til then?"

"Yes, of course, I'm not that old and decrepit, Elsie! See you soon. Bye!"

She told Margaret at once, and could see she was relieved at the news.

"I don't want you to go Elsie, but possibly it is for the best. You are needed back home, and I'm sure Arthur will be glad if we are on our own again. When will you go?"

"First thing tomorrow morning Margaret. Could you order me a taxi for nine o'clock, and I shall be home by lunchtime. It will give me time to clear up the flat before going back to the shop on Saturday morning."

There was no more discussion on the subject, but Elsie detected an easing of tension in the house. She felt rested and ready for work again. With Jim in trouble, she had to be there to work in the shop, and get all the information she needed to look after it if he went to hospital immediately. Later in the evening, Joan called back just before she left for home. "I left a message for Jane, and she called me back just now. She understands, and will see you on Saturday some time. She sends her love and hopes you are better."

"Thanks Joan," replied Elsie, "See you tomorrow."

On Friday morning, she was up early. Margaret cooked her one of her 'special' breakfasts as she did for Arthur, which she enjoyed. He politely said good bye and wished her a safe journey. She could see he was pleased to have his wife all to himself again. Margaret said very little. When the taxi came to take Elsie to the station, she shed a few tears while Elsie thanked her for all she had done to help her. Then she said that Elsie must come and see them again in a few months time, but Elsie knew she wouldn't, and suggested Margaret come up to Sidhurst for the day and spend it with her. Margaret promised she would, and that was that. Getting in to the taxi, she kissed her sister and waved her goodbye as it sped down the road. By half past twelve, she was opening the front door of 8a St Marks Parade. There was still a huge cold lump in her stomach, but to all intents and purposes she was ready for work and for Jane to arrive tomorrow! The break had done her good, and although her grief was prominent in her mind, she felt she could face life again!

****

Chapter 9

*H*ome again in her flat, Elsie washed out her dirty clothes, and re-placed the crockery Margaret had helpfully tidied up and put most in totally the wrong cupboard! She needed some more food, so did a little shopping for lunch that she made and ate, before going down to the shop.

She was greeted by a smiling Joan. "Elsie, you're a sight for sore eyes! How are you? I don't know how we could have carried on if you hadn't returned! Jim is so ill, poor man! It's pitiful to see him, and I wish he would forget the shop. You know how he is!"

Elsie smiled back. "Yes, I do, Joan, but what triggered all this off?"

"I don't know for certain, but I know he was terribly upset, as were we all, when he heard the news about Brian. I shouldn't say this, I suppose, but Jim has always loved you, I'm sure you know, ever since or even before, Bill died. This and the extra work together with the excitement of getting Boot's trade until they re-open, brought it on."

"Yes, Joan, you could be right." She ignored the comment about Jim loving her. "Has he been to the shop today?"

Joan shook her head. "He spoke to me this morning to say he was not well enough to come in, so I have had to cope on my own. I shut for lunch, but I have hardly been able to tackle the new prescriptions. Still, most customers are being very

understanding, and don't mind waiting until the next day. So I
have been making them up in the evening."

Elsie studied Joan while she was talking. She looked very
tired, and it was obvious she had been carrying the shop virtually
on her own. Jim was able to keep in touch, but otherwise could
do very little.

"You've had a very hard time, Joan, and I'm sorry I wasn't
here. Why on earth didn't you 'phone me earlier? I could have
been back last week or even before if I'd known he was ill!"

"Jim wouldn't hear of it!" said Joan. "It wasn't until I told
him I would shut the shop as I couldn't manage it on my own,
that he agreed I should contact you. So here you are!"

Elsie took charge. "I'll look after the shop. You get on with the
prescriptions. I'll telephone Jim and tell him I'm back, and in the
meantime I'll put the kettle on! I know I need a cup of tea!"

"Good idea, Elsie. Glad to have you back!"

Joan went in to the dispensary and seeing no one in the
shop, Elsie called Jim. It took a long time before he answered,
and she almost hung up before his voice answered. "Hallo, Jim
Shaw here," he sounded sleepy and weak voiced. "Who is it?"

"It's Elsie, Jim, I'm back in the shop and helping Joan. How
are you? Not too well apparently."

His voice perked up immediately. "I've missed you Elsie, I
really have. I've been thinking about you every day and wondering
how you are."

"It's not like you to be at home on Saturday afternoon. Is it
your headaches?"

"Yes, Elsie" his voice sounded tired and grim. "Except when I
take some heavy painkillers, it is almost continuous. I know you
have only returned a few hours ago, but could you come to see me
after you shut this evening. Come early, if you are quiet. I must
see you as soon as possible. The hospital could telephone any time
for me to go in, and there is much to tell you before I go!"

"Yes Jim, I understand. I'll be there before six o'clock. Try
and get some rest until then. I'm fine, and ready to get down to
things again."

"Thank goodness Elsie. It is a relief to know it. See you later."

She put back the telephone. He sounded in a bad way, but she was here now to do what she could.

Her immediate thoughts were manning the shop. If she had to spend time on the booking etc., there would only be Joan in the shop. An extra assistant as Jim had suggested before she went away, is becoming essential. Did she know anyone?

As soon as she put down the telephone, she mentioned it to Joan, "Yes, we certainly will need extra help if Jim is going to be away semi-permanently. Nothing springs to mind, but I'll think about it and see if I can think of anybody suitable."

Later in the afternoon, Elizabeth McIver came in. Seeing Elsie back, she was obviously embarrassed over her last meeting with her, but Elsie greeted her warmly, and saved her any confusion.

"Hallo Elizabeth, How good to see you again. I'm so sorry about the last time I saw you. I'm much better now. Thank you for not staying last time. I couldn't help it, I'm sure you understood."

"Of course I did, Elsie. So glad to find you back in the shop. They've missed you. How are you? Is it any easier yet?"

"Yes, it is, although, of course, I am like a stone inside. Work is what I need now, to keep my mind occupied. Now, have you come in for a refill of your usual medicine?"

"Yes please, my dear. By the way, we never had that tea together. How about coming round this Sunday about 4.00? Is it possible?"

"It's most kind of you to ask, but I am sure Jane is coming on a 48 hour pass if she can, so I must refuse this time, but perhaps I could accept on another occasion?"

"Yes, please do. I quite understand, let me know as soon as you feel like it. Now, how much? The usual?"

"Yes, please." said Elsie, and handed her the receipt for the payment. "Oh, and one more thing. I don't know if you have any ideas, but we are in desperate need of an extra assistant in the shop. I don't suppose you know anybody suitable?"

"I think I might, Elsie. Let me give you a call when I have spoken to her Mother. I will speak to you later."

"Oh, thank you. If you can, it would be a life saver for the shop. Don't 'phone until tomorrow if you don't mind, or, I may see you in church. If so we can talk about it then."

"Good idea, see you tomorrow." Mrs McIver left the shop, and Elsie just hoped she had someone of interest. Mrs McIver was a positive lady, and if she knew anyone, they would be a real possibility. She must mention it to Jim when she saw him later.

The autumn evening was closing in as she knocked on Jim's door. He was slow coming to answer, and she saw the difference in him as he ushered her into his hall. His face was drawn and pale, and he looked twenty years older than when she last saw him. She pretended not to notice.

"You are looking better than I thought, Jim. It's good to see you again." He held his hand out for her to shake it.

"You're not a good liar Elsie, I have a mirror you know!" He led her straight into the drawing room and waved her to sit in the chair next to his desk. She saw he had spread lots of papers, invoices she thought, on it.

"Sit down, Elsie. Now, are you still happy to be my Manageress? It will be a lot of work you know."

He was checking her out, as he must in view of what they were going to discuss.

"I'll have to show you as much as I can of the books, the suppliers, the prices, paying the invoices, ordering and paying the staff, dealing with the bank, and so on. I have decided to throw you in at the deep end. Well, I have no choice really! One of the first things is to introduce you to Fred Miller the Bank Manager, and arrange for you to have the power to sign cheques. We'll do that on Monday. So, will you take an early lunch, and come with me to meet him at one o'clock. It's the only time he can manage, so it has to be then. I hope I will be well enough to make it!"

Elsie hadn't realised how much authority he was giving her until now.

"Yes, Jim, I'll be ready. In the meantime, I have some spies out looking for a new assistant in the shop. A young person I thought, preferably a lady, possibly an older teenager. What do you think?"

"Sounds a good idea. You'll have to train her, you realise."

"Yes, I know, but I would rather have someone who will learn than someone with bad habits I may not have time to break. Anyway, Joan will help a young assistant, I'm certain."

Jim said nothing except. "Fine, Elise, I'll leave it to you. You are the one who will have to work with her. Now, here is the bought invoice file. In here you will find all the invoices for goods we have purchased this year, so far. These are all paid, as you see them marked. Now I will show you the Purchase Ledger where you will see the cheque paying the invoice, and the entry in the Cash Book, here, which is the double entry."

It started to come back to Elsie. She had helped Bill in the dairy sometimes, and although he had the responsibility, she interested herself in the books, and what Jim was telling her was not entirely new.

For over two hours, Jim went through every detail of the shop, the turnover, the discounts he obtained from suppliers, and by the time half past eight came, they were both becoming very tired. Jim was driving himself hard. As his drawing room clock struck the half hour, he suddenly closed the Cash Book he was discussing with her, and announced. "Can't manage any more tonight. Let's call it a day. Have a quiet day tomorrow, and I'll speak to you on Monday in the shop about half past ten."

He got up, swayed a little, and quickly took her to the front door. "Thanks for coming tonight, Elsie. From now on you are in charge. I will leave all the decisions to you. While I'm around, ask me anything you are uncertain about. I would like you to arrange to come to my house and make up the books of account, whether I'm here or not, every Thursday. You can come when you like, and you can fit it in when you can leave the shop. My housekeeper will let you in, and she will open the desk for you. Anything else, speak to me on Monday. Goodnight, and have a pleasant weekend."

He was obviously in pain, and dead tired. Elsie did not argue, just replied. "Fine Jim, speak to you on Monday." She went out and the door closed behind her.

Left on his own, Jim held on to the banisters, and slowly hauled himself up the stairs to his bedroom. After taking two of the tablets to kill the pains in his head, he lay down on his bed, and moved his head back and forward until the pain eased, and fell asleep. He was in a bad way, and he knew one way or the other, his time was running out.

Elsie walked pensively back to her flat, her mind buzzing with all the details he had thrown at her. She was to be 'mistress 'of the business! She had control of the money, and it was up to her. Jim trusted her completely, and she must do her absolute best for him. She resolved to throw herself into the shop. It would keep her mind occupied, and could not have come at a better time!

On Sunday, after an early breakfast, she dressed in her best outfit, and went along to the morning service at St John's. The vicar, who had heard of her loss, and knew she had been away, greeted her back with enthusiasm. "Delighted to see you here again, Mrs Winter. Another fine autumn day, isn't it. I hear you are back in the shop. I shall be coming in shortly, I expect." Elsie replied. "Thank you, Vicar. I shall look forward to seeing you."

She went into the church, realised she was a bit early, and sat in her usual pew. A few minutes later Elizabeth McIver came in and seeing Elsie, came across the aisle to sit next to her.

"I think I have found someone you'll like, Elsie," she whispered. "Tell you about her later. Can you come back with me and we'll have a glass of sherry together while I give you the details?"

"Thanks Elizabeth. I shall be every happy to. Is your husband well?"

"Yes thank you. Very busy, as usual, and a bit bad tempered, but not surprising considering how hard he is working."

At that moment the procession appeared at the back of the church, and conversation finished.

Elsie sat in one of Elizabeth's comfortable chintz covered arm chairs, and sipped her glass of rich sherry, while Mrs McIver gave her details of the girl she thought might fill the vacancy in the shop.

"She's nearly eighteen, left school last term, and wants to be a 'chemist' as she terms it. In fact what she means is a pharmacist. Her parents are not well off, and can't afford to pay for at college, so she intends to qualify in her spare time, and earn a wage working at a chemist. When her mother told me, I immediately thought of Shaw's, and your enquiry came only two months after she told me of Ann's ambitions."

"How do you known her, Elizabeth?" asked Elsie.

"Her father works in the factory in the yard, he is a labourer. Honest as the day is long, but not very intelligent. Her Mother is a real gem. Quite plain, but bright as a button, and straight as a die. Ann inherits her Mother's brain, and looks like her Father. Has the best of both!" she laughed. The only thing, she is not terribly well spoken, but otherwise I think you will find her ideal. She is keen to learn, and when I mentioned the opportunity to Mrs Simpson, she wanted to tell Ann immediately. I said wait until I have spoken to you, as you might be wanting someone older and with experience. What do you think?"

Elsie was delighted. It seemed too good to be true.

"Ask her to call in at the shop next week as soon as she likes after ten o'clock so Joan will be there, and I'll have a talk with her and show her what she will be doing. Did you say her name is Ann Simpson?" "Yes, "said Mrs McIver. "I'll tell her, and you can expect her at five minutes past ten on Monday!" She laughed again! Ann, she knew, was very keen.

After a few pleasantries, she concluded the visit." Now, my dear, I must get on with Sunday lunch. I'll look in during the week and you can tell me how you get on. I think you will like her."

Elsie got up, thanked Elizabeth for the sherry, said goodbye to her husband who was working in the garden as she went out, and walked back to her flat. Could it be that she had a new assistant? Monday would be interesting, and she could introduce her to Joan so they could compare notes.

At ten o'clock on the dot, a smartly but poorly dressed young girl entered the shop, and came straight to the counter and Elsie. "Good morning. Are you Mrs Winter?"

"I am," replied Elsie, "Are you Miss Ann Simpson?"

"Mrs McIver said I should come 'ere this morning, as you 'ave a vacancy at the shop. Is that 'ere?"

Elsie winced a bit at the missing 'h', "Yes, it is, Miss Simpson.. Please sit there, "She pointed to the chair by the counter, "and as soon as my colleague comes in, any time now, we can have a talk, and show you what you would be doing."

She deliberately ignored her, and went on cleaning the counter and dusting the front of the glass cupboards. Ann was looking about the shop, taking it all in. Elsie could see she was, as Elizabeth said, like her Mother, 'bright as a button'. Joan came quickly in the door.

"Good morning, Joan, have a good day yesterday?"

"Yes, thanks, good morning Elsie! What's this, a young customer already?"

"No, let me introduce you to Ann Simpson. She has come for interview this morning." Joan held out her hand. "Hallo Ann, pleased to meet you. Haven't I seen you in the High Street?"

"Yers," replied Ann. "bin living 'ere all me life. Always wanted to work 'ere!"

Joan ignored the accent, but winked at Elsie. "Well, I'm the pharmacist, and make up the medicines for the prescriptions from the Doctors. We'll have a chat when Mrs Winter has talked to you. "

"Righto," replied Ann.

"Joan, could you be kind enough to stay in the shop while I have a talk to Ann in the dispensary?" said Elsie. Joan nodded, and Elsie said

"Come on young lady, come in to the back, and we'll see what you can do." They went into the dispensary, and she sat Ann on the stool." She saw hr eyes bulge at the sight of all the huge coloured bottles, and shelves stacked with medicines.

"Now, let's ask you a few questions, first, and then you can ask me what you want to know. Right, how old are you?"

"Oi'm seventeen and an alf." replied Ann quickly.

So it went on. Every question Elsie asked, Ann replied quickly and honestly. She began to like her. Not only did she answer smartly and obviously innocently, but she also had a happy manner and ready smile. When Elsie made a small joke, she giggled, quite naturally.

"Now, Miss Simpson, what do you want to ask me?"

"Can I 'ave time off to go to school for me heducation?" asked Ann.

"Yes, you can, in fact I want you too. If you want to be a pharmacist, which I think you do, it is essential. You can ask the college to write to me, and I'll give you the time off. No pay for those days, of course, you must understand that."

"Tha's O.K. Now wot abart me wages? 'ow much?"

"Well, at your age, you are on sliding scale. You start at, and she mentioned the scale figure for seventeen, and you have an increase on your birthday every year until you are twenty one, of five shillings each week. Is that O.K.?"

Ann was overcome, and her accent lapsed even further. "Cor, that's a fortune, Mrs Winter, me Mum said you were a toff! When can I start? Will I be able to wear one of them coats what you've got on?"

She pointed at Elsie's white coat.

"Yes, you will. In fact, you will always wear one in the shop. As soon as you arrive in the morning, at nine o'clock, you will put it on and wear it until you leave at 5.30. We also work Saturdays, but you will have one afternoon off in addition, on a day when you are not at college."

"Cor, sounds smashin'!"

"Right, now, go and talk to Mrs Summers, and see if she likes you."

She opened the door and called to Joan. "Over to you Joan. Come and have a chat with Ann, and see how you get on."

As she passed Joan on the way to take over the shop, she gave a slight sign to indicate she liked Ann, Joan went in and soon she could hear them both laughing.

Fifteen minutes later, they both came out. "She'll do!" said Joan, and grinned at Elsie

"When would you like to start, Ann" asked Elsie. "Soon as I can. T'morrow if you want?"

"No, that's a bit quick. Let's make it Thursday morning. It's half day, and not usually so busy. It'll give you time to learn the basics so you will be a help to us as soon as possible. Now, off you go, and we'll look forward to seeing you at nine o'clock on Thursday, O.K.?"

"Yes, I'll be 'ere. Doan 'ee worry!" She went out and they watched her dancing for joy along the pavement!

Elsie looked at Joan. "Well?"

"If we train her right, she'll be fine. Could be a real help and asset to the shop, but her accent!! Can you correct it d'you think?"

"I think I can. She's young, keen to learn, and will copy us, or we'll copy her!" They both laughed.

Elsie prayed quietly to herself that Ann would be what she wanted. If she proved a mistake – Elsie dared not think of the consequences to Shaw's

Early Tuesday morning, the shop had a visit from Mrs Simpson. She came in warily, and introduced herself to Elsie.

"I'm Mrs Simpson, Ann's Mum. Now, wot you bin saying to 'er. She says you offered 'er as good wages as I get! She's only seventeen yer know!"

"Hallo, Mrs Simpson, I'm Elsie Winter, the Manageress. What's the problem, do you want me to pay her less? She seems very bright young lady. I have great hopes for her if she likes it here, and works hard. She will be getting a lot more, especially if she becomes a pharmacist!"

"She'll work 'ard, I'll see to that. She says she can go to school. Is that right? When will that be?"

"I don't know yet. It is up to Ann to approach the college, and tell me to whom I should write, and the course she will be studying. I'll give her any help she wants, once she works here, so long as you're happy about it!"

"Cor, she's fell on 'er feet, that girl. Thank you for bein' so kind. Tell me if you ever need some work done. My Harry's a dab 'and at labouring. How about yer garden? Need anything doing?"

"I'll keep that in mind Mrs Simpson. Now I have to go. We're looking forward to seeing Ann on Thursday. It was really nice meeting you. Goodbye, and call in anytime and I'll tell you how Ann's progressing."

"Thanks very much. You are a toff, I've always said so. Like when your Bill was killed. We was all so sorry. What a gen'lman. You must miss 'im."

With that last telling remark, Mrs Simpson left the shop as she had come. Joan had been listening in the dispensary. "You've made a friend there, Elsie. Wouldn't want to cross her though. She could be a nasty woman treated wrongly!"

Ann started on Thursday as agreed. Elise had delayed sweeping the front of the shop until she arrived, a few minutes before nine o'clock. She looked happy and keen. Elsie took her in the back and sorted through the coat cupboard until she found one to fit her. Slightly taller than Joan, she was a lot slimmer, and Joan's size proved to be a good fit. Soon she was outside with Elsie wearing her clean white coat looking as proud as a peacock in her 'new uniform'. She was used to sweeping, and had the job completed in half the time it took Elsie.

She started by showing her where everything was, and after each section, tested her. Soon most articles were sorted in her mind. Elsie told her that as a customer came in she would ask them what they wanted, and Ann would get the goods and bring them to the counter. This would improve her geography of the stock. It worked well, and by the time they finished for early closing day, Elsie was satisfied she could move on to teaching her the operation of the till.

That evening she reported to Jim what she had done. He did not know Ann Simpson, but gave his approval." I hope she proves to be useful," was all he said except to say he thought she had taken on a brave task to employ such a young lady. Her accent didn't worry him at all. "If she's got a pleasant and willing personality, the customers will soon get to know and like her." That was what Elsie thought.

In the morning she set about showing Ann the till. Her arithmetic was good, even if she spoke badly, and at the end of the day when they checked it together as past of her training, the totals were exact, with no errors. Then Ann admitted she had given three pence too much change, and made it up from her pocket. Elsie was well pleased with her honesty, and immediately gave her it back from the till, but didn't show her how she entered the three pence she gave her back. Joan liked her and she Joan. As soon as she was free in a quiet moment, Joan asked her to help her in the dispensary. Ann went in like a shot!

It proved to be another successful day for Ann Simpson, and already, Joan and Elsie felt less stretched .

On Saturday, a customer rang about four o'clock and said she had left her small bottle of flu' mixture on the counter by mistake. Elsie looked quickly and found it next to the till. Ann said she found it, but didn't know what to do, so held it there waiting for the customer to return. When she knew who it was she offered at once to take it round to her house on the way home. Elsie was so pleased, and so was the customer when Elsie told her, that she told Ann to go home at a quarter to five, and drop it in on the way home. Ann was delighted, and even more so, when Mrs Roebuck, the lady who left it, gave her sixpence for delivering it! Before she went, Elsie gave her the pay for the three days, and it was a very happy Ann who went home to show her Mother her wages. Elsie knew it was a good start, and just hoped it would continue when Jim was in hospital.

Ann settled in to become one of the team very quickly. Joan was able to get her prescriptions completed on time, and Elsie could let her resume her part time hours except on Mondays when there were many and it was a rush to complete then by the end of the day.

As the weeks passed, Elsie went to see Jim regularly. She noticed his head pains came and went. When the shrapnel moved, he was in agony, and only survived on heavy sedation from Dr Hargreaves. Other times, he seemed almost normal when the metal remained static. The operation was becoming urgent,. Jim was losing weight rapidly, not eating well, and all he was interested in was seeing Elsie and talking about the shop. Elsie began to make up reasons to see him twice some weeks. She knew how it bucked him up to have a chat, and once when she met the Doctor, he said how much good her visits did him. So, she lied more and more frequently to visit the little square house and made his tea while they talked, often at his bedside.

The autumn moved towards winter, and November brought wet and cold. One afternoon, Jim asked Elsie if she knew anything about the 'gas main' explosions. He showed her an article in the paper that talked about them. One, particularly, at Chiswick seemed mysterious, and Jim couldn't understand why there had been several in the space of a few weeks. Damage to the mains, he supposed, due to the blitz, and only just coming to the surface – literally. Then one particular afternoon, he was waiting to tell her some news, and it really worried him.

"My friend, Jack, the Warden, you know, came today, and told me some interesting but worrying news." Elsie listened attentively.

"You know those gas explosions," "Yes," replied Elsie

"Well, they aren't gas at all. They are a new German rocket. They're calling them 'V2's'. The Germans are launching them from Holland and the unoccupied parts of France and Belgium. They travel through the air until they crash on London. There's no warning at all, and the first thing you know is when they explode on hitting the ground!"

Elsie was appalled. "I thought we had finished with these things when the doodle bugs stopped. Have any fallen near here?"

"Not as far as I know. It is all been kept hush hush for the moment, but they are increasing, so soon everyone will know!"

"Please God none fall on Sidhurst," said Elsie. "Surely we've had our share of bombs."

"Amen to that" replied Jim. "Now, what's been happening in the shop? How's Ann getting on, still doing well?"

"Yes, very well indeed, Jim" she responded. "I haven't been able to move her accent yet, but you were right, the customers don't mind. She is so helpful, and delivers their prescriptions if they are late bringing them in. I think they like her and are amused by her cockney voice and mannerisms."

"Knew she would do well if she has personality. Told you so, didn't I!" said Jim triumphantly.

They continued until Jim was falling asleep with tiredness. Elsie bid him goodnight and walked home. The V2's as Jim had referred to them, worried her. No more problems, she hoped.

The one thing Elsie really wanted was to see Jane again. She had heard nothing until she rang up well into November full of apologies, and said she would like to come on Friday for the weekend. Elsie at once said "Yes, Jane, please come. Wherever have you been?" Jane was quite nonchalant. "Just been so busy, haven't had a minute to relax. Finally, I said I had to have a 48 hour pass, or I would take it anyway. The Captain i/c my section wasn't very happy, but agreed reluctantly. It is O.K. to come isn't it?"

"Yes, I said so Jane. Come as early as you can.!"

"See you on Friday evening then, bye Elsie!"

Of course, as soon as Elsie put down the 'phone, all the grief about Brian returned. In her enthusiasm and caring for Jim, and his business, it had been pushed to the back of her mind. Jane will be the same, particularly if she's working hard. We must try and get out together, perhaps into he country if the weather holds. I know, we'll go chestnutting on Sunday!

For the second time in four months, Jane sat in the train on the way down to Sidhurst in a worried frame of mind. How would she find Elsie? She was conscience stricken for not having spoken to her, but her work was never ending. When not working she was either sleeping, or trying to blot out the memory of Brian from her mind. Was Elsie doing the same? In addition there was another worry, and it was imperative she had a long serious talk to Elsie. How would she take her news? Would she be shocked when she heard? The journey slipped past without her realising, and the shout of "Sidhurst, Sidhurst" from the platform porter only just prevented her missing her stop. Ten minutes later she was knocking on the door of No. 8a. Elsie came running down the stairs to meet her!

"Jane, how lovely to see you again! Come in, I have the supper ready. You'll eat some won't you?"

Jane studied her, not believing how well she looked. No sign of grief. What had she done to deal with it so well? "How are you, Elsie? How is Jim, and the shop? "

"It's very busy, Jane, and I'm the Manageress now. But how about you? You must have been very busy too, otherwise you would have called me before."

Jane wanted to tell her news, but for the time being thought she would wait and see how Elsie was when the initial meeting was over. "I'm working very hard to take my mind off the past, Elsie. You must know what it's like! Sometimes I am in despair, and then I work all the harder. Then I get better again, until the next time! What about you?"

"Yes, the same, really, but the shop is so busy, Jim's ill, and we have a new girl to train. I don't have, or try not to have, time, to think. I find it's best that way. Let's have supper, and we can sit and talk after."

It was not a big meal, but Jane didn't want much anyway. After they had washed up together, and it was dark, they sat round Elsie's fire in her drawing room, and settled themselves comfortably, one in each arm chair.

Jane decided now was the time to reveal her news and the reason why she had not contacted Elsie earlier.

"Elsie, I have some important news to tell you. I don't know if you will be shocked, pleased, think I am a naughty girl, or what. The reason why I have not been in touch with you is that before Brian left for France, we were married! I'm Mrs Winter!. That's the reason why the War Office sent the details of his death and belongings to me. You got the telegram because I put my address as being 8a St Mark's Parade!" Elsie sat up astonished. "Have a look at the telegram if you have it handy!"

She moved quickly to her bureau, and opening the lid, took it out from the top of the pile of letters, and read it. The address was to Mrs B. Winter – and she never noticed in her shock at receiving it! She thought for a moment. Jim hadn't noticed either!

"Why did you do that, Jane?"

"Because I knew if anything happened, being at the War Office, I would be informed immediately anyway. In fact, I knew before you did!"

"Why didn't you telephone and tell me?"

"Well to be honest, we thought you would be shocked. You said it was too soon, but Brian wanted us to be secure before he went away. That's not all. Now, I know you will be shocked, but I have to tell you. I'm going to have Brian's baby! I thought I was a month ago, but wanted to be sure before I told you. I am almost certain, now, as I've missed two periods, but I intend to see your Doctor while I'm here to get it confirmed. Now, can you see how bad I've been?"

Elsie was totally shocked, horrified, and delighted, all at

the same time! Only nineteen, she was pregnant with her dead son's child! Brian must have had a premonition. Did he know something?

"Jane, why so quick? "

"Brian almost knew he would not be coming back from his last action. He was sent behind the enemy lines in advance of his unit, to organise the resistance. They had been sent some 25 pounders, and his task was to show them how to use them, and liaise with the allied forces. He got caught in an ambush, that bit is correct, and his truck blown up. They couldn't report the exact truth, but I found out. He wanted to have a family if he could, and perhaps, he still will. Are you very ashamed at what we have done, and not even told you?"

Elsie did not know what to say. She was going to be a grandmother! Something she never thought could happen after Brian's death. Now she had a future, and maybe a grandson! God had forgiven her!

She stood up and held out her arms to Jane. "Jane, never mind whether you were naughty or not. This is the happiest I have been since I heard of Brian's death."

With that she burst into tears, and the two Mrs Winters', old and young, held one another with tears streaming down their faces! After a while, Elsie recovered sufficiently to say. "What are your plans Jane? What will the Army do when they know about the baby?"

"They will discharge me. There's no place for a pregnant Sergeant in my unit! Once again, Elsie, can I ask for your help?"

Elise knew at once, the only family she had was Jane, and she would bear her grandchild. Boy or girl, it didn't matter. Jane was now 'family', and as such would get all the help Elsie could give.

"I will telephone Dr Hargreaves this evening before surgery finishes, and we'll go together to see him tomorrow morning!"

Jane smiled. It had gone as she hoped. "Fine, Elsie, anytime will be O.K. I have to be sure before I tell my C.O." Elsie went over to the 'phone, and asked for the doctor's number, and made the appointment. In her surprise and delight, she had completely forgotten the shop!

"Is it alright if I come with you, Jane? You don't mind do you?"

"Elsie, you are the only Mother I shall have now. I want you to come. We can share the final confirmation together!" Elsie had to sort out the morning in the shop. She was sure good old Joan would hold the fort for an hour while they went to Dr Hargreaves. Ann also, could be trusted for an hour in the shop, so it would be alright.

"Jane, I have to work most of the day tomorrow. What do you want to do? Rest, or perhaps do some shopping? Have you had any sickness yet?"

"No sickness yet, and I feel very well, just a bit tired because of the work load."

"That will have to stop. You must have plenty of rest. I'm sure the doctor will insist you stop work as soon as possible. I did. You cannot take even the slightest chance."

"I don't intend to. Now, Elsie, looking to the next few months. Can I come and live in the flat when I get demobbed? I shall have nowhere to live, and a pregnant single lady will not find digs easy to get?"

"You must, Jane. I shall be in the shop most of the time, and I go round to Jim's twice a week in the evening, but if you don't mind that, I should love you to stay here."

Jane was relieved. The thought of being thrown into Civvy Street with nowhere to go or live, frightened her. She had visions of staying at the Salvation Army hostel.

"I shall try and get some work for a while at least; any ideas?"

Nothing occurred to Elsie, but she said. "I'll have a think, and we can look in the local labour exchange and papers. You will find something, I'm certain!" but in reality she was not so sure. Not in her condition when she was discharged. Maybe after the baby was born.

"Now, Jane, I'm going to ask Jim if we can visit him tomorrow evening. The news will buck him up. He is quite ill now and still waiting for a date for his operation." She picked up the telephone again and Jim answered the call.

"It's Elsie, Jim. How are you today?"

She heard him mumble an answer, but he was obviously half asleep. "Would it be alright if I came round to visit tomorrow evening, Saturday? I'll bring Jane with me. She is here for the weekend. "

"Yes, Elsie. Am going back to sleep now, it's been a bad day!"

She said goodbye, and said to Jane. "That's organised, now let's hear all your news!"

For the first time, the two ladies chatted woman to woman in a way impossible to do when Brian was present. Jane learned all about Brian's young days growing up in Sidhurst, building up a fund of knowledge that she could keep and savour. Elsie told her about Bill, the babies grandfather, the Winter family, all her relatives, now passed on, until Jane knew that Elsie and she were the only relatives either had still living. It was a sobering thought, and would bind the friendship and respect one to the other as time moved on.

The next day, Jane with Elsie in attendance, walked into Dr Hargreaves surgery, to be greeted by Elsie's doctor in a careful fashion. Elsie introduced Jane, her daughter-in-law, and it sounded strange. The doctor thought she had probably come for herself, and had brought Jane along for comfort, and was, therefore surprised, when Jane said,

"Doctor, I am almost sure I am having a baby, but just to be absolutely certain, and so I can inform the Army officially, would you please examine me and confirm I am pregnant."

He looked at Elsie and smiled. "Of course, just take a few clothes off behind the screen, and I'll examine you."

"While Jane undressed, he said to Elsie. "What marvellous

news for you. I suppose you are hoping for a grandson?" Elsie smiled. "Yes, Doctor, I am thrilled. I only knew yesterday, but it will make all the difference. They were only married three months ago, just before Brian went back from leave."

The Doctor examined Jane thoroughly, asking all the appropriate questions. After only a few minutes, he announced.

"I can confirm, as well as I can ever do, that you are pregnant, About three months I would guess. Does that fit your own thoughts?"

"Yes, it does," smiled Jane. "Now I can tell my C.O., and we can start to plan things!"

"Back you go and get dressed. I want to see you again, as soon as you are back in Sidhurst. You are going to live here, I assume?"

"Yes" replied Jane. "I shall .be living with Elsie, so would you please be kind enough to include me on you patient list from now on. I expect to be discharged in about a month."

"Why. Yes, Mrs Winter, I'll be pleased to. Come and see me when ever you need."

As soon as they got outside, Jane said "There you are, I knew it! All being well, you will be a grandmother next May. Probably around the 15th I estimate."

Elsie was full of happiness. Brian had done her proud. Another Winter was on the way, and she never thought there would be anyone to continue the family!

In the evening, they walked round to Jim's house about seven o'clock when it was almost dark. Jim was up and ready to meet them. Elsie had seen him earlier in the week, but Jane hadn't since her last leave. She thought he looked very ill, but tried not to show her concern.

"Hallo, Uncle Jim, How are you? Better than I thought you would be from what Elsie told me."

"So nice to see you again, Jane. I am so sorry about Brian. How are you bearing up? Anything I can do, you only have to ask Elsie!"

"Thank you Uncle Jim. but I have some news to tell you." Elsie left it to Jane, and said nothing.

"You have to address me as Mrs Winter, now, Uncle Jim. We were married just before Brian went back off his last leave, and what's more, I am going to have a baby. Elsie will be a grandmother next May, all going well!"

"Jim visibly brightened, and sat up in his bed. "Now, that is some news!" Then he was as usual, immediately practical. "I expect the Army will throw you out right away, won't they? Where are you going to live? Have you anywhere planned?"

"No, I am afraid I have asked Elsie if it is O.K. for me to live with her, certainly for the time being."

Jim said nothing for a few moments, and Elsie thought he was going to refuse to have her in the shop flat. Then to her horror he said,

"No, that won't do at all. There is not room for you both in the flat, and when the baby comes, it will be impossible trying to get a pram up and down the stairs."

"Yes, I know," said Elsie, "We've thought of that, and together we can manage."

"Oh, so you've got it all planned, have you!" said Jim. "Well, I'm going to change your plan whether you like it or not!" Elsie and Jane sat wondering what he was going to say.

"What I want you both to do, but especially Elsie, is to move at the end of November into my house. If you particularly want to have your own place, Jane, you can stay in the flat, but I suggest you accept my offer, and both come to live with me. There is plenty of space for us all, and I would really like you to come. Now, I have some news of my own. In early December I shall be going into hospital for quite a long stay. So you see, it is quite perfect. You can look after my house until I return, and if I don't, well, it's yours!"

Jane was non-plussed, but Elsie knew he meant it. "Thank you very much for the offer, Jim, but you must let us have until tomorrow to make up our minds. Don't think me churlish, but it is a big decision, and we must sleep on it. I hope we can accept."

Jim could see she was embarrassed, and wanted to reassure her, but decided to let her make up her mind with Jane. He knew what he really wanted, and so, he thought, did Elsie, and that was why she demurred. Don't push her, and all may work out as he wanted.

After hearing about the details of the operation, and seeing Jim looking tired, they quietly made their farewells, and Elsie said she would telephone him tomorrow. "Ask anything you want, Elsie. You will have charge of the house anyway, at least until I get out of hospital."

Jane and Elsie walked slowly back to the flat. Neither said much, until Elsie spoke her mind. "You know what this means Jane, don't you!"

"I think I have an idea, but enlighten me."

"It means Jim wants me to marry him. I know he has always loved me even before Bill died, but I never gave him any encouragement. If we move in to the house, I will have to, in order to stop any gossip, if for no other reason. You know what Sidhurst is like!"

"Yes, I thought so. I saw your face when he suggested it. It must be your decision, Elsie. Do you love him? Even a little?"

"He has done so much for me, Jane. I owe him more than I can ever repay. I don't believe I am likely to meet another man like Bill, and Jim is very kind. I am going to accept, and as soon as he gets near to coming home from hospital, I will propose. I know he will never propose to me because of his damaged face, but what's wrong about a scarred face. If it hides the man underneath, which it does in this instance, why not marry him. I hardly see the scars now anyway just through working with him. Yes, I shall ask him, and yes, we will move into his house. Oh dear, sorry Jane! I haven't asked you if you are happy to do it?

"Elsie, it's marvellous. We will thank him tomorrow and accept before I leave to go back to barracks."

Elsie thought about his old and loyal housekeeper, who had

looked after him for many years. She must talk to him about her. There would not be room for her as well as the two of them, and especially with Jim in his own room when he comes out of hospital. Yes, she must clear that before she finally accepts the offer!

By the time they sat down in the flat, both Jane and Elsie were becoming excited at the prospect of living in Jim's big house. It was a class above any house that Elsie had lived in. Although the Dairy had excellent accommodation, it was company property, and attached to the shop. This would be a home with it's own garden!

Later in the evening she asked Jane if she had heard of the new V2 weapon in London.

"Elsie, I wasn't sure if you knew about them, so didn't mention it. I have heard several in London, but thankfully none near. They are much more frightening than the doodle bugs. The bomb it carries is bigger, and they strike without warning. People who think about them finish up unable to go out, or even leave the shelters. The best thing is to ignore them, and get on with your normal day's work. If one has your name on it, well, that's it!" Apparently, you hear two bangs. The first when the rocket enters the atmosphere, and a second when it explodes on hitting the ground. They are almost instantaneous. Bang, bang, just like that!"

Where have they fallen, Jane, do you know?"

"No, it is still kept confidential, but they have all been in London or the suburbs. They fall quite indiscriminately."

"Can we do anything to stop them? The RAF managed to deal with the doodle bugs?

"No, nothing can be done, except to overrun the launch sites, until they are too far away to reach us. When that will be no one knows. The advance is slowing down, and as they are launched from Holland, it may be some time."

"Let's change the subject," said Elsie. "I don't want to know anymore. Let's hope they don't fall here!"

On Sunday morning, after coffee, they went round to Jim's again. He had risen early to see them, and looked better than yesterday. Elsie told him immediately their combined decision, and he nodded,

"I'm very pleased, neither of you will regret it. Elsie, you anyway would have had to come round at least twice a week once I go in, so you will save time on that. The walk to the shop will do you good! So that's settled. Move in when you like!"

"One thing we have not mentioned, and it's very much on my conscience, Jim. That is, about your housekeeper. There won't be room for us all, will there?"

"Trust you to think of her, Elsie. I have already talked to her. She has been with the family for many years, my Father before me, then after my Mother died. She wants to retire, and live out her years on her own in peace and comfort. I have rented a small cottage outside Sidhurst on the way to Bromley, and she will live there supported by me. It is already in hand, and the only reason why she has not already moved, is because of looking after me. Once you are here, I hope she will only be needed on the odd day each week. She is quite prepared to do that as soon as I say the word."

"Thank you Jim, you have covered everything, I think. Once you have a definite date for hospital, I will move in a few days before. How does that suit you?"

"Fine, Elsie, I will let you know as soon as I know for certain. Now, some coffee before you go?"

"No, thanks very much Jim, we are on our way to church, and if you will excuse us, we shall just make it!"

"Of course, see you both soon, I'll try and make it to the shop on Monday, and meet Ann. She sounds quite a character!"

They went out of his front gate and down the road towards the church. It had been an excuse to get away, and once they were out of Jim's sight, she turned back to the flat.

For a while they discussed plans for the future, and to let events take their course, then act accordingly. Elsie took Jane to the Black Horse for dinner, to give them free time until Jane had to return to London. She caught the early evening train, and travelled back a very happy and relieved young woman. Now all she had to do was break the news to her officer in charge on Monday!

On the home front, nothing moved for several weeks, but over London, the threat of the V2's was becoming real. Not a sudden burst of missiles coming over, this was a more insidious menace. The number of explosions steadily grew in number. In early December one morning about ten o'clock, Elsie heard one hit their area. She knew what it was when she heard the double bang, just as Jane had described. That was all, until a customer told them it had hit a school at Catford, and many children had been killed and injured without warning.

Shaw's The Chemist was prospering. Although Boots was open and back to normal, their trade was steadily increasing. Ann was becoming very quick and the customers found her amusing. Many of the older ones came in for a laugh as well as to have their prescriptions made up. Elsie began to see that Joan was becoming hard pressed to cope, and feeling the strain. She should have retired, and Elsie decided to take action to get help for her before she was forced to stop. Jim was still waiting, so she mentioned it to him one December afternoon when she went round to do the accounts.

"You will have to get a part time pharmacist, Elsie. Have a word with the Association; they may be able to help."

"Thanks, Jim, I knew you'd know what to do. Do you have the address and 'phone number?"

"Not immediately to hand, Elsie, but you'll find it in the miscellaneous file in the cupboard under the stairs."

Elsie knew he must have the old files and accounts somewhere, but she had not been shown where. When she opened the door, what looked like a small broom cupboard, was in fact, much larger. Someone had taken down the wall at the back, so it was enlarged to more than double it's original size. After some delving she found the papers she wanted, with the address and telephone number..

Next morning she got on to the Association early, and after being passed around a few times, spoke to a useful lady who said she would see if she could find somebody. Later in the morning, she called back, and said she had someone in Crayford, and if Elsie would pay her the cost of travelling on the bus to Sidhurst, would be interested. Her name was Mrs Joan Loveridge. Elsie obtained the details, and spoke to her that evening.

Joan Loveridge answered the 'phone and Elsie explained what she wanted. Joan sounded very efficient, and Elsie wondered if she was taking on more than she bargained for. Nevertheless, it was decided she would come to Sidhurst on Wednesday and discus what Elsie required. Elsie felt she was on trial rather than the other way round! She arranged with her trusty Joan to help her interview the new lady, and to test her experience and knowledge as it was beyond Elsie's expertise

Joan No.2 as Elsie dubbed her, arrived on time, and was obviously as Elsie thought, efficient and a 'no nonsense' lady. However, Joan 1 said she was good deal more up to date than she, so Elsie hired her on a monthly basis, and promised that if she fitted in, a long term position would be available. She didn't tell Jim. She made the decision. Accounts calculations told her the shop could well afford her. Profits were up, even with both 'Joans', Ann, and her own increased salary. The shop was growing and the future looked rosy.

****

Chapter 10

$\mathcal{N}$ ovember had gone, and the first fog of the winter shrouded Sidhurst High Street. It was cold, very cold, and people felt it in their houses. The damage from the doodle bugs had reopened cracks and holes, and the frost seemed to penetrate everything. Shaw's was getting even busier. Prescriptions for flu' medicine, cough mixture, and aspirins competed with lemon pastilles and juice for top selling position. Jim was still at home, and Elsie worried about him. Luckily as he did not go out, he didn't catch any winter ailment, but he was losing heart waiting, and Elsie wondered if she could do anything to hasten his hospital visit.

Elise was so glad she had taken on Mrs Loveridge, now known by everybody as Joan 2! She kept good hours, was idolised by Ann, and dispensed the medicines with speed and efficiency. Ann was to start at night school after Christmas, and was still happy and keen as mustard. She respected Mrs Loveridge, and called her Ma'am! Even better, she was copying her 'posh' voice that had an imperiousness everyone noticed. Joan 1 was happy to take second place to her, and no doubt hoped she would be able to retire completely in the spring when the pressure eased.

The V2's were becoming a constant threat. Elsie preferred not to think about them as Jane had advised. Sometimes the double bang as one landed in the vicinity troubled her, but she tried to ignore them. Jane had telephoned her early in the month to ask if it was alright to come for Christmas. She still had no date for her demob, and she thought it would be towards the end of January, but was keeping well, still very busy, and so Elsie tried not to worry about her. The war was not going well. The Germans had launched a counter attack in the Ardennes on the back of the cold weather, and pushed the allies back. It was all a bit depressing, and Elsie felt she needed to do something to raise her spirits.

She wondered what to organise for the Christmas Holiday. Ann was getting so excited, and kept asking what was going to happen in the shop. It was infectious, and Elsie began to plan something for them to do to welcome Jane on Xmas Eve. The shop would close at three o'clock, and she needed to see if she could raise Jim's mood at the same time. She came to the idea, if Jim approved, that they would all go round to his house on Xmas Eve, and have a small party around his bedside! As they all would want to get home, it could be short, just an extra half hour beyond normal closing time and would not make Jim too tired. For the first time since the war started, this year there was an extra allowance on each ration book, and a few more luxuries in the shops. One supplier, who liked Elsie, not Mr Cheseman, brought in a small box of chocolates he had procured for his best customers, and Elsie hid it at the back of the cupboard in her flat for the party!

Out of the blue, her plans fell into disarray. She had spoken to Doctor Hargreaves about Jim, and his declining health and spirits, and he had acted to press Jim's cause to his consultant. On December 12th just two weeks before the Christmas holiday, Jim received a call to attend hospital that Friday, and to say his operation was scheduled on the Tuesday following. He rang Elsie immediately, and gave her the news. She went round in the lunch hour to see him.

"At last, Elsie, I'm to go in on Tuesday! I'll have the operation before Christmas!" He was in a mixed up mood. Pleased the day had come at last, but nervous for the future and the aftermath of such a serious operation.

"No more headaches" he crowed. "One way or the other!" He knew, of course, it would be a critical operation, and his life could hang in the balance according to what the surgeon found.

"Jim, you'll be fine. I know it." said Elsie. "Just relax until you go in. I'll come round every day and come with you to hospital if you like. The shop can do without me for one day at least!"

The reply was immediate. "No", Elsie. I don't want you with me. I will be better on my own. Afterwards, come when you like, I shall be pleased to see you, of course. This is something I must face on my own, you do understand?"

"Yes, of course Jim. Now, anything I can do while I'm here?"

"No, thank you. Is the shop busy?" Always the shop, Elsie thought he would die if the shop failed!

"I'll have one last session with you and show you the cash book etc., if you feel well enough on Monday, Jim. Now, I must get back to see what they are all up to in my absence! See you tomorrow!"

She went quietly out. That was that. On Wednesday it would be up to her for an unknown time, perhaps for ever if Jim didn't make it. The thought frightened her. She did not realise how much he had become part of her life. Please God the operation is a success!

The news spread round Sidhurst immediately. Everyone seemed to be coming into the shop to wish him well! She had no idea he was so well known. From fellow traders, wardens, customers, and suppliers, all asked after him and wished him a successful operation. He was a war veteran, and it was wartime. Another war, maybe, but the feeling was the same. God help Jim in his hour of need!

An ambulance came and collected him on Friday, and by the evening he was safely and comfortably sitting up in bed in a private room in the neurological wing of the Charing Cross Hospital. His surgeon had already been to see him and increased his painkillers, which left him happier and almost pain free. This he told to Elsie via the Ward Sister when she telephoned on Saturday morning. She was not allowed to see him until after the operation scheduled for Tuesday, as they wanted to do various tests and X rays to determine how best to tackle the metal in his head.

For once, Elsie did not have to concern herself with him. He was in good hands, so she could catch up with things at home that were getting left undone. The first job was to have a long talk to her sister, and she telephoned her on Saturday evening.

"Hallo, .Margaret, how are you? All ready for Christmas?"

"Margaret sounded a bit nettled as she replied. "Yes, hallo, Elsie. About time we spoke. How is everything? Shop going well? And what about Jane?"

"As usual, I've been so busy I haven't had a moment to speak to you." Then she brought Margaret up to date, telling her about the new Mrs Winter, the baby, Jim's operation, the impending move to Jim's house, and so on. By the time they finished, Margaret was flabbergasted.

"Your news is always exciting, Elsie. So I'm to be a Great Auntie now. How is Jane coping? Out of the Army yet?"

"Not yet, but hoping to be demobbed just after Christmas, she will live here until we move to Jim's house. What are you doing for Christmas? Anything grand?"

"Not really. We have several parties to attend. Duty really, and mostly Arthur's customers. Not very exciting!"

She sounded bored,. "How is Arthur? Is he happier than when I visited?"

"No, he isn't! He gets more irritable all the time. I think it's more than his usual stress. I am trying to get him to go to the doctor, but he point blank refuses. I hope Christmas will give him some rest, and improve everything."

Elsie knew it wouldn't! She returned to Jane. "I'll let you know when Jane leaves the Army, and perhaps you would like to come up one Sunday and see her. Neither of us has any relatives left, except you. She would be pleased to meet her new Auntie!"

Elsie heard Arthur. "Who the devil are you blathering to now, Margaret?"

Elsie took the cue. "Speak to you again soon, Margaret! Will call in the day it might be easier for you!"

"Yes, I agree," replied Margaret. "Goodbye, Elsie!"

On Sunday, she went to church to pray for Jim, Jane, and the future. It was the last Sunday service before Christmas and the Vicar had added a few decorations to go with the carols. The church was full, so she was unable to sit next to Mrs McIver, but waved to her as she came in.

Mrs McIver looked across and caught her smile. "See you after" she mouthed at Elsie who replied similarly "Yes, alright!"

On the way out, she shook hands with the Vicar who welcomed her and her news about her forthcoming grand child, and then waited for Elizabeth as she also shook his hand.

"Hallo Elsie, Glad I caught your eye, Come back for a glass of sherry for Christmas. Not that I need any excuse!"

"Yes, I'd love to. Do you know this is the first free day I've had since November! You've heard all about Jim and Jane, I imagine. Everyone seems to know!"

"Well, not the latest. How is Jim? When is his operation? Soon I expect!"

"It is scheduled for Tuesday. They say he is better since he went into hospital, so it will go ahead, I think. I must say I am very concerned for him, and the future, if it's not successful!"

"I'm sure all will go well. I suppose you are in charge for the time being?"

Elsie was not inclined to tell her about the impending move, so just answered. "Yes, I am very busy. You know we have two more staff, Ann, of course, and now Mrs Loveridge, a new pharmacist taking over from Joan."

"And how is Ann getting on? Settling in is she?"

"Yes, I'm delighted. She is very happy, an asset to the shop, and the customers like her. She is so willing and keen about everything. Puts us all to shame!"

"I'm so glad she was a success. Thought she would be, but you can never be sure with a girl from that background."

"She's getting on extremely well. Any news of Gordon?" The question came out quite naturally, and Elsie realised he meant nothing to her now.

"He's out in the Far East, somewhere. I haven't heard from him for some time. To tell you the truth, I am a little worried. I feel all is not well, but have no reason except instinct to tell me. All one can do is wait for news, but I hope it comes soon!"

Elsie's mind turned back to Brian, Not another casualty in Sidhurst, surely!

As they walked back, she suddenly changed her mind about the sherry. "Elizabeth, I forgot. I promised I'd do something for Jim in the shop before lunch. I'm sorry, but do you mind if I refuse your invitation. I must get it done!"

"I understand, Elsie. If I don't see you before, have a very happy Christmas."

"Thank you Elizabeth, and the same for you too. I hope you hear from Gordon in a day or two. Goodbye."

She turned to walk back along to the Parade. She wanted to be in her own flat on her own, and think about Bill, Brian, and her life gone by. Soon she would be trying to have a jolly Christmas, and couldn't do that without spending some time in contemplation with her husband and son, both in a better world.

On Monday she spoke to the Ward Sister, who confirmed the operation would be as scheduled. She said Jim was nervous, and they had given him sedatives to make him rest. "Telephone me in the evening tomorrow, and I can tell you how he is," she said "He will go to theatre for ten o'clock. I have no idea how long it will last. It depends what they find."

"Thank you" said Elsie. "I'll call tomorrow evening."

On Tuesday, she was on tenterhooks all day. Joan 1, and 2 as well as Ann, all noticed her bad temper. They knew, of course what it was, so said nothing. When she went up to her flat for a break, Ann said "Cor, Joan, please God 'e's alright. She's like a bear wiv a sore 'ead!"

"That's enough, Ann." said Joan 2, but agreed wholeheartedly. In her short stay at Shaw's, she had never seen Elsie so jumpy and difficult.

The day passed slowly for Elsie. She couldn't but think about Jim. He was becoming part of her life, and the thought of losing him after Bill, and Brian was terrible! God help him through!

"I think I'll phone about five o'clock," she said to herself. "It won't strictly be the evening, but I can't wait any longer. Once I leave the shop, I shall have nothing to take my mind off him." At ten past four, the 'phone in the shop rang. Elsie heard Joan 2 answer it in the dispensary. "Shaw's Chemists" she replied. Elsie was tidying up some stock she had just got out of it's packaging.

"Just a moment, I'll get her for you."

"Elsie," she called. "It's the Hospital for you!"

Elsie's heart beat faster. She almost ran to the 'phone and took the receiver from Joan. "Elsie Winter here!"

"Hallo Mrs Winter." It was the Sister's voice. Now for it!

"I'm pleased to tell you Mr Shaw has had his operation, is very weak, but it was as far as we can tell, successful. Too early to be sure, but I think he is going to be much better. The surgeon took out two pieces of metal, but he has suffered no damage to his brain, so we are very optimistic. Thought you would like to know as soon as we knew anything."

Elsie burst into tears. "Thank you very much, Sister. When shall I call you again?"

"Phone tomorrow morning. After a good night's sleep, we should know better how he is. Goodbye, Mrs Winter"

She struggled to control her emotion. Both girls were looking at her waiting for the news. "He's going to be O.K, they think. As far as it goes at the moment, it has been a successful operation!"

Ann said "Good thing too. Now perhaps we can get back to normal, and think about Christmas!"

"That's enough, Ann," said Joan. "Wait until you have someone you love very ill, then you'll know what it's like!"

It came to Elsie in a flash! "Yes, I suppose that's what it is. I have got so used to working with Jim, I haven't realised how much he means to me. It is not the same sort of love they talk about in romantic books, or as I thought I felt for Bill or even Gordon, but it's true, I do love him. Or put it another way, I couldn't do without him any more. "

She walked back into the shop feeling happier and much relieved. All he has to do now is recover fully, and I'll just have to wait until he does!

During the days up to Christmas, she occupied herself preparing the small party, which she now had decided to hold in the shop's little room and the kitchen. She enlisted Ann, and she was soon hard at work. Gradually the pile of food and small presents grew. Ann spoke to almost all the customers who came in. Even Mrs McIver didn't escape. Everyone wanted to know how Jim was and many had brought a small present for him and the staff of Shaw's. Sharp at four o'clock on Christmas Eve, they shut the door bolts, turned off the lights, and retired to the little room. While Elsie had dealt with the customers, Joan and Ann had set about turning all the gifts into a spread that filled the little table, and the counter in the kitchen. Elsie got out her only bottle of sherry saved for the occasion, and poured everyone a glass, even Ann.

"Raising her filled glass she announced, "Happy Christmas everyone. Thank you for your work during the year, and now let's drink to the recovery of our owner, Jim Shaw. May he get well quickly, return to good health, and the shop!"

Joan 1 and 2 toasted with Elsie, while Ann had already

drunk her sherry, but managed to add her "Merry Xmas" to the chorus.

"Come on," said Elsie, "Let's all tuck in!" and they did! About five o'clock someone banged on the shop door. "Ignore it." said Joan. "No, it might be important." replied Elsie, going to the door.

"It was the Warden who had spoken to Elsie, and had told Jim about the V2's "Knew you would all be in there, Elsie. Happy Xmas, and pull that window blind close, you're showing a light!" He burst out laughing. Elsie knew he was joking.

"Be off with you," she replied. "Happy Christmas!"

About a quarter to six, Elsie called a halt. "It's time you all went off home. Have a happy day tomorrow, and come back the day after Boxing Day rested and ready for the fray once again. We'll not open until 10.00 o'clock and it's certain to be busy day!"

"Good night, Elsie, Happy Christmas" they said as they trooped out, except Joan 1. "I thought Jane would be here, Elsie. Where is she?"

"Be along later, I expect, Joan. I'm looking forward to her coming. Hope she will not be too late. I want her to come with me on Boxing Day to see Jim."

"Please wish him well, and give him my regards, Elsie. Good night, happy Christmas, and thank you for all you are doing for the shop."

"Good night Joan, happy Christmas!"

Elsie shut the door and went back to clear up the remains of the food, and wash up so the shop was tidy for December 27th. It would be a busy day. It always was after the holiday. Everyone would want prescriptions made up for winter ailments!

Jane arrived about seven o'clock. It was a poor journey from London. The train was full, and most of the passengers inebriated. She and Elsie embraced at the door. "What's the news of Jim, Elsie?" were her first words.. Elsie told her the latest news. "Would you be kind enough to come with me on Boxing Day to

London to see him, Jane?" she asked. "That is unless you have to be back on duty!"

"No, I have three days, so would like to. Guessing you would want to go to London, I noted the times of the trains on December 26th, and there is a Sunday service. One every hour, direct to Charing Cross. What are the visiting hours?"

"Officially two hours in the afternoon, and one in the evening. Whether they relax them over Christmas, I don't know, but in any case, an hour will be enough for the first visit I'm sure."

"That's agreed, Elsie," said Jane. "I've brought a few things for you for our Christmas dinner!" she opened her kit bag, and took out a chicken, some cartons obviously holding cakes, and a bottle of wine."

"Oh, how marvellous, Jane. Where did you get them?"

"The people in my office presented them to me. They said it would be the last time I could have alcohol, and wished me luck with the baby and my future. Look, they have also given me some clothes for the baby!" She showed Elsie a holdall stuffed with baby clothes.

"People are very kind, Jane aren't they? Let's try our best and have a happy day tomorrow."

"Shall we go to midnight service, Elsie? I would love to!"

"Yes, so would I. Let's have something to eat, and sit quietly round the fire until it's time. I must go and pray for Bill and Brian, and I know you will want to do the same."

The two Mrs Winters' spent a quiet, thoughtful, but sad, Xmas Day. Enough to eat, their minds were with Bill and Brian, but with each other to help, they never became maudlin, and went to bed as happy as they could be under the circumstances of the first Christmas without their menfolk.

On Boxing Day they went to see Jim.

Charing Cross Hospital looked grey and forbidding as they walked up to the entrance, but once inside, the lobby and corridors were strung with decorations of every sort. Nurses they passed as they made their way to Jim's ward were joyful and laughing. The atmosphere was relaxed and happy.

Elsie said "Is it always like this, Jane?"

"No, I don't think so. It's Christmas, and everyone tries to enjoy it, even if they are very ill."

They continued along several passages passing nurses all the time, until they reached his Ward. Jane would have walked straight in, but Elsie knew they must check if visiting hours had started before entering. A staff nurse came towards them.

"You can go in,. Visiting hours are extended today. Who are you visiting?"

"We've come to see Jim Shaw." replied Elsie.

"Ah yes, the man with the head injuries, isn't it. He's in the side room over there. Wait a moment, and I'll take you in."

She went off to the end of the ward, where she approached a Sister. They didn't hear what she said, but the Sister immediately walked across to meet them.

"Is it Mrs Winter? She asked looking at Elsie. "Yes, that's right and my daughter-in-law"

"I'll take you in to him. The operation was a success, but he is still very weak. I must ask you not to get him excited, and not to stay longer than half an hour. He has had a bad time, and is on the mend, but must not over exert himself."

They followed her into Jim's room. He was sitting up in bed and smiled as he saw them. His whole head was swathed in voluminous bandages, and all they could see above his mouth were two holes for his eyes. From the little they could see, he looked drawn and his eyes were dull. Elsie hadn't known what to expect, but realized from what she saw it would be a very long recovery.

"She went to him and took his hand. "Hallo, Jim, how are you feeling? The Sister says you are getting along very well indeed. Is it very painful?"

Jim again smiled at her. "A lot better, Elsie. Less ache each day. Not as bad now as it was when I came in. Look, here's what they took from my head. He pointed proudly at two very tiny lumps of silver metal on his bedside table. "Glad to see them there, not in my head still!"

He looked at Jane. "Hallo, Jane, what news from the Army? Got a date for coming back to Sidhurst yet?"

"No, not yet, Uncle Jim, I expect to hear any day now. You're looking better than I have seen you since we met. I bet you're glad it's over aren't you?"

The sister came bustling in. "Are you alright Mr Shaw? Mustn't let this family of yours tire you out. Ten minutes more, that's all I'm afraid today." She bustled out again.

"Tell me about the shop, Elsie. Is all well? Have you got a new pharmacist?"

"Yes, I have Jim. She's Mrs Joan Loveridge. She lives in Crayford, and seems very good indeed. Joan says she's better than her! Ann has settled in and works hard. All in all, it is in good order, and we are getting more business. I think everyone in the town sends their best wishes, for your recovery. I just can't remember them all."

"Good, I'm happy. Now, Jane, how's the baby? No problems? Excellent! The sooner the Army frees you the better. You must both move into the house. As soon as I am well enough I will write to my housekeeper and tell her to expect you!"

The Sister came bustling back again. "Now Mrs Winters' please say your goodbyes to Mr Shaw, he has to rest. Come again tomorrow or when you can, and you can have longer."

"Looks like we must go, Jim. Concentrate on getting strong and well." Elsie bent towards him and gave him a quick kiss on his cheek. Jane saw his expression. He would get better in no time at all was what it said! "Come and see me when you can, Jane." said Jim.

"See you both again soon."

They moved away towards the door. Sister came busily in again, and went over to give him some medicine. "Good bye, Jim!" And they walked quickly down the passageway and out of the entrance to Charing Cross station. Jim had survived the operation, now all he had to do was build up his strength and avoid any illnesses while convalescing!

Elsie and Jane visited Jim twice each week. On the days Elsie didn't go, Jane whose office was not far from Charing Cross, was given permission to visit him during the one hour visiting in the afternoon, while Elsie came in the evening. Jane was inured to the steadily arriving V2 rockets, but Elsie wished Jim had been looked after outside London. He had a number of set backs, and the worst occurred only a week after his operation. Elsie went up one evening to find him looking and feeling unwell. She immediately spoke to a staff nurse who told her he had contracted an infection, and had a fever They were obviously concerned, although they tried to hide the fact from Elsie. She asked how they were treating it, and Sister said they were using one of the new drugs 'M. & B.' she called it. A range of very effective sulphur type drugs recently developed and used widely to treat infected war injuries. Elsie went home worrying, and rang Jane to tell her. However, the crisis quickly evaporated when the drugs became effective. In a week, he was back to continuing his recovery.

Sometimes Elsie would swap visit times with Jane, and go up in the afternoon. It was normally on the half day closing, when she could spend time after visiting Jim, looking at the shops.

Jane heard from her Unit, that her discharge date had come through, and she rang Elsie to tell her about Jim, and also that she would be coming to Sidhurst in early February. Elsie thought it was a bit late, and she ought to have stopped working well before, but Jane was happy about it, and so Elsie asked Jim if they could move in at the end of January.

"At last, you have taken up my offer," he replied when she asked him. "They are letting me out of bed for a few minutes each day now, so I'll 'phone Mrs Daly and tell her to expect you to move in at the end of the month, and you will discuss it with her when you next go round to do the accounts."

"That will be fine, Jim, thank you very much."

Mrs Daly had been most co-operative when Elsie somewhat nervously discussed the move. "That will suit me just fine, Mrs Winter. I shall move out as soon as the young Mrs Winter arrives. We can work together in the meantime. I am sure we shall get on famously, and to tell you the truth, it is a bit lonely without Mr Shaw. Is he still getting on well?"

Elsie reassured her that he was, and went back to her book-keeping. Mrs Daly brought in some tea, which was unusual, half an hour later. So she was obviously pleased to be moving to the new cottage Jim had provided for her!

Towards the end of January, after seeing Jim, she went to look at some of the West End shops where she hoped she might see things needed in the house. She was determined to have it immaculate when he returned from hospital. Consequently it was gone four when she caught the train back to Sidhurst, and getting dark as she alighted at her destination. She handed in the half of her return ticket, and walked happily down the station approach to the bus stop at the end. To reach the 241 bus to the High Street, she had to walk a few yards along the pavement passed three or four shops both sides of Station Road that been built to catch the commuters travelling to London each day.

She passed the first and paused, as she often did, to look at the china displayed in the window, while the passengers who had just alighted, left her behind. Although it was nearly dark, she peered into them to see if anything caught her eye. Turning away, she heard a loud 'bang'. Instinctively she threw herself back into the shop doorway, anticipating the second that always followed as a rocket hit the ground. A massive blast of air hit her, knocking her to the ground half in the shop doorway. As she fell, she turned her face away to avoid the hard concrete. In slow motion, she saw bricks, dust, smoke and a mass of everything flying through the air above her. For a second she watched stupefied, then, to her horror saw a mass of building falling from above. One particularly large block came straight at her! She jerked herself away just in time and it crashed into pieces in front of

her, but the one that followed she could not avoid! Heavy pieces
of masonry, glass, wood, and dust hit her! The last thing she
remembered was a jagged edge like a dagger, hitting her face.
There was no pain, as the world, the noise, and the chaos round
her turned black!

A voice said "At last! I think she's coming round!"
Elsie's' brain slowly returned to life. Everything hurt! She
tried to move, but hands restrained her. "It's alright, Mrs Winter,
don't try to move. You are in the First Aid Station in Sidhurst,
and you are alright." Elsie attempted to sit up, but a stabbing pain
in her side forced her back with a gasp. "Keep still," said a man's
voice. "You have fractured two ribs, have a badly cut face, and
your right arm is broken. If you try to move, it will hurt!"
Elsie's memory came back. The last thing she remembered
was the rocks falling on her, then nothing! She attempted to
move again, and stopped quickly with the hurt. "I told you!"
said the same man. "If you want to ask anything say it where
you are!" Elsie kept still!
"What happened? And where am I!" she said in what she
hoped was her normal voice. As she spoke she tried to open her
eyes. She looked but saw nothing! "I can't see!" she cried out. "I'm
not blind am I?" Now she was in panic. To be blind! She couldn't
bear the thought!
"No, no, you're not blind at all! You have bandages over
your left eye. The cheek around it has been badly cut, and I have
stitched it while you were unconscious" It was the man again!
"I'm afraid you will have a scar, but otherwise in a few days
you will be fully recovered. Just lie still, and once the pain killers
I have given you work, Nurse will bring you a cup of tea which
you can sip. Now I have other patients, so I will hand you on to
Nurse Maxwell. See you again later Mrs Winter. Don't worry
you're going to be fine!'"
The voice of presumably, Nurse Maxwell took over. "Hallo
Mrs Winter, don't rush yourself, I'll be here if you want me."
Elsie was now fully awake. "What happened? " She asked.

"A V2 rocket hit the shops apposite the station. Three were demolished. The First Aid men found you unconscious in the doorway of Johnson's, and brought you here in the ambulance. You have been unconscious for nearly two hours, and have a nasty bruise and concussion on your head."

"Two hours!" said Elsie, and her mind raced. The staff will wonder where I am. Then she remembered. It's Thursday, they would not have even missed her!

She tried to relax and lie still, but the pain was becoming stronger now she was fully conscious. She put her hand up to her face, but the Nurse saw her and gently pulled it down to her side again,. She could see the long vertical cut right down her face, almost to the bone across her cheek, which the doctor had carefully stitched together. It was a wound that time would never erase. He knew the lady would carry it, marring her face for the rest of her life. Nurse Maxwell knew Mrs Winter from when she called in at Shaw's, and had recognised her at once when she was brought in. Her pretty face would be no more, and she felt very sad for her when she used a mirror for the first time!

Elise felt the pain easing, and managed to lie still and doze. Nurse Maxwell came over several times, but Elsie did not notice. She smiled, and went quietly away. Mrs Winter would have to go to the Cottage Hospital to have her arm set in plaster soon, but for the time, the Doctor said "Let her sleep. It will help clear any shock!"

Elsie slept on under the influence of the pain killer for another hour. It was of course quite dark, and as other casualties left, there was just Elsie and another man, still waiting to leave.

The doctor came back a few minutes before Elsie woke up. Nurse spoke to him, and he came across to see her. Perhaps it was the slight sound of his footsteps on the linoleum covered floor that roused her. She opened her eyes, or at least the uncovered one, and half smiled at him.

"Hallo Mrs Winter, are you feeling better? You've had a good sleep. I think you are well enough to move you to Sidhurst

Hospital where they will set your arm. After that, if you feel well enough, you can go home, provided there is someone who can care for you. Your fractured ribs will be very sore for a time, although I have bandaged them tightly to prevent movement."

Elsie considered what he said. "Unfortunately, Doctor, there isn't! I live alone. The only person who could help is my sister at Gravesend. Is it possible someone could speak to her. I am sure she would come up to care for me tomorrow."

"I'll speak to Matron, and see if she can keep you in until your sister comes. Give nurse Maxwell her number, and she'll telephone before you go to have your arm set."

Nurse Maxwell came over. "Have you the number handy Mrs Winter?" she asked.

Elsie replied "It's Gravesend 2116, nurse. When you speak to her, tell her but don't alarm her. She'll come up immediately, I know!"

"Alright Mrs Winter, don't worry, we're used to breaking news like this." Elsie heard her heels click along the floor and knew she had gone to telephone.

Another nurse came in and went over to Elsie. "Here are some more painkillers for you Mrs Winter. Take two now, to help you on the way to hospital. They should work by the time the ambulance comes to collect you."

Elsie obediently lifted her head. The nurse slipped two tablets into her mouth, and raised her head a little more so she could sip some water and swallow. "That's good, now lie back and relax while they take effect."

Nurse Maxwell returned. "Your sister Margaret says she will arrive at your flat soon after the shop opens, get the key, and get it ready for you. I have given her the number of Sidhurst Hospital, and she will telephone about ten o'clock tomorrow. She says 'not to worry', she will do everything."

Elsie found she was starting to cry. She didn't know why, but the nurse did. Shock was coming out, and she did her best to comfort her.

Gradually the tears subsided, and she felt better as the tablets started to help the pain. As if in a dream, two ambulance men appeared wheeling a stretcher on a trolley.

"Come on Mrs Winter, we've come to take you to the Hospital. No dressing gown? Oh well, never mind!" Elsie wondered what they meant. She had no intention of getting on a trolley with only a hospital gown on!

"Nurse" they called. "Mrs Winter needs a dressing gown. Could you get one for her, please!"

"Don't worry Mrs Winter. We'll be ready in a minute."

Nurse Maxwell appeared, and Elsie tried to sit up. Now she could! It didn't hurt quite so much. With the help of the ambulance men and the two nurses, she was lifted and moved to the stretcher. The two men took charge, and wheeled her out through the entrance into the night air. It was cold, and she felt the chill breeze whipping across her face.

Gently she was loaded into the ambulance, and travelled the short few minutes to Sidhurst Hospital, and into Casualty. A nurse came over to meet them.

"Ah, Mrs Winter, we've been expecting you. You are to go straight to be plastered, and then we have a bed for you. Doctor Hargreaves wants to speak to you first."

She and the trolley were transferred to a garrulous porter, who wheeled her off talking non-stop, to a treatment room, where she recognised Dr Hargreaves.

"Hallo Mrs Winter, how are you getting on? You've had a nasty shock and some injuries. Sister will plaster your arm after we have X rayed it, and then you can stay here at least until tomorrow. I understand your sister is coming to help you at the flat?"

"Yes, and hallo, Dr Hargreaves. I am still in a lot of pain." she said. "Yes, and you will be very sore for a time Does your sister realise how incapacitated you will be for some days? The fractured ribs will be painful, and your arm will prevent you doing much at all for yourself. It will be impossible to get up and down the stairs after tomorrow when we shall give you something to get you up them."

Elsie did not know what the nurse had told Margaret, so simply replied "I am sure we can manage once I am in the flat. Margaret will do all that 's needed, I know."

"Right, if you're sure. I'll call at the flat once you're settled, and check all is well, and see if you need more pain killers. Now, I will leave you to Sister. Try and sleep tonight, it will do wonders for your recovery."

A staff nurse appeared, and the two nurses took her off to the treatment room, where Sister got to work. The most painful part was the X ray when they moved her arm to get the right picture, and later when again it was put in place and covered with plaster. After that it still ached, but the pain was bearable.

Although it was gone half past nine when she was finally settled in a lovely clean but small hospital bed, the pain killers still deadened most feeling. She managed to eat some supper brought to her by a young trainee nurse who reminded her of Ann. Soon after, the lights were turned out, and she drifted off to sleep.

Margaret, for the second time, caught an early train to Sidhurst, and arrived at Shaw's at a quarter past nine, to be met by a worried Joan 2. Of course, she did not know Elsie's sister. She was a competent and efficient woman, but was concerned that there was no sign of Elsie, and no response to calls either by telephone or knocking on her front door. When Margaret told her what had befallen Elsie, she became all efficiency.

"I'll see after everything here, Mrs Bushell!. You get off to Mrs Winter, and see she is alright. If you need any help when you get here, just call on us in the shop, and we'll be straight out to help!"

"Thank you Mrs Loveridge, I will certainly do that if necessary. Now, I will go up and prepare Elsie's flat so her bed is ready for her. I don't think she will be up and about for some time!"

As she expected, Elsie's flat was tidy and spotless. She checked to see her bed was ready, put the tea cups out for their return, and picked up one of Elsie's warm coats, before going down to the shop again, where she rang for a taxi.

Arriving at the Hospital, she went straight to reception and asked for Mrs Winter. Within a few minutes she was ushered into Elsie's Ward. The staff nurse spoke to her before she went in.

"Mrs Winter has not seen herself yet. Her face has a nasty cut and is heavily bandaged. You can't see much, but her face is heavily stitched and swollen."

Margaret had been warned which was wise when she saw Elsie was lying back, and obviously sore.

She went up to the bed quietly. Elsie was lying, her eyes closed, trying to sleep while waiting for her sister to call for her.

"Hallo, Elsie, how are you?" Elsie turned to face Margaret. As she knew what to expect, she managed to successfully hide her expression. Elsie's face was red, purple and blue where it was visible, but two thirds was bandaged, and she could only imagine the wound beneath.

"I'm not too bad, I think, Margaret!" she replied. "A bit sore, and can't see out of one eye. The worst is my ribs. They are so sore and bruised. It hurts to breathe, and they have given me something to help make it better. I want to go home!"

"I shall go and talk to the doctor now, and see if I can take you right away!"

Margaret bent over and lightly kissed the top of Elsie's head. "I'll go now and ask. See you in a minute!"

Margaret went down the Ward to the office at the end and asked for someone. The staff nurse on duty came over.

"You're Mrs Bushell?" she asked. "We've been expecting you. Can I have a word, please?"

Margaret listened attentively.

"Mrs Winter has had some nasty injuries, but is taking them very well. She is in constant pain, and although we have given her tablets to help, she will not be able to move for some time until the soreness goes. Fractured ribs are very painful, and without the tablets, she would be in agony. Not only that, her right arm is broken and has been set in plaster, but probably the worst, and long term problem is her face. A piece of glass or something similar must have fallen on to it. The sharp edge has run down her face, and she has twenty stitches to hold it together. The scar will be permanent, although it will lessen in intensity in time. I don't think the bandages will come off for a while, but you should see she can't see her face when the wound is dressed,. She will want to, but until the shock has gone, there is no point in making it worse!"

"I see" replied |Margaret. "Thank you for the warning. I'll do my best to take your advice."

"When she does have to see her face, let Dr Hargreaves be there. He's very good at helping patients on these occasions."

"Thank you again, Staff, I'll see that he is! Now, can Elsie come home?"

"Yes, she can. Before she goes, I'll give her two more tablets to help her on the journey. I'll ask the auxiliary to fetch you both some tea while the tablets take. Then she can go."

"Is there anywhere I can call for a taxi?" asked Margaret.

"Don't worry about that. Dr Hargreaves will help you. He will take Mrs Winter home in his car. Now go and talk to her while we send for the tea."

Margaret went back to Elsie, and filled the time helping her sip the tea, and listening to her account of the V2 and her injury. "I was very lucky, Margaret! God still has work for me to do!"

Just before eleven o'clock, Dr Hargreaves appeared with two porters, and a wheel chair. The porters helped Elsie into it, still in the hospital dressing gown, and wheeled her to the doctor's car that was drawn up at the entrance. Gently the porters helped Elsie into the rear seat,. It was painful, hut she could stand it, and with Margaret beside her, Dr Hargreaves drove her home and parked outside Shaw's. Immediately the shop door opened, and Joans' 1 and 2 came out to the car.

Margaret met them. "Can you help us get her upstairs, please?"

The Joans' pressed forward to help. Dr Hargreaves showed them how to support Elsie. Together they lifted her out of her seat, and stood her carefully on her feet. She felt better standing and stepped forward until she was at her front door.

"Now"said Dr Hargreaves, "Comes the tricky part! Can you lift your feet Mrs Winter?"

It hurt, but she found she could do it as long as they supported her back so she remained upright. Slowly, step by step, they supported her through the door, up the stairs and into her bedroom. The doctor said "Now Mrs Winter, stand with your back against the side of the bed, and while I support you, lean slowly back." She did as he asked, and he took her weight letting her slowly down. The ladies slipped back the covers, and Doctor Hargreaves carefully laid her on her back. She was in bed in her own home!

Dr Hargreaves looked relieved. "I'm glad that's done." he said. "Thank you ladies, for your help. I think we should leave Mrs Winter to recover from that ordeal." He led them out of her room, and down the stairs. Margaret stayed with Elsie, and carefully tucked in her blankets and covered her with the eiderdown. The flat was cold, and some warmth was the next thing.

Elsie felt tired out. Fortunately the pain was slight, and she lay back feeling safe again, and was soon asleep.

Margaret returned from lighting the fire in the drawing room, and switched on the electric fire in the bedroom. Elsie was sound asleep, now what? Margaret was a careful person. She first took the painkilling tablets, and put them in the bathroom cupboard where Elsie couldn't reach them. Just in case!

It had been along and hard day for Margaret. First the shock of the telephone call from the hospital, and then the rush to pacify Arthur, before packing a small overnight bag, and setting off early for the station. She knew she had a real task on her hands once Elsie woke up, and wondered how best to help her. She had not reached any conclusions, when the telephone rang.

"That's not Elsie," said a young woman's voice. "No, I'm Margaret, Elsie's sister."

"What's happened? I'm Jane, Mrs Winter's daughter –in-law. "

"Well it's a long story. So if you don't mind, I'll cut it short, as I badly need a break. Elsie has been quite badly injured at the station by a V2. It fell on the shops by the approach, and knocked down four shops. Elsie was lucky, and had the presence of mind to take cover immediately she heard the first bang, but some of the falling masonry from the building, fell on her. She has two broken ribs, a broken right arm, and a badly cut face. I have just helped her home from the hospital, and she is settled as comfortably as she can be in her bed. "

There was gasp of horror at the other end. "Can I speak to her, Margaret?"

"No, I'm afraid she can't move to get to the telephone. She is asleep, and I won't wake her."

"Yes, I understand, I am coming to the flat next week when I am demobbed. Will you be able to stay until then? Once I am there, I will look after her!"

"That would be great help, Jane. I cannot stay too long because I have a house and husband at home,. He has already been difficult over my coming here at all. He does not like Elsie, very much, I'm afraid!"

Jane did not pursue why. "I have a day off on Sunday that I was going to use visiting Jim Shaw, but now, I'll leave a message, and travel down Saturday night. I can sleep at the Black Horse, or somewhere. Don't worry, I'm used to looking after myself! Give Elsie my love, and tell her I called. Goodbye Margaret, I'm looking forward to meeting you!"

Jane sat shocked at the news. She must to tell Jim. He would, already be anticipating Elsie would be there today, and what about the shop? Jim first!

She decided not to telephone, but to go herself to see him. It wasn't visiting hours! Too bad, she would push her way in! She set off immediately, caught a bus, and was at Jim's ward twenty minutes later. The Sister glared at her as she came in through the double doors, but hesitated as she saw the uniform. She didn't know Jane.

"Good afternoon Sergeant, It's not visiting hours yet you know! She looked curiously as she saw Jane was pregnant. What can I do for you?"

"I'm sorry, but I need to speak urgently to Mr Jim Shaw. Would it be possible, please?"

"It's most irregular, but if you make it quick, I'll allow it on this occasion. Not bad news, I hope?"

"Not serious, but not good either." said Jane as they walked together across to Jim's room. "His closest friend has been badly hurt by a V2, and I need to tell him as he will expect her to visit today. He will be upset, and I wanted to break the news myself, rather than telephone!"

"Just five minutes only. I'll leave you to it."

Jane went over to Jim's bed where he was lying dozing.

"Hallo Jim" she said.

Immediately he sat up. "What's wrong Jane, Is Elsie alright, or why are you here?"

"Now Jim, don't get upset, Elsie's O.K., but she's been hurt by a V2 rocket at the station in Sidhurst. I have just spoken to her sister, and she's home from hospital, and sleeping. She's going to be O.K., but has broken ribs, a broken arm, and a very bad cut on her face. She has had twenty stitches!"

Jim looked shocked. "Oh dear, poor Elsie, and me not there to help. Will you see her Jane?"

"Yes, when l I go to Sidhurst tomorrow."

"Right, As soon as you get to the flat, you must make arrangements to move yourselves to my house. If Elsie cannot move, get Dr Hargreaves to assist her. I will pay the removers. Get a proper firm, and forget the cost. She will recover much better there, and I can telephone her if you put the receiver near her bed!"

Already he had it worked out! "Thank you for coming to

tell me. I do appreciate it. Now you'd better get off before Sister throws you out. Bye Jane, and thanks again. I'll talk to Margaret in the morning."

Jane left the Hospital. She had done what she could for the time being. Now, she would try and get round her Unit to let her have the few days leave she had not taken, and go down to Sidhurst earlier. She would get the earliest train she could on Saturday, as soon as she went off duty.

Margaret was feeling extremely hungry, and she found enough in Elsie's larder to make a light snack, but nothing for later. On tip toe, so as not to wake Elsie, she went down to the shop.

"How is she?" said Joan 1, who was behind the counter.

"Sleeping, thank God!" replied Margaret. "I wonder if I could ask you to look after her for about half an hour while I get some food in for us. I can't find sufficient for us both!"

"Yes, of course," said Joan 1. "I said to call us if you need any help! I'll go up and sit with her. Joan will keep an eye on Ann in the shop. "Thanks" said Margaret. "I won't be long!"

Margaret watched Joan go up to the flat, heard no sound, so walked quickly into the High Street. She managed to get sufficient for their needs, and congratulated herself on having put her ration book in her handbag. Without it she couldn't have bought anything worthwhile. As it was she had bacon, bread, half a dozen eggs, and butter. A whole week's allowance, and a luxury. Elsie needed spoiling and she bought sufficient until Monday. She returned to the flat, just in time to hear Joan reassuring Elsie who was half awake as she entered her room. Elsie was in pain, and she couldn't move into a comfortable position. "Stay still Elsie. Joan, would you get the bottle of painkillers from the bathroom cupboard, please."

Elsie was struggling again. "Elsie, listen to me. Stay still until you have taken the pills. Then you will be able to move a bit better." Joan returned with the bottle. She took out two, and Joan handed her a glass of water. Joan went to Elsie, and carefully raised her a little. Elsie gasped with the pain, but stayed firm. She knew the pills were necessary. With an effort, she managed to swallow and lay back wincing with the soreness in her cheek and ribs.

Joan stayed and talked with them until Elsie's pain diminished. She sat up.

"I feel better now, Margaret. Pass me the mirror from the table, so I can see what my face looks like!"

"Joan went to reach for it, but Margaret quickly stopped her. "No, Elsie, there's nothing to see. Until the bandages are changed, you can't see your face. Wait 'til the doctor calls then it will be worth the pain to have a look."

Elsie lay back again. Joan 1 looked at Margaret. "You look much better than I expected, Elsie. Are you very bruised? When I have time, and you feel like it, you must tell me what happened. Did you know six people were killed in the flats above the shops at the station? That's what I've heard from customers in the shop. You were lucky!" Elsie opened her left eye and looked at Joan. "Yes, I suppose I must have been! Not that I feel lucky at the moment!"

The pills were starting to take effect, and she lay back again and closed her eyes. For a few minutes more, she recalled as if in a trance, the masonry falling, and fell asleep. The two ladies crept out leaving her to rest.

Next morning Dr Hargreaves called just after eleven o'clock. Elsie was looking a little better, and with the help of the tablets, in less pain.

Doctor Hargreaves looked at her as he said. "Now Mrs Winter, you look better this morning. I trust you slept well. Did she?" He looked at Margaret.

"Yes, she did. I had to give her more tablets in the night. I hope that's in order."

"Yes, give her two whenever she needs it to help with the pain. One is not sufficient at the moment."

"Now, Mrs Winter, I want to look at the stitches to see all is going well. It may hurt a little when I remove the bandages, but I will be as gentle as I can. Are you ready?"

"Go on," said Elsie "before I think about it!"

He prepared her for what she would see. "I'm afraid your face is not a pretty sight at the moment, but if you want to look, now's the time. If not, it is not important, as it will only improve."

"Yes, I do! Margaret, please hold the mirror for me."

The doctor slowly and carefully unwound the bandages. Margaret, holding the mirror, saw that Elsie's face was stitched from just above her eyebrow to almost the bottom of her jaw. No doubt the stitching was well done, but the effect was startling. The right side of her face was a line of jagged black stitching in a zig zag line down her bluish, purple cheek, with congealed blood that had oozed through the stitches. Her soft face was no more, and Margaret's attractive young sister was a disfigured wreck! Her hold on the mirror wavered.

"Hold it steady, please," said the doctor.

"Elsie looked in horror as the dreadful apparition that was her face appeared in the mirror.

Doctor Hargreaves had anticipated her reaction.

"Looks pretty bad, doesn't it, Mrs Winter. but it will quickly improve when I remove the stitches next week, but you will always have a scar. But you are alive and will soon be well again to live a full life. You'll see!"

He quickly re-dressed the wound, leaving it so Elsie could see again out of both eyes. She was appalled, but he did not seem at all shocked, and Margaret too, had not been concerned, so she lay back, glad to rest again. The pain would go, and then she could get back to the shop again.

Over the next week, Margaret looked after her to the best of her ability. Elsie could do nothing for herself, and appreciated the trouble her sister took to ease her pain. Jane came on Sunday, and helped as much as she could, and heard the whole story. She made no comment about Elsie's appearance, having been warned by Joan 1 beforehand. Then she was back in London again until the following Saturday when she would leave the Army for ever!"

   In her last few days, she spent much of the time making arrangements and obtaining prices for the removal to Jim's house. She spoke to Elsie's doctor and told him of the plans. At first he was doubtful of the benefit of moving, but once he realised it was Jim's house to which they were going, he saw the advantages, and promised he would help Elsie with more pain relief, if necessary. She went most days to visit Jim, and kept him abreast of her plans for the move. He approved, and wanted to receive a daily bulletin of the news from Sidhurst..

   By the time Jane came home finally to Sidhurst complete with her packed kit bag and civvies, Elsie was showing the first signs of feeling less pain. Her arm no longer ached as much, and the fiery soreness in her cheeks, was lessening by the day. Only her ribs were still very sore. She was tiring of being ordered about by her sister, but because she could do little without her help, stayed her temper! For the first two nights, Jane had to sleep at the Black Horse until moving day
   In the morning, just before the van came to move them, Doctor Hargreaves gave Elsie an injection to help her when she had to move. She felt pain free nearly all day, and he took her over to No. 6, Amhurst Square, Jim's house, in his car. Once there, Mrs Daly saw to it she went straight to her new bed that had already been brought down into the Drawing Room. She felt relieved and elated, all at the same time, because she knew all would come right eventually. All she had to do was get well again!

****

Chapter 11

*F*or Elsie the month of February 1945 was one of the most difficult she had ever faced. The excitement, if she could call it that, of her injuries, and the tale of how she received them soon palled. For weeks the pain continued. Her stitches were removed, and her cheek began to feel less sore, but her ribs! Even after three weeks they hurt, but less now, as she breathed and moved. Margaret returned to her angry husband as soon as Jane came to Sidhurst. Elsie was able to cope with visitors to keep her amused. Slowly and steadily she was able to ignore the soreness, and get back to more activity.

The day she remembered was when Jim, who rang every day from hospital, and spoke to Jane for the latest news, received a surprise. Jane, guessing when he would telephone, had encouraged Elsie to get up for a while for the first time. She felt better once she got to her feet, and insisted in helping Jane who was washing up the lunch dishes. The telephone rang, and she heard Jane say "Would you like to speak to her, Jim?" She handed Elsie the telephone receiver.

"Hallo, Jim!"

"Elsie, is it you? You must be up at last! It is wonderful to hear your voice again. How are you now you're out of bed? A bit unsteady I expect!"

""Never mind me, what is more important is what about you? Any idea when you can come home? The house is wonderful, and I get up for a bit longer each day. We shall be together again soon, I am sure, and then we can talk about everything that has happened."

"That will be marvellous, Elsie. The doctor wants me to spend a few weeks at a special convalescent home. They are still not sure about all my reactions. I don't know what they expect at my age! It looks as if it will be early May before I get home, but I'm feeling better than I have done for a very long time. Be patient, and we'll be together soon!"

"Jim, as soon as I can, and it will be in a few weeks now, I am coming to see you. Never mind where you go to convalesce, I shall come! That's a threat, not a promise!" She laughed, and Jane looked at her with joy. It was the first laughter she had heard from Elsie almost since she knew her!

"Alright, Elsie, I'll keep you to that! Now, you relax, while I talk to Jane. Is she well? She never tells me, but now I can ask you, I shall get the truth!"

"Yes, she's very well. Looks after me like a baby! I have just helped her do some washing up. It's the first time I have been allowed to lift a hand since my injuries!"

Jim was about to ask her about her face, but thought better of it.

"Damn, sorry Elsie, someone else is waiting to use the 'phone. I'll call you tomorrow!"

"Alright, all my love, and also from Jane!"

Jim put down the telephone and nodded to the lady waiting to use it. "Over to you" he said to her, and moved away from the kiosk. Elsie had been delighted to hear from him, and he was thrilled. He would call her tomorrow.

It was as if Elsie had been drinking a tonic! She ignored the sore feeling in her ribs and cheek, and turned to Jane. "Jim sounds better than I have heard him for ages! I must start doing more. From tomorrow you must see I am up and about as early as possible. I'll start the books again immediately!"

Jane wanted to make her take things slowly. "I have a lot of papers that Ann's brought round from the shop, and there are some that were here when I arrived. Mrs Daly put them in the desk for you as soon as you can deal with them again!"

Elsie went slowly across to Jim's desk. It was crammed with bills, bank cash slips, letters, in fact a mass of things all to be dealt with. "Who has been looking after the cash for the shop, Jane?"

"It must be Joan 2. Ann brings all the paperwork round every afternoon at closing time. You'll see her if you stay up."

"I'll have a quick look through, but not be too long today Jane. I think bed after tea. What do you think? You know how I am getting on."

"I agree Elsie. That will be more then enough for the first time. One extra day won't hurt after so long!"

"I'll get us some tea. Jane. You go and sit down until I bring it in, or better, I'll call you, and you can carry the tray!"

Elsie was back in the fray. From that day onwards, she never took her pain killing tablets, and steadily improved. She never mentioned her face and it's horrid appearance. She ignored it like the residual pain.

In the middle of March, the whole world was agog with the rapid advances by the Allied Armies across Europe. Stories were appearing about terrible camps where prisoners were being found half dead with starvation and maltreatment. Elsie was horrified that the Germans would do such things. She had always thought, like most people, they were a civilised race, but now she was not so sure. Meanwhile V2's were still coming over, but less in number. One fell near Sidhurst on the 21st. Elsie and Jane heard the explosion, and found out later it fell in Hither Green, about 4 miles away. There were casualties, but how many they never found out. When could they be stopped? Surely the Allies had almost overrun the launch sites?

At the end of March, Elsie and Jane went to see Jim, who had moved to Epsom, where he was having the final exercises for his health. He looked well, fit and happy. Jane and Elsie had to help one another from the train and taxi. Jane was seven moths pregnant and Elsie still stiff, but almost free from pain. Her plaster cast had been removed earlier in the month, and she felt well again,

Jim rose from his easy chair where he had been relaxing, as they came in the door. He hadn't seen Elsie since her injuries, and steeled himself to give her a warm normal greeting as she came over to him. He got up meet them..

"Hallo, Jim, at last we're here to see you. I didn't know whether we would come to you, or the other way round. When are you coming home?" She went over to him, and kissed his cheek.

"In early April, they say. They will have done all they can for me by then, and I must say I feel like a new person. What a success!"

Elsie knew him of old. "Jim, you haven't mentioned my face! Is it that bad?"

"No, I haven't Elsie. It is a nasty scar, and to be frank, it doesn't improve your beauty, but who am I to comment!? Elsie, I wonder if Jane would leave us for a moment or two. She can get us some tea from the canteen. It's just over the way," and he pointed to a long low Nissan hut across the road outside.

Jane took the hint and got up carefully. "Yes, I need to spend a penny, anyway. I'll bring some back on a tray."

Once they were alone, Elsie said to Jim. "Now we are alone, I want to ask you something serious Jim." He looked at her sternly. "No, Elsie, it's me first, I suggested it!"

"Go on then, Jim."

He took a deep breath which said now for it!

"I have been thinking about you the whole time I have been in hospital. I know what you have said whenever I have wanted to take our friendship further, but now I am asking you outright.

Elsie, it's time we got married! I will propose to you properly if you like, but now I've said it. Will you please marry me? I love you; I always have, even before Bill died. Will you accept, please?"

Elsie, she was ashamed to admit later, bust out laughing.

"Jim, I was going to ask you exactly the same question! I thought after all the brush offs I have given you, you would never ask! What about my face. It is dreadful. Can you bear to live with it all your life?"

"Elsie, I love you. You have the temerity to worry about your face? What about my awful scars that have been with me since the last war. Can you bear to live with that all your life?"

With that they both laughed again. "It took me a while to realise, and a lot of care and help from you, Jim, but I finally came to my senses when I was injured. It made me realise how much I missed you when you were in hospital, and I knew I could not go on without you beside me, and to take care of me. Then I had to go and get hurt myself. Yes, Jim, of course, I'll marry you, as soon as you like when you get home!"

She went over to him and taking his head between her hands, kissed him on his cheek, where the scar was still etched deep into his face, on his head where the new operation scar was still red, and finally on his lips.! He took her in his arms, and kissed her gently, and knew they were really together, at last!

Jane came back with a Nurse, who carried a tea tray with cakes and a large of tea, and put it down on the small table between the easy chairs.

"Do you want me to pour out, Elsie" she asked them, noting their flushed faces.

"Before you do that, Jane, meet my fiancé, Jim Shaw. As soon as we are both back at Amhurst Square, we are getting married!"

Jane's face broke out in a broad smile of happiness.

"Now, I shall have a Father as well as a Mother again, for me and baby. Many congratulations. I am really delighted. Wait until I tell the girls at the shop!"

Elsie looked at Jim for agreement before replying. "If Jim agrees, we'll let that be your job to enjoy!".

The three sat together on the armchairs, and it was the happiest tea Elsie could remember since she lost Bill!

When visiting finished, she kissed Jim again, this time on his lips, and he hugged her, before they left him. He kissed Jane, and Elsie could see he was already acting the father for his grandchild!

On the way home, Jane and Elsie talked excitedly about plans for the wedding and her baby. Which first? Would Jim be home in time before it was born? After a while, each sat in happy silence. Elsie thought about Bill, what he would think. Would he approve? Of course he would. What about Brian? Would he? Of course he would! He liked Uncle Jim as he always called him. So now it was the two of them plus Jane plus another! What would they think in the shop, and Mrs Daly, would she be pleased?

They decided to keep it confidential until Jim came home. That way, Jim would be able to share in the celebrations and they could hold a party for the staff and their friends to make the announcement.

In early April, Elsie went back to the shop. The two Joans and Ann all gave her a great welcome, although Ann could not help grimacing at Elsie's face. A look from Joan 2 stopped her making any comment! The customers similarly, welcomed her back. She wanted to tell Elizabeth McIver her news, but when she asked about Jim, Elsie kept her counsel, and simply said he would be home soon.

"You are living with Jane at Amhurst Square, aren't you Elsie?" she enquired.

"Yes, that's right. It was the best place to recover from my injuries. I suppose I shall be back in the flat once I have fully recovered my mobility!"

It was a lie, but it silenced Mrs McIver, and would stop any gossip in the town. No doubt Mrs McIver had been asked to find out what she could!

Jane continued to keep well and active. She came to the shop during the day to have a little exercise, and found she was getting interested in the work. Ann, the little scamp, took her under her wing, much to Elsie's amusement, and Jane played along. Ann soon showed her what she did in the shop. Jane picked it up instantly, and enjoyed chatting to Ann, who was fascinated by the details of the coming baby.

Elsie was now not arriving until after nine o'clock. Ann was trusted with a shop key, and by the time Elsie came, the front was swept, and the shop tided for customers. In the middle of April, she arrived at the shop, to be met by Ann, who had a letter for her. "It came registered post this morning, Mrs Winter, I had to sign for it."

Elsie took the letter. It was addressed to Mrs W. Winter, at the flat, and she read the top with interest. It was from Wilson, Wyatt and Foster, Solicitors. Must be something Jim has organised she thought, and put her thumb under the sealed top and opened it.

Dear Mrs Winter,

I would be grateful if you will be kind enough to contact the undersigned as we have a matter of some importance we need to discuss with you as soon as possible. It is concerning a matter very much to your advantage.

Yours sincerely
T. Wyatt, *Solicitor*

What could it mean? Then she thought. "It's one of Jim's ideas for the wedding or a present. I'll call him as soon as I have the shop settled, and Joan is here."

She forgot all about the letter until she had her morning break, and then remembered and sought it out from where she had put it under the counter. She looked at the number, called the operator, and a woman, obviously the switchboard, answered. "Wilson, Wyatt and Foster. Can I help you?"

"I wish to speak to Mr Wyatt, please." said Elsie "Hold on, and I'll put you through."

"Wyatt here." said a very refined voice of a man, obviously of some class.

"It's Mrs Winter, here," she replied. "I have received your letter asking me to telephone you. Can you tell me what it is about, please?"

"Are you Mrs Elsie Winter, wife of Mr William Winter who managed the Dairy in Sidhurst?"

"Yes, I am,. Bill Winter was my husband."

Mr Wyatt said," Before I go on, Mrs Winter, would you be kind enough to tell me what happened to your husband. You said 'was' so I assume he has died. Could you tell me when and how, please?"

Elsie began to be annoyed. What he was asking was private. Why should she tell this man for no apparent reason!

"I can, but not until know what this is about!" she sounded irritated.

"Please bear with me, Mrs Winter, all will be explained in a minute. Please just tell me how and when your husband died?"

"He was killed in an air raid in the Blitz in 1941." she said "Why?"

"It has to be confirmed, but it is almost certain if you are who you say you are, you could have a sizeable sum of money left to you in a legacy. I assume you are at the address to which I sent the letter?"

"Yes, I work in the shop below the flat."

"I should like to visit you and tell you about this inheritance. Would it be convenient for me to call upon you tomorrow at about 11.00am? It will take about an hour, and I will need to see some documents. Would any records of your husband be there?"

"Yes, I have them all in the flat. Oh no, I forgot, they are at 6 Amhurst Square now. Could you call there?"

"Yes, I'm sure I can find it without difficulty, as I know Sidhurst tolerably well. I will be there at 11.00am. Is that convenient?"

"Yes, Mr Wyatt," said Elsie, "I'll see you tomorrow."

She put down the telephone. What on earth was it about? She did not know anyone who had money, and neither had Bill to her best knowledge. It puzzled her, but she didn't mention it too anyone in case it was a hoax of some kind.

Next morning, she put on her best dress, and stayed at home until he came. At five minutes to eleven, the doorbell rang, and as Mrs Daly was there, Elsie sent her to see who it was. She came back immediately and sad. "There's a Mr Wyatt here to see you, Mrs Winter. Shall I bring him in?"

"Yes please, Mrs Daly, don't keep him waiting."

A tall well dressed man in a dark suit was ushered into the drawing room. He was very much a 'city gent' and came forward to meet her as she stood up. "You are Mrs Winter?" he asked.

"Yes, I am. Would you like some tea or coffee?"

"No thanks very much" he answered in a cultured and gentle voice. "I'm Tom Wyatt, a partner in Wilson, Wyatt and Foster, who wrote to you and spoke to you yesterday. What I have to tell you, subject to final proof, is that you have been left in the estate of Mrs Mary Windlesham, a considerable sum of money, perhaps as much as one hundred thousand pounds!"

Elsie gasped. "I don't know anyone with that sort of money! Are you sure it's me?"

Mr Wyatt smiled. "You can blame your husband. Did he rescue an old lady from her bombed house in November 1941 and die saving her?"

"Elsie remembered suddenly who Mrs Windlesham was. She was the lady who Bill rescued from the house in Black Horse Road! "Of course," she exclaimed. "but the old lady had no money.

The house in Black Horse Road was tiny, and it is not a wealthy area."

"It's a long story, but it was Mrs Windlesham. She died a few weeks ago, and we have been trying to contact you to tell you of the bequest to you in her Will. When probate is granted, you will receive the money in full, but in the meantime, I am authorised by the Executors of her estate to make you an advance of ten thousand pounds any time you wish to accept it! It was her written wish that you should receive this amount immediately in case you are in hard circumstances since your husband died!"

Elsie sat back astonished. Once again Bill had looked after her! She couldn't believe it! "But where did her money come from, Mr Wyatt," she asked.

"From a relative of hers, who died in South Africa about two years ago, just after she was rescued by your husband. Now, she too has died, and left a large amount of her considerable fortune to Mr Winter's wife. Now, one more detail. I must see the birth certificate of your husband, your wedding certificate and his death certificate, if you have them here, to prove you are who you say you are. Can I see them?"

Elsie still couldn't believe what she was being told. Whatever would Jim and Jane say? She would be a wealthy woman! Could it really be true or was she dreaming!

"Yes, Mr Wyatt, I'll get them now. Please wait while I go up to the bedroom and find them in my deed box."

She had put them away carefully when Bill died, not for any particular reason, but because she wanted to keep them safe for the rest of her life as part of the past she never wanted to forget. She brought the box down with her to the Drawing Room and opened it in front of him. Her hands sorted through the papers until she found a brown envelope with all the details of Bill, his life and death, untouched since 1941."I think you will find what you want to see in here!" she handed it to him.

He took the envelope, and opened it removing the contents. "Ah," he said, "These are what I want!" In his hands he had the certificates. After perusing them he nodded and returned them to the envelope and handed it back to her.

"That's fine," he commented. "All as I hoped. Thank you for your time Mrs Winter, I can return to London now and confirm to Mrs Windlesham's Executors that I have found you, and the monies I mentioned, will be forthcoming when Probate is confirmed. In the meantime, do you wish to have the advance of ten thousand pounds I mentioned earlier?"

Elsie was still stupefied!

"Well, yes, I would Mr Wyatt. Are you certain this is not all a dream?"

He chuckled as he rose to his feet. "No, it's real enough. You will soon be a rich widow, Mrs Winter, and you can thank your late husband for it. Mrs Windlesham did not forget what he did for her that cost him his life, and you your husband. It has been a pleasure to meet you. The first cheque in advance, will be sent to you here, in a few days time, once I have cleared it with the Executors. I will write to you concerning the settlement of the full estate, and enclose payment at the same time. Now, I must get back to London. I wonder if you would be so kind as to call me a taxi to take me back to the station?"

Elsie came out of her spell with a start!

"Yes, of course, Mr Wyatt, I will call one immediately. Are you sure you won't have some refreshment before you go? It won't take a minute and the cab will not be here for a quarter of an hour?"

She went to the telephone and picked up her personal telephone list where the local firm was listed, and called them for a taxi to Jim's house.

"Five minutes, they said." she relayed to Mr Wyatt. "Are you sure about not having refreshment before you go? Mrs Daly can get us both something if you have the time before you return to town?"

"No, thank you for the invitation, Mrs Winter, I have a busy afternoon ahead, and must get off as soon as the taxi comes! I hope I shall see you again when the full settlement is made. I will telephone you then, and make a longer appointment, or perhaps, you would be good enough to come to my office. You will, I hope, by that time, be fully recovered from your injuries. I heard about them from Mrs Jane Winter. That's partly the reason I came to Sidhurst, rather than asking you to bring the documents to my office."

He seemed to have found out a lot already from his contact with the shop, and his talk to the staff.

"You seem to know a lot more about me, than I do of you, and your company! How long have you been looking for me?"

"Since November, when Mrs Windlesham died, the contents of her Will were known, and my company were appointed to act on behalf of her Executors of her Will. All they knew to tell me was what was written in it, and the reason for her bequest. That was the wife of Mr W. Winter, who used to live at Manor Dairies, in Sidhurst, and that her life was saved by your husband, the local Air Raid Warden, who lost his own life at the same time! The police informed us of your present whereabouts, knowing you live above Shaw's the Chemist. You are well known in the town, you know." He smiled at her, and they heard a knock on the front door. "That will be my taxi I expect. It has been a pleasure to meet you Mrs Winter, and I hope you will have lunch with me when we meet again in my office in London!" There was a knock and Mrs Daly came in. "The taxi is here Mrs Winter, for your guest."

"Thank you very much Mrs Daly. It's for Mr Wyatt. Would you be kind enough to show him out?"

"It has been a great pleasure, Mrs Winter," said Mr Wyatt again "to be the bearer of such happy news! I look forward to our next meeting." He held his hand out to Elsie. "Goodbye."

"Thank you for your courtesy and I am still in a daze over the news, but it will sink in quickly, I'm sure, and I'll expect the first money soon. Goodbye." She stood up, and Mrs Daly led him to the front door, and saw him to the taxi waiting at the kerb..

After he went, Elsie sat thinking. It all seemed a dream! Had a Mr Wyatt really just visited her? She decided to say nothing to anyone until she had considered what it meant. From what Mr Wyatt had told her, she was about to inherit a very large sum of money. The thought frightened her, yet the possibilities of what she would be able to do excited her. What would Jim and Jane think? She decided to do nothing, tell no one, and wait until Mr Wyatt's letter came. By then she would have had time to decide how best to break the news.

Mrs Daly came in to the Drawing Room. "Would you like some coffee before you go back to the shop Mrs Winter? I hope nothing is wrong? Mr Wyatt seemed a very important man!" She was fishing to know why Mr Wyatt had visited!

"Yes, thank you very much, Mrs Daly, I can spend a few more minutes before I go back to the shop. Some coffee would be very much appreciated." She did not answer the other question.

She drank her coffee, and by the time she had finished it, her mind was a little calmer. She would say or do nothing until Mr Wyatt's letter came. She wondered where Jane had gone this morning. Probably for a short walk if she felt well, and Elsie worried because she walked on her own. Her time was getting near, and she really should have a companion when she went out! Now, it looked as if she was out on her own again! As Mrs Daly came in to clear the coffee things, she asked her

"Do you know if Jane has gone out, Mrs Daly?"

"Yes, I think she has. Left about half an hour ago, I think. She didn't want to interfere with your guest!"

"Of course," thought Elsie, "Typical of Jane. Not her business and she made sure she kept away while he was here! "Oh dear, I hope she isn't too long. We can walk to the shop together!"

Elsie picked up the paper to make it appear as if everything was normal, and Mrs Daly went back to the kitchen with the tray. Soon after, Elsie heard Jane come in the back door.

"I'm just off to the shop, Jane, shall we go together, or are you too tired after your walk?"

"Yes, Elsie, I'd love to. It's a beautiful morning, and getting warmer. I feel fine, and can sit down in the shop when we get there."

Normal routine was under way, and although Elsie was still excited over the news, she put it to the back of her mind, waiting for Mr Wyatt to contact her again.

Jim came home from hospital in the middle of April. He looked and sounded fine, and Elsie had not seen him look healthier. He hired a taxi to bring him to Amhurst Square, very sensibly, for he was tired by the time Elsie greeted him at the front door.

"Welcome home, Jim!" as he came in his front door.

"Elsie, my dear, at last! I'm home, and we have so much to do! First, I want to see how you have organised the house!" He put his case down, and waited while the driver brought in the second with all his belongings.

"Before you get any ideas, come and sit down. Mrs Daly's been waiting to see you again and welcome you!" He didn't wait, but walked straight into the kitchen and hugged her. "I'm home Mrs Daly! How good to see you again!"

Mrs Daly was quite overcome. "Why, Mr Shaw!" and went quite pink with embarrassment. He had obviously never hugged her since he was a little boy!

"You are looking really well. Now, shall I make you all some tea?"

"Yes, and lets have some cake as well, if you have some?"

"I'll bring some in, and Mrs Winter can pour out. I'll tell Mrs Jane you're here!"

Minutes later, a very large Jane came in. "Home at last Uncle Jim!

"And isn't he looking well, Jane" said Elsie.

"He certainly is, he'll be trouble now Elsie! You'll have to watch him!"

"That's enough of your cheek, young lady. Now, how's the baby? When is the great day? It can't be long now!"

"No, It's due in early May. The date is the 12th as near as we can tell. I will go into the Nursing Home at the beginning of the month. That's what Dr Hargreaves has arranged."

They sat chatting for a few minutes and then Jim asked "Now Elsie, when can we go and select an engagement ring? Any ideas what you would like? And where do you want to go to get it?"

Elsie had the answer. She had thought about it for many days waiting his return home.

"I would like to go to Woolwich, to the shop where Brian and Jane got theirs. I have some ideas, but I don't want a flashy looking affair, just a neat circle, but enough to make it clear I mean it!"

"You'd better, my dear." said Jim, "If not, I'm wasting my time!" And they all laughed with him!

"We'll go on Monday afternoon. You can forget the shop after eleven o'clock. We'll have some lunch in Woolwich, and find the ring afterwards. How does that suit you?"

"Sounds marvellous, Jim!"

"Right, that's settled. Now, what arrangements have you made for my return? Is there anywhere for me to sleep?" he grinned. Glad to be home and to have two ladies around him. Elsie had never seen him so animated.

He wanted to go to his shop immediately, but Elsie persuaded him to wait until tomorrow, which eventually he did, grudgingly. It was a good thing, because by five o'clock he was exhausted, and Elsie helped him up to his room, and unpacked with him. She insisted he went to bed, and brought him up some high tea at six o'clock. He was already yawning when she went to get the tray, so she kissed him and told him to lay back and rest for a few minutes. When she returned he was already fast asleep. Home at last, and ready for the fray!

They went to Woolwich next day, having checked to see the shop was the one Jane went to. Brian was in her mind the whole time, and as she looked at the excellent selection, she felt him at her back with Jim. She made her choice, a modest sapphire and diamond circlet, with alternate stones. Jim wanted her to have a more expensive one, but she knew what she wanted, and he accepted her choice. As they looked at various pieces, a small four leafed clover brooch caught her eye. Where had she seen one like it before?

"I don't want to buy it, Jim, but could we look at that brooch? I'm sure I've seen it somewhere before!"

The assistant took it from the case. "It came in a few weeks ago, madam, it is second hand." Elsie looked at it, and suddenly she knew where she had seen it! It had been her friend Betty's! She remembered Betty showing it to her. A present from her first boyfriend! It had a flaw on the back of one of the petals, and Betty and remarked that it had been less expensive and that was why he had bought it for her! "Could I have a look at it please?" she asked the assistant.

"Yes, madam, of course." He took it from the case and handed it to her. She looked at it, turned it over, and knew immediately it was Betty's! The flaw was the same!

"Thank you very much, but it's not quite what I want!" The assistant took it and returned it to the case.

Jim put the engagement ring on her finger and kissed her. She turned it in her hand and saw it sparkle as it caught the light. She kissed him back. "Thank you very much Jim, now it's official! We are engaged!" He took her hand, and together they left the shop with the congratulations of the assistant in their ears.

As they walked up the road, Jim said "You didn't want the brooch then?"

"No Jim and I didn't want to say anything in the shop. That brooch belonged to Betty, you know, she was murdered in the park! I wonder how they came by it? I know it's hers, that's why I looked at the back. It has a flaw! I can only be hers!"

"You must go to the police Elsie! It could be very important!"

Nothing more was said and they chatted like every newly engaged couple on the way back to Sidhurst on the bus. Elsie wondered what he would say if he knew about her windfall! All in good time!

The next morning she went to Sidhurst Police Station and walked up to the counter.

"May I speak to the officer concerned with Betty Manner's death, please?"

"The station Sergeant looked her curiously. "Just a moment madam. It's Mrs Winter, isn't it?"

He remembered her, much to her surprise. She didn't realise she was well known in Sidhurst.

"Would you like to sit here and he'll be with you in a few minutes." said the Sergeant after calling someone on his desk telephone. She sat in the chair and waited.

A plain clothes officer came in from the back. "Hallo, Mrs Winter, what can I do for you? I am Detective Constable Palmer. Would you like to come through to my office?"

She followed him through to a small room and he sat her down in a chair, then took his place opposite. "Now, how may I help?"

She told him about seeing the brooch in the jewellers in Woolwich.

"I know it was Betty Manner's" she said. "I've seen it many times when we went out together. It was a present from her first boyfriend, Bill. The same name as my husband, that's why I remember it so well. It has the same defect. I turned it over and examined it. I'm absolutely certain it's the one!"

"That's very interesting Mrs Winter. Thank you very much for coming in. Yesterday you said you saw it in the shop?"

"Yes, I went to buy a ring, and noticed it in a case on the counter. The assistant showed it to me. It's priced at £25, and they said it was second hand and they purchased it a few weeks ago."

"This could be important, Mrs Winter" said Detective Constable Palmer. "Would you be kind enough to come with me, I would like you to make a statement of all you have told me."

He took her to a desk, and selected a Statement Form. "Now, tell me again, exactly what you saw and did, and all the details of the brooch that you can remember, where you saw it, how much it was priced, and anything else that might be of value in tracing it's previous owner. I will write it down, for you to sign when you are satisfied it is correct." He began to write, then waited for Elsie to dictate her statement. Every so often, she had to wait for him to catch her up, or to answer a query about the account. It took nearly four pages, but finally, she said "That's it as far as I can remember."

"Right, thank you Mrs Winter, I'll now read it back to you, to see you agree and then you can sign it""

Elsie made two small corrections that he initialled, and asked her to initial as well, and then she signed at the bottom of each page and at the end.

"Thank you very much indeed, Mrs Winter. What you have told us will be investigated immediately." He saw her to the door, where the station Sergeant said "Goodbye, Mrs Winter, thank you for coming in!" and she was walking back to the shop. Whether it would help she had no idea, but she had acted correctly, so it was off her mind.

After leaving the Police Station, she went directly to the shop. They were all there, Joan 1 and 2, Ann, but not Jim, who was having a late start on his first morning back. She said nothing as she walked in, except her usual "Good morning, Ann," then followed by the same to the Joans' both hard at work, one in the dispensary, and the other in the shop. Ann noticed her ring instantly and said nothing, but Elsie could see her bright eyes examining it!

"Everything alright Ann? No problems yet today?"

"No, Mrs Winter. Is Mr Shaw coming in today? I know he is out of hospital, at last. I am looking forward to meeting him!"

"And him you, Ann." replied Elsie She thought she would give Ann time to tell the others. "I'll just go up to the flat to get something, Ann. Carry on until I come down, and make us all some tea, if you will?" She went out of the shop again, up the stairs in to the flat, and checked it was secure, tidy, and nothing out of place since she was last there. Then she returned downstairs.

As she went in the door, Joan 1 came up to her and took her left hand. "What's this I see, Elsie?" her face was smiling. "So you've done it at last! I'm so glad for you both. When did this happen?"

"We agreed a little while ago while Jim was still in hospital, Joan, but decided to wait until he was home again so we could celebrate our engagement together!"

The second Joan heard and came out in a rush!

"You crafty thing, Elsie, never said a thing did you!" She was smiling and Ann said. "Told you she 'ad a ring! Can I congratulate you too, Mrs Winter. Will you be Mrs Shaw soon?"

"Not until we are actually married, Ann. We haven't set the date yet, but it will be very soon I know! Now, where's the tea and biscuits?"

About half an hour after, Jim appeared through the door. Elsie was in the shop, and deliberately went up and kissed him. "How did it go at the Police Station, Elsie?" he asked. "Were they interested?"

"They certainly were. The detective who took my statement said they will investigate the brooch immediately!"

"I should think so. Now, do they all know?" he grinned impishly at the three ladies waiting respectfully at the back. "

"May I introduce the two ladies you haven't met. Firstly, our new pharmacist and dispenser, Mrs Joan Loveridge." Jim shook her hand. "I have already heard how efficient you are Mrs Loveridge. Please call me Jim, and I will, if you agree, call you Joan 2, as we all know you."

"Of course, Mr Shaw. But I would prefer to keep to that name if you don't mind. It is more respectful!"

"Yes of course, but I shall still call you Joan!"

"That's fine, thank you, and very pleased to meet you."

Elsie beckoned Ann to come forward. "This is Miss Ann Simpson. She's been helping us for several months now, and very quick and bright she's proving to be. I have agreed for her to have day release to study at the local technical college for her exams. I'm sure she will pass them quickly, as she's keen as mustard. Wants to be a pharmacist too, don't you Ann?"

Jim saw Ann recoil a bit at his appearance. "Now, I know what I look like Ann, but I don't bite!" he smiled charmingly and shook her hand.

"Pleased to meet you Mr Shaw." said Ann, and went back to her work behind the counter.

"Now I know everyone," said Jim, "Let's see what the shop looks like. He went round examining everything, noting new products, and obviously happy to be back. "I would like to check on the flat, Elsie," he said after he had finished his inspection. "I'll walk up with you and just check all is well."

They left the shop, and went up the stairs again.

"I like the look of the new girls, Elsie. Joan 2 is obviously in charge, and Ann has bright eyes and seems quick and alert. Joan 1 needs to retire. Has she made any mention of it?"

"No, she hasn't since I was injured, Jim. I imagine she will say something now you and I are back. She wants to retire, I know, and I think, if you agree, we shall not need her now. Also, Jane is showing an interest in the business, and perhaps eventually she will want to be part of it."

"Yes, let Joan 1 have a quiet spell helping and going back to her part time hours for a while, and I can work out a pension plan for her. From what I have seen, we are busier than ever. What a good thing you found two excellent staff when you did. I am very proud of the way you have been running the shop. I couldn't have done as well myself! Shaw's is growing."

"I have some ideas about that, Jim, and I will discus them with you at home, when we are undisturbed, and you can tell me what you think."

"I am intrigued, Elsie, but, as you say, not now!"

Jane did not make an appearance that day, and Elsie thought it was because it was Jim's first day back, but when she went home for lunch, Mrs Daly said she should go into hospital. Elsie talked to Jane, and she was obviously feeling things were getting near, although not yet imminent. She rang Dr Hargreaves, who reserved a bed for her in the Sidhurst Nursing Home. Elsie walked with her down to the old Victorian building in Haybury Road, where practically all Sidhurst's residents had their babies, carrying a small case with her clothes. She saw her safely established in a comfortable bed. The baby was not expected for another week or more, but Elsie felt happier with her safely in the Nursing Home where she could be watched.

At the end of April it was apparent that the war was coming to an end. Berlin fell to the Allies. It was now just a question of time before Germany agreed to unconditional surrender which was Churchill's only acceptable deal with them.

On the 3rd May, Jim noticed the postman call, and collected the letters from the box in the hall. "There's one for you, Elsie, from a solicitor! What have you been up to?" he grinned at her.

"Wait until I have opened the letter, Jim, and I'll tell you!" He watched with interest as she opened the letter from Wilson, Wyatt and Foster. It was, as she had anticipated, his confirmation of the bequest. As she pulled the letter out of the posh looking envelope, a cheque enclosed with it fluttered to the floor. Jim, looking half over her shoulder with great interest, picked it up. "Elsie," he said in a startled voice. "It's a cheque to you for ten thousand pounds!"

"Yes, Jim, I've been expecting it. Now I can tell you what I wanted to talk to you about last week in the shop, if you remember!"

He didn't remember, she knew that, otherwise he would have mentioned it before, but he said vaguely,

"Oh, yes, I do seem to remember you saying something."

"Well, you remember the lady, Mrs Windlesham, who Bill saved from the house that collapsed on him and killed him?" Jim remembered the incident only too well, but not the lady's name.

"Ten days ago, I had a call and a visit from the solicitor dealing with her Will. You were still in hospital. Mrs Windlesham died and left a huge estate that she inherited from a relative in South Africa, and included a bequest of one hundred thousand pounds to me. This is the first payment in advance! Jim, I'm a well off widow you are marrying! What do you think of that!"

Jim's reaction was mixed. He was pleased for her, but was well off himself. "But we don't need it Elsie. I have more than enough for us both. What do we need with more, although, of course, it makes you a wealthy woman in your own right!"

"Now, that's why I wanted to talk to you. Let's get married first, then make Shaw's a limited company. As soon as the shop next door comes on the market, or even before, we'll buy it, and even one in another nearby town. We have the staff to run it, and can recruit some more." She paused out of breath and Jim said "Hold on Elsie, that's enough for the moment. Let's discuss that bit. Firstly, who would own my shop?"

"You and I would, Jim. I would put money in and we would both become Directors." She paused to let him consider what she had put forward

"Perhaps I am going to fast, Jim. What I'm saying is, this is the time to expand. Shops are for sale at low prices in this area. That won't last. If we bought the shop next door, we could enlarge our stock, compete better with Boots, and get more discount from the suppliers. What do you think?"

"What about our wedding, Elsie!" He was thinking one step at a time." When will it be? "

"I think June would be the time, Jim. Jane will have had her baby by then, and we shall have time to prepare and think about what I have been saying. Now, what do you think?"

"Then, how about Saturday 17th June in St Mary's Church? Can we agree to that day? It would seem ideal. There's a lot to do, your dress, the reception, who to invite, and more. Isn't that enough to think about for now?" asked Jim.

"Yes, I agree, let's confirm the day, and I will see the Vicar and ensure we can have the church. Until that's certain, we can do nothing."

That afternoon, Elsie spoke to the Vicar and received his agreement for 2.00 pm on the 17th June. All was set for the day of their wedding. Elsie did not want a grand affair, but when she saw Jim's guest list, all Sidhurst seemed to have been included! Elsie was sad because in the whole list, there was only one family member, and that was on Jim's side. His brother who he didn't like, and never saw, had to be included. Preparations began.

One Tuesday evening, 7th May, Elsie and Jim came home as usual from the shop after a particularly busy day. Elsie went up to her room, and feeling tired, lay down on her bed before she had a bath. The shop was always dusty when they unpacked new stock, and plenty was arriving these days. She lay down and became aware of noisy sirens on the river Thames Her window looked east, and far away she could hear them sounding continuously. Whatever was going on? It was curious and then she recognised the sound, it was the Morse code for 'V'. Everyone knew three short blasts and one long, is the signal 'V for Victory', and the ships were all sounding it! It must mean something important, and the noise increased. More and more ships were joining in!

She went to the top of the stairs. "Jim," she called. He came from the Drawing Room in answer. "Listen!" He came up the stairs and together they looked out at the quiet May evening. "It's the 'V' sign. The war must be over, Elsie!" She looked at him and he hugged her. "At last Jim, no more war. Peace at last!"

They went outside to listen, and soon they heard cheering coming from the High Street. Everyone knew. It really was over at last! They went back into the house and turned on the wireless. The announcer was repeatedly breaking into programmes to announce Germany had surrendered unconditionally, and Mr Churchill later in the evening, announced that the next day, the 8th May would be a holiday. VE Day he called it – Victory in Europe!

They sat together in the Drawing Room, looking out on the beautiful spring flowers in Jim's garden as the evening closed in. Jim suggested they had a glass of something to celebrate, but Elsie could not find any enthusiasm. "Maybe tomorrow, Jim. I only feel relief tonight. Tomorrow, when we have the holiday. Just think what the war has cost us, and what changes it has brought!" She felt a light tear on her cheek. Bill gone, Brian gone, and next a grandmother! How Jim had helped her!

At that moment she thought of Jane! They were supposed to be on their way to see her in the Nursing Home! "Jim, come on, we are due to visit Jane. I had completely forgotten listening to the news!"

"I'll get a coat, Elsie, it could be chilly coming back!" At that moment the telephone rang. Elsie answered it.

"Is that Mrs Winter?"

"Yes, Elsie Winter here. "Mrs Winter, this is Sidhurst Nursing Home. Mrs Jane Winter has gone into labour. If you come this evening, it is possible you may not see her. I'll call you immediately there is any news!"

Elsie's reaction was to rush off immediately, but Jim stopped her. "We might be there a long time, Elsie. Let's eat something first and them go. If we are there all night, at least we'll be prepared!"

About half past nine, they arrived at the Home, to find Jane well advanced in the birth of her first child. Together, holding hands, they sat until two o'clock in the morning waiting for news. Just at the darkest hour, it was ten past two exactly; Jim said later, Sister came through the doors from the Ward to announce "Mrs Winter, your daughter-in-law has a baby boy! She especially wanted you to know immediately!"

Elsie's dream had come true! It would be she knew, another Brian. "Can we see her yet?" she asked the Sister.

"Yes, you can! In fact she's asking to see you! Follow me!"

Jane was sitting up in bed with young Brian in her arms looking pink and wrinkled! Elsie went over and kissed her. Jane, you are a clever girl!" and to the Sister, "How much does he weigh?"

"Six pounds seven ounces!" said Sister. "I'll leave you with her, but not too long please, she is very well but extremely tired."

"Well done, Jane!" said Jim, "What will you call him?" he asked mischievously.

Elsie looked at him and realised he was joking.

Jane smiled. "I dare not name him anything but Brian! And his second name will be after my Father, Marco. Are you happy with that Elsie?"

Elsie was crying with emotion,. Everything she ever hoped was coming true. "Do you realise he was born on VE day, Jane?"

Jane looked at her. "What's that, Elsie?"

"Of course, you don't know. Germany surrendered unconditionally yesterday evening, and today will be a holiday. It has been named VE Day!"

Jim leant towards Elsie and Jane. Elsie was sitting on the side of her bed. "Many congratulations Jane, the house will be all ready for you when you come out. You need to sleep, so we shall see you in the morning." He kissed her on the cheek, and lightly touched Brian's head. "Cute little chap isn't he! Now, come on Elsie, leave Jane to sleep. Plenty of time tomorrow!"

Elsie, who had been feeling emotional anyway, managed to hold back her feelings until they were walking home. People were still everywhere in the streets celebrating before VE Day had really started. Then her emotions came flooding out in a stream of tears. Sobs of happiness and relief combined with all the memories of the year mixed with Bill, Brian, and the war. She had a grandson! Another Brian, and if Bill could not be here, this was the next best thing. Bill had seen her through just as he always did. Now, she was even going to have enough money to be an independent lady, and a new husband. Jim would not be an easy man to live with, she knew that, but he was kind and generous, and together Elsie and Jim Shaw, would battle on through life together. Jane could come with them as long as she wanted, or until she found another partner. That was in the future and too far ahead to contemplate!

****

Chapter 12

$\mathcal{T}$wo weeks later, Jane and Brian junior came home from the nursing home. Mrs Daly had happily retired to her new cottage, and Jim and Elsie had refurnished her room to turn it into a nursery. It was next to Jane's room, and still left the other two rooms for Elsie and Jim. Elsie had spent some of the money to outfit it with the best she could get in spite of the war restrictions still in force.

Brian thrived from the start and was soon putting on weight because Jane was able to feed him herself. Elsie, for the time being, was at home preparing for the many items to be arranged before the wedding. Jim went back to his shop full time. The staff were agog with baby Winter and the forthcoming marriage.

Jim and Elsie, as planned, married on the 17th June, and a reception was held in St Mary's Church Hall afterwards. It seemed all Sidhurst was there. Elsie had the best dress she could find in the circumstances, using the extra clothing coupons that were issued for a bride about to marry She kept the whole ceremony low key, and would have minimised the reception afterwards, but Jim wanted everyone to attend who could.

The local paper came out every Friday, and had a long report with pictures. "Local Shop Proprietor marries V2 Victim!, was how it announced the wedding and there were several not very flattering pictures of them both outside the church! Jane was the Matron of Honour, and Jim had his brother as his best man. Elsie greeted him for the first time just before the ceremony, and didn't find him as unpleasant as Jim had made out. Nevertheless, Jim really only had him, because there was no one else in his family left alive! There was no honeymoon. Elsie didn't want one. She had the highest regard for Jim, and loved him. But nevertheless, he was not Bill, who was her first love and would be forever her sweetheart in her mind. She would never forget him. Luckily, Jim respected his memory, and had overcome his guilt at Bill's death. After it was all over, the family, for now it was, returned to 6 Amhurst Square. Elsie and Jim had invited the three shop staff to have supper with them after the reception, and meet Jane and her new baby They both met them in the doorway, and thanked them for all the help they had given to them both during the last year of turmoil. Each received a special gift of an extra week's wages, and it made the whole evening a very happy occasion. After the meal, they all toasted 'Shaw's The Chemists, Peace, and the future'

The next morning, Elsie and Jane were looking at the local paper again, laughing at the pictures of themselves, when a report at the bottom of the page caught Elsie's eye. The headline announced –

"Local Man Charged with Murder!"

"Look, Jane! You must read this!"

The article went on to report that a local man Charlie Taylor had been charged with the murder of Miss Betty Manners, whose body was found in Sidhurst Park in the autumn. He was remanded in custody, and the case would be held later in the year.

"Well I never," said Elsie, "So it wasn't Douglas Armstrong, after all. I wonder how they found out?

"Now Douglas will be able to come back cleared of suspicion. I must admit that I thought he had done it, and so did everyone else! I wonder if he knows yet and where he is?"

No doubt it would all become clear, and she knew the forthcoming case would create huge local interest in the town.

1948

Elsie and Jim settled down to run and expand their business. By 1948, they owned two premises. Firstly, Shaw's Sidhurst had been doubled in size, as Elsie wanted. The shop next door had lost trade steadily, and the owner, whom Jim knew, accepted a reasonable offer, and retired. It was now Shaw's Ltd. Secondly a shop had been purchased at Bexley.

Jim was Managing Director of Shaw's Ltd with fifty five per cent of the shares, Elsie had twenty five, and Jane fifteen. Joan Loveridge, had been appointed Manageress, and was making an excellent job of Shaw's Bexley, setting it up and establishing customers. To give her an incentive, Elsie insisted she had the remaining five per cent of the shares. She had earned it! Jim was starting to feel the pressure of his long and suffering life, and the second operation had aged him. He didn't want to spend so much time now in the shop, and handed more and more on to Ann. She passed her exams with flying colours, and was the mainstay of the shop when Elsie was not there herself.

One afternoon, she and Jim were looking back to their wedding day, and she thought it would be a good idea to make a before and after comparison of her face. Jim said "I don't know why you worry. I don't!"

"But you're a man Jim Shaw! It is much more important to a woman, and I want to see the comparison for myself!"

"Well, all I know is your face is almost back to where it was. O.K., you have a long scar line, but it is no longer red, which made it so unsightly at the beginning. In some lights it is not even visible at all. The only feature that still shows is a small amount of puckering and wrinkling along the scar line where the stitching pulled the skin a little. Really, your recovery is amazing, and a credit to the skill of the Doctor at Casualty who did the neat sewing! Don't worry about it! No one else does!"

Nevertheless, she was not satisfied until she made a direct comparison. Jim took a close up picture of her face on his camera, and when it was developed, they examined it carefully. What Jim said was true. A little of the skin was pulling to one side just above her cheekbone, but otherwise her face had recovered almost completely to where it was before. The long scar would never disappear, but was slowly changing into a silvery line down her face, and in a few years more would be all that could be seen to remind her of that awful day the V2 fell on Sidhurst! She was not too dissatisfied with what she saw, and still thanked her lucky stars it had not been worse!

The flat above Shaw's was now rented by a friend of Joan 2.. She was a woman separated from her husband who had returned after the war and didn't want her. There was some scandal, but Elsie did not pry into the precise reason as to who was to blame for the separation! She was a quiet and well behaved lady, and paid her rent on the dot. She worked in the Council offices at Sidhurst Park, and helped the staff in the shop occasionally with errands . They said she is very lonely, but Elsie found her pleasant, and was grateful to have a good tenant in the flat. Jim was happy with her too, but that was mainly, Elsie thought, because she paid on time each month, and never had to be chased for her money!

It was fortunate for Elsie, that she had the company and love of a kind and generous husband, because in the next few years, several of her friends passed away. Whether it was the relaxation of the stress of war that triggered off failures in these persons, no one knew, but she was not unusual in losing close friends, relatives, or associates just after the end of the war. Two such examples close to her occurred in 1946 and 1947

In March 1946, Arthur, her sister Margaret's husband died. His earlier bad temper, and irritability with his wife, became even worse. In February he suffered a sudden severe stroke while working in his office at the bank, and was rushed to Gravesend Hospital. There he lingered for nearly two months without any improvement, and then suffering a further attack, died on a Sunday morning. Elsie had a sad call from her sister, and immediately went to comfort her, and stayed with her a week. She felt very sorry for Margaret. They didn't have any children, but fortunately she was left with an excellent pension, and a large house, but was soon very lonely. Elsie tried to get to Gravesend once a fortnight to see her. Now a well off woman, with a new husband, the comparison was striking to when Brian was killed and Margaret had, it seemed, everything. Now Margaret was the one in a parlous situation!

Her friend, Mrs McIver, passed away quite suddenly. She had been coming into the shop for many years for her angina pills and quite unexpectedly in October 1947, she had a severe heart attack. She was taken to the hospital, but died two weeks later. Elsie was very sad. She had been a good friend and customer, and Elsie missed seeing her at church, where Jane and she went taking young Brian, if it was a children's service, or at Christmas. Gordon McIver had returned from the Far East just after his Mother died. He came into the shop one morning looking much the same only older. He knew, of course, about her marriage, and congratulated her. He had heard, as had everyone in Sidhurst, of her good fortune, and could see for himself how the business was expanding. The day he came in they had just taken occupation of the next door shop, so it was very evident to him that Shaw's was growing. He still lived in Sidhurst, and had taken a post in his Father's business working in the Export Division, where he could use his overseas experience and knowledge. He was out of the country most of the time!

A new pharmacist had been engaged to take over from Joan Loveridge, and Shaw's had become the established Chemist in

Sidhurst. Boots in contrast had not flourished, and although they were still open, it was only a matter of time, Elsie thought, before they closed the branch.

In the autumn of 1945, Charles Taylor was found guilty of the murder of Betty Manners, and hanged for his crime in January 1946. Elsie followed the reports of the trial meticulously every day in the paper. He had been traced by a brooch which the police had established he had sold to a jeweller when he needed money. The police traced him to an address in Woolwich, and he was apprehended during a search of his digs. Being unable to account for his possession of the brooch, the Police arrested him on suspicion, and under severe questioning he confessed. It appeared he had seen Betty walking tearfully through the Park on her way home alone, after being dressed down by Douglas. It was the noise they were making that attracted his attention. When Douglas stormed off and left her, he followed her until she was well away and then assaulted her. Betty was never the one to give up without a fight, and in his attempt to rape her, had screamed so loudly that he panicked and strangled her to silence the noise. Once he realised what he had done, he fled back to Woolwich, and laid low. Then he ran short of money and sold the brooch to the jewellers for £5! The jeweller remembered the seller, and picked him out from a picture book of suspects. He already had a criminal record for assault, so the Police knew they had the right man. In due course under pressure he confessed the crime, and suffered the ultimate punishment!

Elsie felt pleased she had contributed to finding Betty's killer. Always a flighty girl, nevertheless, she had been a good friend, and didn't deserve to die like that! Justice had been done, and Elsie had done her bit!

Her fiance, Mr Perkins, had risen from Foreman to Works Manager at Klingers, and considered himself a very important member of society! A view not shared by many people, and especially not by Elsie and Jim, or the staff at Shaw's! On the occasions when he came in to purchase something, he was

abrupt, aggressive and generally rude. They served him politely
and carefully, as he had a reputation as a trouble maker. He met
Elsie and Jim when they were out walking one Sunday afternoon,
and just managed to find sufficient grace to acknowledge them
with a curt 'Good afternoon!' He looked quite hard at Elsie, in
her smart well dressed attire, and she felt very satisfied with her
position in life. Whether he had found another bride, she never
knew, but for certain, bride or not, he would always have a lady
somewhere on tap. He was that sort of man!

In the early part of the year, Jane was invited to visit her
husband Brian's grave at Arnhem. Elsie could have gone, but
decided to leave it to Jane. Although he was not an airborne
officer, she was his widow, and he had been killed close to
Arnhem The invitation came from the Airborne Regiment who
were organising a special visit for close relatives of those killed in
the battle for the town. The officer who sent Jane the invitation
was an acquaintance of hers, and had specially made sure she
was invited

Jane decided to go, and take Brian now nearly four years old,
to see his Daddy's grave. Elsie saw them off from London, and
they travelled with a group all visiting the graves where their
relatives were buried. It was a sad journey, but Jane wanted to
go to see where Brian was resting for herself.

Elsie was not sure how much Jane enjoyed the experience,
because she was very quiet and sad after she returned. It was not
until the third day after she came back to Amherst Square that
she was able to tell Elsie about the visit and Brian's grave. She
said it was beautifully tended by the Dutch people who kept it
immaculate, and how it was laid out in many rows. Thousands
of identical white headstones all etched with the soldier's name,
rank and date of death. The local people had planted flowers
on each grave, and made sure they were always watered and
properly cared for.

After some searching, she found Brian's grave with a number of other officers killed at Arnhem, and took a snapshot of it for Elsie to see. The picture was in black and white, but she could see the flowers in bloom on the top of the grave where the local people had planted them. As she was showing Elsie, the pictures, Jane said, "I wanted to bring you back something as a memento, so took these photos, but in addition, the grave had one rose blooming on it, looking very beautiful. I'm afraid I cut it and took it so you could have it. Here it is!" She opened her bible that always went with her since Brian was killed, and took out an immaculate pressed white rose!

Elsie sat back in surprise and astonishment! Her mind raced back to the afternoon in Gravesend when she and Margaret went to the séance just after Brian had been reported killed. She still remembered as if it was yesterday, the message he sent to her via Irene Haskell, the medium who relayed it on to her, that he would send her a white rose! Elsie knew she had never told anyone, not even Jane. The only one who knew apart from herself was Margaret, and she was sure she had not passed it on to anyone! Brian had kept his word! She knew now, he was at peace in Heaven and together with his Father. A great tide of emotion, guilt, love and remembrance, came over her. She held her arms out to Jane and they put their arms around one another and let all the grief and emotion flood out!.

For a while she was unable to tell Jane why she had been so badly affected. Jane wondered if it was something she had done or if by returning with the rose, she had done something wrong. Once Elsie recovered her composure, she retold the episode with her sister. Jane was amazed. "There was just the one bloom, Elsie, nothing else. Most of the other graves had several, and they were all red or pink roses. Brian's was the only white one, that's partly why I brought it. I had a feeling there was something special about it! It must be more than coincidence. You always said Brian and Bill look after you. Do you think that as you have married Jim, they feel free to depart?" Elsie said nothing for a while thinking about what Jane was saying.

"I think you are right, Jane. This can only be Brian telling me he is happy where he is and with his Father, and that now it is time for us to move on, and start living a new life bringing up his son in the way they would want!" A great weight had lifted from her mind. Brian had released her, and Bill was with him, so must have agreed!

She felt peace at last. Everything had worked out, and she could move on with Jim and Jane, her new daughter, and her new grandson, into a new life. God would decide when it is time for her to join Bill and Brian waiting patiently somewhere in his world far above.

THE *End*

ISBN 141209831-9